Praise for Ellie ries

"Delectable." *views*

"Quirky . . . intri your stomach growl." *Reader*

"Delicious." —*RT Book Reviews*

"This debut culinary mystery is a light soufflé of a book (with recipes) that makes a perfect mix for fans of Jenn McKinlay, Leslie Budewitz, or Jessica Beck."
—*Library Journal* on *Meet Your Baker*

"Marvelous." —*Fresh Fiction*

"Scrumptious . . . will delight fans of cozy mysteries with culinary delights." —*Night Owl Reviews*

"Clever plots, likable characters, and good food . . . Still hungry? Not to worry, because desserts abound in . . . this delectable series." —*Mystery Scene* on *A Batter of Life and Death*

"[With] *Meet Your Baker*, Alexander weaves a tasty tale of deceit, family ties, delicious pastries, and murder."
—Edith Maxwell, author of *A Tine to Live, A Tine to Die*

"Sure to satisfy both dedicated foodies and ardent mystery lovers alike." —Jessie Crockett, author of *Drizzled with Death*

Also
by Ellie Alexander

Meet Your Baker

A Batter of Life and Death

On Thin Icing

Caught Bread Handed

Fudge and Jury

A Crime of Passion Fruit

Another One Bites the Crust

Till Death Do Us Tart

Live and Let Pie

A Cup of Holiday Fear

Nothing Bundt Trouble

Chilled to the Cone

Mocha, She Wrote

Bake, Borrow, and Steal

Donut Disturb

Muffin but the Truth

Ellie Alexander

St. Martin's Paperbacks

First published in the United States by St. Martin's Paperbacks, an imprint of St. Martin's Publishing Group.

MUFFIN BUT THE TRUTH

For information, address St. Martin's Publishing Group, 120 Broadway, New York, NY 10271.

www.stmartins.com

ISBN: 978-1-250-85423-0

Our books may be purchased in bulk for promotional, educational, or business use. Please contact your local bookseller or the Macmillan Corporate and Premium Sales Department at 1-800-221-7945, ext. 5442, or by email at MacmillanSpecialMarkets@macmillan.com.

Printed in the United States of America

St. Martin's Paperbacks edition / January 2023

10 9 8 7 6 5 4 3 2 1

Dedicated to the wildland firefighters who risk their lives to protect the wild spaces along the Rogue, and throughout Oregon's vast forestland.

Chapter One

They say that family can be more than our family of origin—that family can also be found. I had found my family in the foothills of the Siskiyou Mountains where I'd spent the last few years carving out a new home and a new future in my childhood town of Ashland, Oregon. My small family of Mom and me had expanded dramatically. Carlos, my husband, had recently joined me in the Rogue Valley and his son, Ramiro, was taking a year away from his studies in Spain to do an exchange program here in Ashland.

It felt like an abundance of riches to have Ramiro with us for an entire year. And as if my heart weren't already overflowing, my circle had expanded to include so many more people whom I adored. Like Doug, aka The Professor, Mom's husband, who had become a second father to me. There was my best friend, Lance, my childhood friend Thomas, and his wife, Kerry. Plus, there was my entire team at the bakeshop. Sometimes it was hard to remember how small I'd made myself on the *Amour of the Seas*, the cruise ship that had taken me from one far-off port of call to the next. Ironically, even though Ashland could hardly be considered a major city, my network of friends and family continued to grow, like a rising yeasty bread dough spilling over the top of a metal bowl.

Bread had been on my mind as of late. After a full summer of baking and traveling, we were settling into the shifting seasons. Carlos and I had flown to Spain to pick up Ramiro for the start of his summer holidays. From there we ventured to Italy for two weeks with Mom and the Professor and Lance and his paramour, Arlo. It had been the stuff of dreams and the vacation I hadn't realized I had desperately needed. Carlos surprised me at the Trevi Fountain with a new ring to symbolize our recommitment to each other. Our travels took us to the lapis waters of Lake Como, wine tasting at old-world vineyards in Tuscany, and all of the historical sites in Rome. Seeing Italy through Ramiro's eyes had been an utter delight. We ate way too much gelato, devoured pasta, and drank copious amounts of espresso. For fourteen days, my mind wasn't filled with recipes or staff schedules. I checked out in the best possible way, savoring the time together with the people I loved.

On the flight home, as my head had fallen on Carlos's shoulder, he had whispered in my ear, "Julieta, you are more relaxed than I have ever seen you. Let's make a pact to get away more often, sí?"

"Yes," I had replied as my eyes fought to stay open. "You'll get no argument from me on that." It was true. Since I had returned home to Ashland, I hadn't had much of a break. I'd been so focused on Torte, our family bakeshop, my staff, and managing our other endeavors—our boutique winery, Uva, and summer pop-up ice cream shop, Scoops—that I hadn't taken time for myself. Italy had changed that. It had served as a reminder that I needed to take my own advice. I was constantly checking in with my team to make sure that they were practicing good self-care, but I didn't afford myself the same grace. When we returned to Ashland, I made a pact to change that. Even if it was a quick getaway to the coast or a weekend trip to San Francisco, Carlos and I needed to preserve time for ourselves. Time to recharge in order to be fully present for our customers and staff.

Don't forget that promise, Jules, I told myself on an early September morning as I arranged yeast, sugar, flour, and salt on Torte's expansive kitchen island.

We had been home from our vacation for just under a month and Ramiro was starting school tomorrow. I couldn't believe how fast summer had flown by. It was probably because we had soaked up the time together, taking Ramiro on day trips to the Oregon Coast, Crater Lake, and the mountains.

Now it was time for routines again. School for Ramiro and baking for me. Torte had been hired to cater a corporate event that was quickly turning into much more work than I had originally anticipated. It had begun with a call from Miller Redding, a personal assistant—or as he called himself, a PA—for Bamboo, a tech company from Los Angeles. He had reached out to me before we left for Spain and Italy about the potential of hosting an event in Ashland in September. His boss had tasked him with finding a venue and caterer for Bamboo's annual corporate leadership retreat. Ashland and Torte were at the top of his list, thanks to Arlo.

Arlo was the interim managing director of the Oregon

Shakespeare Festival (OSF) and Lance's boyfriend. Apparently, Bamboo had been a corporate sponsor at the last theater company Arlo had managed in LA. Miller hadn't taken much convincing. He flew up for a long weekend in early August and signed a contract on the spot for Torte to cater a "lit" (his word, not mine) corporate retreat.

The leadership team would arrive on Friday. We were hosting a dinner here at the bakeshop for them that evening. Then we would head to the Rogue River, where we would prepare meals while the team went on a rafting trip. Miller had arranged for glamping yurts and a full kitchen to be set up at the campsite on the banks of the Rogue River. We would be responsible for breakfast, lunch, dinner, and snacks for the weekend rafting trip. I had catered plenty of off-site events over the years, but this was going to be a new challenge: creating high-quality, artisan fare over open flames and on camp stoves.

My team had helped sketch out menus. The goal was to prep as much as we could at Torte, like bread that could be sliced for decadent raft sandwiches and breakfast French toast, as well as cookies, pies, and brownies that we could bake ahead and pack into camp. It was a bummer that the event was coinciding with Ramiro's first week of American high school. He had promised me that it was no big deal.

"Jules, I will come for the weekend when school is out and go tubing in the river. The Professor says he will teach me how to raft. It will still be warm, yeah?"

"It should be. September is my favorite month for weather," I had told him. "Warm days and cool evenings with a touch of a breeze and the first hints of changing leaves. Yes, it will be perfect for floating the river."

The Rogue River had been deemed a Wild & Scenic River in the 1960s. The vast wilderness canyon was known for its breathtakingly rugged scenery, salmon runs, and whitewater rafting. Adventure seekers like the group from Bamboo could raft the upper sections of the river and get their adrenaline pumping with some class III and IV rapids. But there were also plenty of lazy spots on the river for floating in inner tubes, swimming, and fly fishing. It was the perfect opportunity for both solitude and team bonding.

Having Ramiro come with us for the weekend sounded like an ideal compromise.

With that thought in mind, I turned my attention to bread. I had been the first to arrive at the bakeshop this morning and had already gone through the opening checklist—lighting the bundles of applewood in the wood-fired oven, setting the other ovens to proofing temps, and most importantly starting a strong pot of our Torte signature fall roast.

I tied on one of our custom fire-engine red aprons with blue stitching and a chocolate torte in the center. Not only did I want to get a head start on our bread orders for the day, but I intended to use a few loaves to test sandwich recipes for the weekend and for Ramiro's first day of school lunch. Okay, I was probably going a little overboard with packing a lunch for a high schooler, but this was my first time being a stepmom (a term I was not a fan of, by the way) and I wanted to do everything in my power to make sure that Ramiro knew this was his home, too.

Once the kitchen had hummed to life, I started the bread dough by pitching yeast, adding a touch of sugar, and warm water, but not too warm. If the water temp is too high the yeast will start to die off. And no one wants a dead yeast.

While the yeast began to bubble, I measured flour. One tip that I always taught new staff members was to measure flour with a spoon. Most home bakers tend to scoop flour with a measuring cup, which doesn't give a precise measurement and can lead to packing too much flour in the cup. Instead, I would demonstrate how to spoon flour into our large measuring cups and then level the top with the edge of a knife. This would ensure a proper reading and not alter the recipe with too little or too much flour.

Once my yeast had doubled in size, I added flour and a touch of sea salt and set the mixture to knead in our industrial mixer with a dough hook. Trust me, I love to knead dough with my hands. I've found that one of the best ways to work out life's stresses—literally and figuratively—is by getting your hands deep in the dough. But sometimes on busy days, like today, letting the mixer do the heavy lifting had its advantages.

My first batch of bread was our classic white bread. I would form the dough into loaves and brush them with a generous amount of melted butter and a dusting of sea salt before they baked in the pizza oven.

Andy, our resident barista turned expert coffee roaster, arrived as I shifted my attention to sourdough and honey wheat bread.

"Morning, boss." He took off his puffy vest and hung it on the coat rack near the basement door. His youthful face was bright with energy. Andy was an anomaly. Most of his peers would be in bed until noon. I knew that like me he'd probably already been up for an hour tinkering with his latest coffee roast. "You can tell that fall is on the horizon. It's getting chilly out there in the morning."

"I know; I love it." I shot him a grin.

"Same." He lifted a canister of beans he had brought from home. "You're really going to love my new roast."

"What is it?" I strummed my fingers together in anticipation.

"I haven't landed on the name yet but think of it as an ode to September." He swept his muscular arms toward the basement door. "If September could be a coffee, this is it."

"Ohhh, I can't wait to try it."

"Give me ten minutes and I'll have a taste ready for you." Andy motioned above us. He had finally grown into his height. When I had first met him, he used to walk around in a permanent slump, but as he had matured his posture had, too. It was nice to see him transforming and becoming a more confident version of himself.

He went upstairs to fire up the espresso machine and prep the coffee bar. I brushed flour from my hands and adjusted my ponytail. As I placed racks of bread in the oven to proof, I reflected on how much Andy had grown since I'd known him. He'd gone from being a slightly goofy college student to a mature young man who had a pulse on the latest trends in the coffee industry and an innate ability to create delicate and intricately flavored roasts.

The rest of the team trickled in slowly over the next hour. Marty, our resident bread expert, ambled over to my workstation after he had washed his hands and tied on a fire-engine red Torte apron.

"Uh-oh, is there something you need to tell me, Jules?" His bright cheeks matched the apron. Marty was in his sixties with silver hair, a gray well-trimmed beard, and eyes that had experienced plenty of sorrow yet still held a bright spark of joy.

"No, why?" I wrinkled my forehead and looked up from the next batch of dough I had started.

"I was worried I'm going to be out of a job." He pointed to the loaves resting on the island. "After all, you're baking my bread."

I let my mouth hang open and shook my head. "Never. No way. This place would crumble without you. I was just trying to get a head start and help you out because I'm going to use some extra loaves for testing recipes for this weekend's Rogue event."

"Whew." He wiped his brow. Some of the heat faded from his face.

"Marty, seriously, you know how much I appreciate you, don't you?" I met his eyes.

He smiled and winked. "I do."

Marty had come to us after his wife died. He had been a bread baker in San Francisco and moved to the Rogue Valley to be closer to family. A fortuitous ad placed at the right time had brought him out of semi-retirement and to us. I'd never been more grateful. Marty was such an asset to the team, for his bread-making skills, but also for his wisdom.

Our staff swayed younger, which was a good thing in my opinion, but Marty and Rosa, our front-of-house manager, had balanced that. I liked the mixing of ages on our team. Bethany, our social media superstar, was constantly trying to convince Marty to set up an online dating profile and he was teaching everyone how to play bocce.

"Good, because I would be lost without you, like lost out in the dense Siskiyou Forest without you." I poked my finger in the bouncy sourdough. "I will also gladly hand this dough off to you and get a batch of breakfast pastries going."

He tipped an imaginary cap. "Many thanks, my lady."

I chuckled and brushed flour from my hands.

Andy appeared from upstairs carrying a tray of coffee tasters. "All right, who's ready for some morning Joe?"

"Me." I raised my hand. "Always me."

Andy passed samples around to Marty, Steph, Bethany, Sterling, Rosa, and me. Then he stood back and appraised us like a zoologist studying animals in the wild. "Okay, be honest. It's a brand-new roast, so don't hold back. Give me the truth."

"What are we drinking?" Sterling held his taster beneath his nose.

"It's a bourbon, pecan Torte blend with touches of caramel and low acidity. It should be sweet with a full body." He motioned for us to try it. "That's why I want your honest opinions, though. I'm not sure if I need to tweak it a bit. Maybe add more nuttiness? Spike up the dark notes?"

I took a sip of the roast. As promised, it tasted like September in a cup. The pecan flavor came through first, followed by a hint of the sweet, buttery caramel. Rich bourbon undertones finished off the coffee. "This is incredible. I think you nailed it," I said to Andy.

He blew me off with a wave. "Come on, boss, I want the dirt. Give me the gritty feedback, too. Don't hold back. I can take it."

"I am." I looked at everyone else. "I swear, it's delicious. It tastes like fall. There's nothing I would change. The sweetness is balanced by the bourbon, and the pecans give it a nice earthiness."

"Agreed," Bethany chimed in. "It's my new favorite."

"Everything is your favorite." Andy gave her a fake scowl.

"That's not true," she protested. "Remember your pepper coffee? I wasn't a fan of that, and I told you it was a bit too much." She stuck out her tongue and grimaced. "So much pepper."

Andy gave her a sheepish look. "Yeah, okay. That's fair. I guess I just want this one to be a winner."

"Are you going to use it in a latte?" Steph asked. She had neatly arranged a stack of custom cake orders at her decoration station.

"I'm not sure yet. I'm going to play around with a couple of ideas," Andy replied. "I feel like this roast stands alone. It's called Ode to September and I'm not sure I want to dilute it, you know?"

Steph stared at her taster like she was examining a crime scene. "I actually saw a recipe last night for a cake with almost these exact flavors. It might be cool to try to pair this roast on its own with a slice of cake."

Bethany clapped. "Now you're speaking my language. That's the kind of stuff that goes viral on social. Let's do it."

"I'm intrigued by your recipe," I said. "I still want one more dessert option for the event this weekend."

"I'll find the recipe for you," Steph said as she tucked her violet hair behind her ears. "You bake it. I'll decorate it."

"Oh yeah, we could do something super cute for fall," Bethany agreed. "Like a luscious beige buttercream with sweet bright red and green apples and fall leaves. What do you think?"

Steph nodded. "Yep. I'm with you."

Marty had moved next to the speaker system. "Since you mentioned Ode to September, how about if we kick off the morning with some 'Ode to Joy'?"

The swelling sounds of the melody reverberated through the kitchen.

"It's settled." I finished my coffee. "We'll collaborate on a dessert to pair with your blend."

Andy grinned. "I better get brewing, then."

He went upstairs and the rest of us gathered to review the morning schedule. September brought a slight reprieve from the crush of summer tourists. The Elizabethan stayed open through the end of October, when OSF would go dark for the winter, so Ashland still saw its fair share of out-of-town visitors, but not to the same level that we experienced during the peak of summer.

"What are you thinking for today's special?" I asked Sterling. He had taken on the role of sous chef over the last couple of years and was thriving in the position. Like Andy with coffee, Sterling had a discerning palate. Food combinations came naturally to him. The only thing he lacked was professional training. Carlos, Marty, Mom, and I had all helped mentor him in that area. He was a sponge when it came to taking in knife techniques or how to mise en place. I knew that soon he would be ready to strike out on his own. I was equally excited for him and dreading the day he would come to tell me he had landed a position running his own kitchen. It was evitable in the business. If I did my job correctly, then there was a high likelihood that some of my staff would eventually grow their wings and fly away from Torte's nest.

I sighed.

Don't think about that now, Jules.

"I was thinking of a creamy tomato Parm soup with cheese tortellini," Sterling said. He had rolled up the sleeves on his hoodie, revealing a collection of tattoos that stretched across his forearm. "We can serve it with Marty's roasted garlic and herb flatbread."

"Count me in for that." I gave him a thumbs-up.

Bethany went through the list of custom cake orders, which she and Steph divided up. Rosa offered to make her grandmother's cinnamon sweet potato pastries as one of our breakfast specials. I took on our daily cookie and muffin offerings as well as the bourbon pecan torte, and Marty would be responsible for finishing each of our signature breads.

Within a few minutes the kitchen was alive with the aromas of fall and the sound of happy chatter amongst our team. I quickly fell into a calming rhythm as I whipped vanilla cake batter until it was light and fluffy. After a summer of adventure, I was lucky to be home and in the place I loved with people I adored. What could be better?

I added a healthy splash of bourbon and toasted pecans to the cake batter. Then I spread the batter into greased cake pans and placed them in the ovens to bake. While they baked to golden perfection, I started on a filling. Since Andy's roast had caramel undertones, I decided on a caramel buttercream.

For that, I would use our classic buttercream base. We made vats of French buttercream daily. I wanted to fold in caramel sauce to give it a richness. I melted butter in a saucepan and added sugar, whisking the mixture until it turned golden brown. Then I removed it from the heat and stirred in sea salt and heavy cream by hand. The caramel thickened to the point that it stuck to the back of a spoon—a telltale sign it was ready.

I folded half of it into the buttercream, turning the frosting into a glossy beige color. I reserved the rest to use between the cake layers.

When the cakes had cooled, I spread on a thin layer of the caramel, followed by chopped toasted pecans, and the caramel buttercream. I repeated the steps for all four layers. Then I frosted the entire cake with the remaining buttercream and placed it in the walk-in to firm up before Steph and Bethany put the finishing touches on it.

"Bread is ready for you, Jules," Marty said as I returned from the fridge. "How many loaves do you want before I stock the upstairs and start packaging our wholesale orders?"

"Can you spare four or five?" I asked. "I want to try a few different sandwiches and see which ones hold up the best."

"Consider these yours." Marty ran his hand over a row of bread fresh from the oven. The loaves' buttery tops glistened under the overhead lights.

"Where to start?"

"I'll leave that to you." Marty reached for a stack of our Torte paper bags and began placing loaves inside.

I went over the notes I had taken from my last call

with Miller. He had been adamant that the lunches needed to be "worthy of executives." I had asked him for clarification, but he had just repeated the statement twice and reminded me that the leadership retreat was for Bamboo's top executive team, who were used to the finer things in life. "It cannot be bougie enough, understood?" he had repeated at least a dozen times.

I had to ask Steph for an official definition of "bougie."

Last year their retreat took place on a private island in the Bahamas. "Think luxury. We need this to be top-of-the-line," Miller had said on our last phone call.

I had tried to reiterate that rafting and camping on the Rogue wasn't exactly the textbook definition of "luxury."

"You realize the Rogue River is pretty rustic, right?" The river was one of the most gorgeous places on the planet, in my humble opinion, but it was hardly glamorous. A haven for backpackers and adventure seekers, yes. But a luxurious escape, not so much.

He had scoffed. "Listen, what I'm trying to tell you is that I need you to impress this executive team. They're used to the very best. Soggy tuna sandwiches or basic peanut butter and jelly aren't going to cut it. I hired you because I was assured that you can elevate food. I saw the photos of the park wedding you catered, and Arlo has been telling me that you're the best in town, but I cannot stress enough that no detail or expense can be spared. Got it?"

We could definitely elevate food. That was my mission in life, but the problem was that Miller would be arriving with the team. There wasn't time to do a traditional tasting and get his feedback and make any adjustments. I had been emailing him sample menus with photos, but it wasn't the same as having a client sit down and actually taste the dishes we were preparing.

After much back-and-forth, we had settled on dinner for the first night. We would be serving a distinctly Northwest spread—a pear and Gorgonzola salad, grilled salmon served with hazelnut rice, and marionberry cobbler for dessert. Dinner on the second day would be prepared at the campsite. For that we had landed on a cowboy cookout with an assortment of sausages on handmade sourdough buns, rosemary and bacon baked beans, herb and butter grilled corn on the cob, pasta salad, and chocolate chip skillet cookies with scoops of our vanilla bean concrete on top. Breakfast would be French toast over the campfire with late summer berries, spicy egg and black bean burritos, and a fruit salad.

It was just lunch on the river that we were still trying to finalize. The main challenge was that the lunches needed to be packed because they would be taken on the rafts in coolers. At some point the river guides would steer the boats to shore and let everyone stretch their legs and take a lunch break before continuing downriver to the campsite. I wanted to make sure the lunch fare was hearty but also up to Miller's high standards.

Today I was trying a third attempt at a chicken hazelnut salad sandwich with dried cranberries, tart apples, and celery. I wanted to serve it on our grain wheat bread. Then for a simpler, yet elegant, option we would do a French ham and cheese on sourdough, and finally a chickpea and sweet pepper sandwich on our honey wheat. Along with the sandwiches, we were going to pack oranges, bags of kettle chips, mini carrots, and our giant cookies and brownies.

"It's like grown-up lunch boxes, Jules," Bethany said as she peered over my shoulder.

"Good, because I'm going to send one of these to school with Ramiro tomorrow," I replied with a grin. "I need him to report back on whether or not the bread gets soggy from the chicken salad."

"Oh, that's adorable." Her dimples creased as she smiled. Bethany was our in-house cheerleader. Her upbeat attitude made it nearly impossible to be in a bad mood around her. I appreciated her authenticity. It was never a forced joy with her; it was simply her easygoing style that rubbed off on everyone. Additionally, she was an incredible baker in her own right. Mom and I had brought her on after discovering her Unbeatable Brownies at a chocolate fest. She continued to bake daily brownies for Torte, along with teaming up with Steph for custom cake designs.

"As long as he doesn't get stuffed in a locker for bringing a packed lunch," I teased.

Bethany laughed. "I highly doubt that. I'm pretty sure that's an eighties movie thing. I don't think that happens anymore."

"Whew." I pretended to wipe my brow. To help protect the slices I placed romaine lettuce between the bread and the chicken salad mixture. I also made sure to let the chicken salad chill completely before scooping it on the sandwiches.

I had Bethany take some shots of our school box lunches for social media and for me to email to Miller. They would go on today's special board, too. As always, I was sure our faithful customers would give us constructive feedback on their favorites.

"I'll head upstairs and add these to the chalkboard," I said to her. After a quick check on how things were going in the main dining area, I went to my office to send a final email to Miller. Assuming the chicken salad held up well, I felt confident we had finally landed on a menu. It might not be Michelin-star worthy, but it was going to taste delicious and fit the brief for a picnic on the banks of the upper Rogue.

Miller responded right away, but not through email. My phone rang mere minutes after I had hit SEND.

I recognized his number. "Hey, great minds think alike. I just sent you an email."

"I know. I read it." His voice was like he was on the brink of a panic attack.

"Is everything okay? How does the lunch menu sound? Like I mentioned, we're going to do a less than scientific poll today with our customers."

"It's fine. It's fine." His tone was dismissive.

"Okay." What was his deal?

"That's not why I'm calling."

My stomach dropped. I hoped he wasn't calling to tell me that the event had been canceled. We had spent two weeks preparing for this weekend, and I already had four fillets of salmon on order.

"Some stuff is going down here, if you know what I mean."

"No, I don't know what you mean."

He sighed, then lowered his voice. "Look, I can't talk right now, but let's just say that there is a lot of drama at the moment, and I need you to assure me that everything is going to be perfect when we arrive on Friday. I'm going to be tied up with other business and can't afford to have to worry about any catering details."

Miller was probably in his late twenties. I'm not always the best judge of age, but when he'd come to Ashland for our initial meeting, I guessed him to be mid- to late twenties.

He was talking as if I were a child, or this was the first time I had ever catered an event.

I tried to keep my tone calm and professional. "Understood. I wouldn't expect anything otherwise."

"Good. I'm glad we're on the same page. I don't have the bandwidth to worry about cookies and sandwiches. Bamboo is imploding and right now I'm the only person attempting to keep it together."

I wanted to ask more, but he ended our conversation abruptly.

"Look, I have to go. I'll be there at four sharp on Friday. You'll have exactly thirty minutes of my time."

I stared at the phone after he hung up. I wanted to give him the benefit of the doubt. He was working in a high-stress environment, after all. Hopefully once he arrived in Ashland, he would be able to relax and soak in some of the Rogue Valley's low-key vibe.

But what did he mean that Bamboo was imploding?

I wasn't looking forward to spending a long weekend on the river with a dysfunctional team, and I didn't like the sound of a company imploding. What had I gotten us into?

Chapter Two

My alarm blared early the next morning. Typically I don't need an alarm to wake up before the sun. Blame it on years of working bakers' hours, but this was a monumental occasion—Ramiro's first day of high school in the US. I silenced my alarm.

"Are you awake?" I scooted closer to Carlos and nudged his arm.

Carlos rolled over and brushed a strand of dark hair from his eyes. "How could I not be with that terrible sound? Why don't you have something kinder to wake up to, Julieta?"

I chuckled. "What do you suggest?"

"Anything but that." He sat up and blinked hard, like he was trying to force his eyes to function. "You know Ramiro does not need to leave for nearly two hours."

"I know, but I want to pack him a lunch and make him breakfast before I go." I rubbed my hands together and bit my bottom lip. "I feel like it's my first day. I'm so excited that he's going to get to follow in my footsteps and be a Grizzly for a year."

Carlos reached out for me and pulled me into his

arms. He kissed me slowly. "This is why I love you. You are too good to him. He's almost fully grown, you know. I think you will end up spoiling him."

"I'm okay with that. I'd rather spoil him than end up with the title of horrible stepmother." I shuddered.

"You could never be a horrible stepmother." Carlos reached for my hand and caressed it. His fingers were callused from long days spent tending the grapevines. "And I am not really worried about Ramiro getting a big head."

"Seriously, that could never happen. He's the best kid ever. I'm not even biased," I teased before leaving him with a kiss. I got dressed in a pair of jeans, a T-shirt, and a sweatshirt. Layering was necessary for September. It was chilly now, but by later this afternoon, it was supposed to be warm in the low seventies. I tied my long blond hair in my typical work fashion of a ponytail and applied lotion and lip gloss.

Carlos followed me downstairs. He was dressed for a day in the vineyard in a pair of well-worn jeans, boots, and a buttoned-down shirt. Fine lines creased the edges of his eyes. His olive skin was naturally tan from working in the fields.

Pinkish light filtered in through the kitchen window, which offered a view of Grizzly Peak in the distance. I loved that we had made my childhood home our own with artwork and pottery from our travels around the globe, family photos, and my collection of vintage cookbooks.

Carlos brewed a pot of French press while I made a batch of chocolate chip pumpkin muffins and packed Ramiro's lunch. I had brought a container of the chicken salad home, so I layered it between butterleaf lettuce and slices of thick-cut bread. The reality was that Ramiro would probably do what most Ashland High School students did—leave campus for lunch and walk down to the grocery store for deli snacks and sodas. He might not even consume a bite of the lunch that I packed for him, but I wanted him to feel welcome and ready to tackle his first day of school in a foreign country and the best way I knew how was through food. My point of connection has always been through baking. Blame it on growing up in Torte's kitchen and my parents' deep affection for infusing everything they baked with love.

"Coffee?" Carlos poured dark French roast into a warmed mug.

"Is that even a question?" I mixed oil, sugar, eggs, vanilla, pumpkin purée, a trio of spices, baking powder, and flour by hand. Then I folded in chocolate chips, after coating them with flour. It was a trick I had learned in culinary school. Dusting chocolate chips or blueberries (anything that was being added to a cake or muffin batter) with flour ensured that they wouldn't sink to the bottom of the muffin or cake pans. There's nothing worse than a soggy mess of chocolate chips on the bottom of a muffin.

The batter came together easily. I scooped it into muffin tins and placed them in the oven to bake for twelve to fifteen minutes.

Carlos stirred his coffee and massaged the side of his eye with his index finger. "I still do not understand how you wake so early and so easily. You are bright and cheery, and I must have at least three more pots of coffee before I can even form a full sentence."

"You're doing pretty well now." I added a splash of cream to my coffee. "It's muscle memory at this point in time."

"And the Capshaw genes, yes? Helen is the same."

"It's true. It's a blessing and a curse." I grinned. "You knew what you were getting into when you married a pastry chef. Don't say I didn't warn you."

His voice became husky. "Julieta, I would never need a warning about you, unless it was to guard my heart. I couldn't take losing you again."

"You don't have to worry about that."

He sat at the breakfast nook. I joined him. "After the time we spent apart, I can't think about not being together. It is so easy. With Ramiro, too." He reached for my hand and laced his fingers through mine. "Maybe soon we will be adding to our family."

"Maybe." I smiled, letting him massage my ring finger. When we had made the decision to give our marriage a second chance, we had exchanged new rings as a token of our love and our fresh start. I had opted for a simple silver band. Jewelry has no place in a commercial kitchen. I've never been a fan of fancy diamonds or sparkly rings anyway. Maybe it was from years of getting my hands sticky in dough. The clean, uncomplicated band felt like the ultimate symbol of our life in Ashland together. It might not be as dazzling or sexy as waking up at a new port of call every few days. Our new life had a permanence I had never realized I desperately needed.

A feeling of warmth spread through my body that I couldn't attribute entirely to the coffee or the heat from the oven. We sat drinking in the quiet and the view of deer and wild turkeys meandering through our backyard. I loved these stolen moments, when we didn't even need to speak but could enjoy the tenderness of a touch and simply being together.

Carlos was right. We were so lucky to have made it. For a while I never would have imagined that he would end up here, in my childhood home, with us making a new life together. Our struggles had made us stronger, and our time apart had given us the space to grow and reflect on ourselves. If you had asked me when I left him on the *Amour of the Seas,* I wouldn't have believed that spending a few years apart could lead to something this good. In hindsight, it had been such a rash decision to leave. Part of me wished that I had thought the decision through more at the time, but then again, if I had stayed maybe we wouldn't be here today. The truth was I needed space, even if I didn't understand why at the time. What I had come to learn was that I had been unhappy on the ship for a while. Carlos not telling me about Ramiro had been the excuse I needed to escape.

I used to blame my romantic tendencies on the fact that my parents had named me after one of literature's most revered romantic heroines. The name Juliet had come with extra weight, and perhaps unrealistic expectations about romantic love. What I had realized since being home was that my ideas about how love was supposed to look had shifted.

Those first days and weeks and months in Ashland when I had been trying to figure out what I was meant to do had felt so lonely. And yet Ashland had welcomed me in, nestled me in, and allowed me the gift of learning who I really was—flaws and all.

Ashland had changed me. Or maybe I had changed myself. Either way, I was so grateful for where we were now.

The oven timer dinged, signaling that my muffins were done. I broke the meditation of our morning coffee and went to get them from the oven.

"Oh, that smell is wonderful." Carlos used his free hand to waft the aroma to his nose. "Your muffins will make Ramiro stir. Who could resist the scent of warm cinnamon and nutmeg on a crisp autumn morning?"

"I thought you weren't a morning person? You're starting to sound like the Professor, waxing poetic and it's barely light outside." I glanced at the clock. I had made arrangements with the team to come in later. I wanted to be able to have time to enjoy breakfast together as a family and take Ramiro to school.

The sound of footsteps echoed overhead. My muffins had done the trick. I could hear Ramiro heading for the shower.

Carlos refilled my coffee. I removed the muffins from their tins and set them on the counter to cool. Muffins and cupcakes will continue to bake in their containers, so it's imperative to remove them from any additional heat immediately.

"Should I cook some eggs and potatoes to go with your muffins?" Carlos asked.

"How hungry do you think Ramiro will be?"

"It is a mystery." Carlos threw his hands up.

We both laughed. I had yet to figure out Ramiro's eating habits. Some days he devoured everything in sight. He was like a goat given free rein over the sweet, juicy blackberry bushes that grew wild throughout the neighborhood. On other days he would barely eat anything. I supposed that was the challenge of being a growing teenager. I was learning to keep the fridge and pantry stocked (not a skill I was used to after years of working on the ship and living by myself).

"I think eggs and potatoes are a good way to start a school year, sí?" Carlos got up from the table and made his way to the stove.

I wouldn't turn down a breakfast scramble.

While Carlos diced garlic, onions, and peppers and chopped rustic potatoes, I took a minute to check my email. Besides not having my own kitchen to keep stocked when I was working on the ship, I had also missed the digital revolution. Cell service at sea had been spotty at best. It was only in the last couple of years that I had broken down and joined the world of social media. Bethany in particular, as well as the rest of my team, had practically forced me to get with the times. I was glad that she had taken on the role of styling photos for Torte's social channels. Baking was my happy place.

I scanned my emails and noticed five messages from Miller, two marked "urgent."

"Oh no," I said out loud.

Carlos stopped chopping. "What is it?"

"This client." I told him about my phone call with Miller. "Bamboo sounds like a dumpster fire. It's an endless sea of requests that make Lance's extravagant productions seem like high school theater."

"That isn't good. And we're going to be spending a weekend with these people?" Carlos returned to his scramble.

"I'm afraid so."

"Maybe I will have to put together one of my special 'Italian' crème brûlée tastings for them." Carlos gave me a devilish grin. He was a known prankster in the kitchen. On the ship his pranks were the stuff of legend. It was all in good fun. He truly believed that a happy kitchen impacted the food.

One of his go-to tricks was to serve a mayonnaise crème brûlée to new sous chefs and line cooks on their first day in the kitchen. He used to swap the cream in the classic dessert for a hearty scoop of mayo and then sit back to watch the reactions when his new recruits took a bite.

Somehow I didn't think that Miller would find much humor in that prank.

I read Miller's messages. He wanted a detailed ingredient list for each recipe so that he could provide that to any of the sensitive eaters in the group, which was absolutely fair and reasonable. We always made accommodations and went out of our way to make sure that any of our customers with food allergies or sensitivities were well cared for. However, I'd already sent him the ingredient lists—three times. He also requested two additional desserts for the campfire dinner. Speaking of teenagers, how much were these executives planning to eat?

Miller's email spelled out that Josie Jones, the owner and CEO of Bamboo, was extremely unimpressed with the menu. According to Miller, she found our offerings to be "pedestrian" and wanted to glitter things up a bit. I wasn't sure how to "glitter" our food, short of edible sprinkles, and it was too late. We'd solidified the menu, and preordered specialty ingredients. I hadn't met Josie yet, but given the way Miller talked about her, I wasn't exactly looking forward to it.

"I don't understand what they want," I said to Carlos as I sipped my coffee. "Miller insisted that they wanted a 'rustic cookout vibe'—his words exactly—but they also want it to be elegant, high-end, and *not* bougie. We're grilling everything over an outdoor fire. I'm not sure how that translates to high-end or glittery."

"This is ridiculous. Food is about the flavors and how it is prepared. Yes, presentation is important, too, but everything Torte creates is made with love. This comes through. What exactly is an elegant cookout?" Color rose in his olive skin as he spoke.

"Your guess is as good as mine. Honestly, I think they're impossible to please. I'm beginning to regret saying yes to this event and dreading this weekend."

"Do not worry. It will be fine." Carlos poured olive oil into a cast-iron skillet.

"I hope so." I sighed as I read through the rest of Miller's emails.

Ramiro joined us shortly. He was dressed in a pair of tapered khakis with a graphic T-shirt. He looked like a younger version of his dad. They had the same dark hair, mischievous eyes, and natural confidence.

"Good morning. You look ready for high school. How are you feeling?" I asked.

"So strong." He flexed and then grinned. "No, I'm good. Excited and maybe nervous."

"That's totally normal," I assured him. Then I patted the chair next to me. "Come sit. I made muffins."

"I smelled them upstairs." Ramiro's dimples became more pronounced when he smiled. "You didn't need to make muffins for me."

"I wanted to. It's your first day in a new school." I pointed to the French press. "Coffee?"

"Sí, thank you."

I poured him a cup. When I had met Ramiro the first time, I couldn't get over the fact that he drank espresso and knew more about food than some of the pastry chefs I had trained on the ship. Then again, it shouldn't have surprised me. Food was in his DNA.

"Soccer practice is after school, right?" I handed him a cup of coffee and a muffin.

"Yes. The coach said it should be an hour or two, but I will text when it's done."

"One of us can pick you up," I offered.

"It is only a few blocks. I can walk." He brushed his dark hair, which matched his dad's, from his eye. He wore his hair slightly longer, so it swept across one side of his face.

I appreciated Ramiro's independence. It reminded me of me. Growing up in a small town like Ashland had provided me with plenty of freedom. I was glad that Ramiro would get to experience that, too. He was already self-sufficient and cultured and now he would have a chance to embrace small-town life in our little remote corner of southern Oregon.

"The coach is going to do backflips when he discovers your skills." I took a seat next to him and helped myself to a muffin.

"Jules, you are too biased. I don't know if I will even be able to earn a role as a starter. I am new."

"And you're an amazing soccer player and all-around kid." I paused. "Sorry, young man."

Ramiro made a face. "You sound like my mom."

"Your mom is a smart woman." I peeled the wrapper from my muffin. "How is she? Did you get a chance to Facetime with her yesterday?"

"Sí. She is good. She says to tell you hi and they are seriously considering coming next month."

"That would be great." I meant it. When Carlos and I had separated, I had been blindsided by the fact that he had a son. It wasn't that I was upset that he had a child; it was that he hadn't told me. But once I had calmed down, gotten some space and distance, and really opened my heart, I realized that he had his reasons for keeping me in the dark. The pregnancy had been unexpected. Ramiro's mom had discovered that she was pregnant after they had broken up and Carlos had taken the job on the ship. She had kept the news from him. Her family hadn't approved of their relationship, and she had decided that the best option was for her to raise Ramiro on her own.

Fortunately, things had changed. She had grown, too. We all had. We'd become a modern, blended family and I had genuinely enjoyed getting to know Ramiro's mom, younger sister, and stepfather on our weekly Facetime calls.

"Maybe they can come for Halloween," I suggested. "The costume parade is so much fun."

"I will check." Ramiro finished his muffin and went in for a second.

Carlos set steaming plates of his breakfast scramble in front of us.

"Thanks, I could get used to this." Ramiro gave his dad a twisted smile as he stabbed the potatoes and eggs with his fork.

Carlos ruffled his hair. "Do not get used to it. Tomorrow it is toast and jam for you."

Ramiro smoothed his hair back into place. "And coffee, sí?"

"Always coffee." I held my cup in a toast.

We finished breakfast and gave Ramiro time to gather his things. The high school was just down the hill, across the street from the campus of Southern Oregon University. Usually on a sunny September morning like this, I would walk to Torte. Honeydew-hued morning light illuminated the waxy oaks and giant sequoias as we drove down Mountain Avenue.

"You can drop me off here." Ramiro pointed to the corner across the street from the high school campus.

"But we can take you to the parking lot," Carlos said, staring at him in the rearview mirror.

"No, no. This is fine. I will walk."

I caught Carlos's eye. "I think he's right. It's not cool to show up with your parents anymore, right?"

Ramiro grinned. "I didn't say that." He opened the door and blew us kisses. "Thank you for the ride. See you later." He was out of the car in one quick, fluid motion. I watched him mingle with a group of kids who were about to cross the street. I felt a swirl of nerves in my stomach for him as he introduced himself.

"He's so brave," I said to Carlos. "Look at how confident he is."

We watched as he vanished into the pack of students chatting happily as they embarked on their first day.

"I think he's going to be just fine," I said, pulling my gaze away.

Carlos turned onto Siskiyou Boulevard with one last glance toward Ramiro. "Sí, I know. I hope he has fun."

"He will," I assured him. "It's Ashland. He'll be a hot commodity. New blood. A Spanish exchange student, who's handsome, kind, and intelligent, like his father. We're going to have to stock up the pantry and fridge. I have a feeling our house is soon to be invaded by packs of hungry teens."

"I hope so." Carlos kept his eyes on the road as we waited at the crosswalk for more students and a family of deer to pass. "It would be nice to be the place where his friends gather. I want to take in this year with him."

"There is one easy way to ensure that will happen," I said with assurance.

"What is that?"

"Food." I smiled. "Lots and lots of food."

He laughed as we drove along Main Street. Both sides of the street were lined with glossy oak trees and vintage cottages with large porches and grassy lawns.

I changed the subject as we continued toward the plaza. The neighborhood shifted into Elizabethan-style businesses with half-timbered siding. "How soon do you think the grapes will be ready for harvest?"

"It feels like it is going to be soon. I check them every day. The volunteer list is ready to go and maybe we can pay Ramiro and any of his new friends to come harvest, too."

"That's a great idea. I'll make muffins and coffee for the morning shift, and we can order pizza for lunch for the volunteers." I couldn't believe it was almost time to harvest the grapes at Uva. Carlos had put every ounce of his soul into tending the vineyard this past year, and I was eager to see the results of his labor of love.

Harvest in the Rogue Valley was always a frenzy as vineyards and pear orchards vied for help with picking the season's bounty. At Uva, our boutique organic vineyard, we had made harvest a party of sorts every year. Volunteers arrived at the vineyard at daybreak to pick rows and rows of Cab Franc and merlot grapes. We provide gloves, special scissors, and plenty of coffee and food. No volunteer left empty-handed. We sent them home with bottles of wine and packages of Torte cookies.

Suddenly a thought invaded. "I hope harvest doesn't line up with this weekend's event."

"I don't think it will," Carlos replied. "My guess is that it will be next week, but we will have to wait and see what the grapes say."

He pulled in front of Torte. "I will come by later and go over the final menu with Sterling, okay?"

"Sounds good. Enjoy the vines."

I left him with a kiss.

Torte's cheery front windows brought a smile to my face. Our red and blue awning had been freshly washed. Rosa and Steph had decked out the front windows with a vintage camping display for the Bamboo event. A canvas tent had been constructed in the center of the window. Its flaps were tied back with pretty pale green gingham ribbons to reveal its interior. Inside the tent was a flameless birchwood fire surrounded by cushy pillows and rolled-up sleeping bags. They had set a delicious scene on a log stump, used for a dining table with thermoses of hot chocolate, s'mores, a rustic apple pie, and camp mugs and plates. Bunches of wildflowers, a large rug, and glowing lanterns completed the look.

I snapped a couple of pictures to text Miller. If he was looking for rustic elegance, our window display was the only proof he needed that my team was up to the task.

I headed inside, feeling a sense of momentary calm. Ramiro was off to school; Carlos had his eye on harvest at the vineyard, which meant I could focus on baking and prepping for a weekend on the Rogue.

My calm was short-lived. When I stepped inside, Andy waved me over to the espresso counter.

"Morning, boss. They need you downstairs ASAP. Apparently, Miller's been calling all morning. He's on his way here now."

"From LA?"

Andy handed me a cup of coffee. "I guess."

I took the drink and went downstairs. Miller had texted me a couple of hours ago. Why would he be on his way to Torte days before his event? I had a bad feeling that I was in way over my head with Bamboo and about to regret it.

Chapter Three

As it turned out, Miller and his boss Josie showed up later in the afternoon, a full three days before the Bamboo retreat. Needless to say, not only had my moment of temporary Zen vanished, but my plan for a leisurely day of baking and prepping for the weekend had as well.

I was putting the finishing touches on a batch of bear claws when Rosa peered into the kitchen. "Jules, sorry to interrupt, but the clients are here." She raised her eyebrows twice and motioned upstairs. Rosa was one of our more recent hires, who had quickly become invaluable to me and the team. She had a calming, centered presence that put everyone she met at ease. She also had incredible baking talent and an eye for design, which meant that she and Steph often paired up to dress our front window display and decorate for our Sunday Suppers.

"Got it." I took off my apron.

"I put them in a window booth and Andy is making them coffee," Rosa said.

"I'll be right up." I smoothed my ponytail and took a deep breath. Why they had shown up three days early was a mystery to me, and I had a bad feeling that it wasn't to take in the sights.

I recognized Miller right away. He was in his mid-twenties with short hair, hipster glasses, and contagious nervous energy. Josie wore all black leather—skintight leather pants, four-inch heels, and a leather jacket. She barely acknowledged me when I went to join them.

"Welcome to Ashland," I said, extending my hand.

Miller stood and offered a sweaty palm. "We couldn't wait. There's so much to go over." He looked to Josie, who rolled her eyes.

I took a seat next to him and waited for him to introduce us. Since he didn't, I took it on myself. "I'm Jules Capshaw, owner of Torte. We're excited to have you here."

She took a minute to give me a once-over and then let out a bored sigh. "I was under the impression this was an artisan bakeshop."

"We *are* an artisan bakeshop. Everything you see in the pastry cases is made by hand with locally sourced ingredients."

Andy arrived with two lattes. "Here you go. The Torte classic."

"One of these should be skinny with oat milk," Josie said, going out of her way to avoid eye contact with anyone.

"That's right." Andy nodded.

"I ordered the same as you," Miller jumped in with a reply.

"Oh God, you're such a suck-up." Josie shook her head in disgust and took one of the drinks.

"Do you need anything else?" Andy looked at me.

"No, I've got it from here. Thanks."

Miller reached for his satchel and pulled out an iPad. "We've got a lot to go over here; should we dive right in?"

"Please." I nodded.

He scrolled through his notes. Josie sipped her latte and stared out the window. "This place is much, much smaller than I was led to believe. I thought the Shakespeare campus was going to be more impressive."

"Have you already made it up to OSF?" I asked.

"Not yet," Miller answered for her. "That's on our agenda later. We need to firm up details for our theater experience once we return from the rafting trip and our wine-tasting tour."

"Rafting. Seriously, rafting." Josie practically spit out the words.

Miller flinched. "You said you wanted adventure."

She scoffed in response and muttered something under her breath that I couldn't make out.

"I think you and your team are really going to fall in love with the Rogue Valley. *The New York Times* did a piece a few months ago about how this region is the new Napa. I'm sure you'll be in good hands with Lance, the artistic director at OSF, too. I know my team has been working around the clock on the campout menu and Friday's welcome dinner." I tried to keep my tone light and upbeat, but it was challenging given the daggers Josie was shooting at Miller.

"Yes, about the menu." Miller tried to refocus, but I noticed he was having trouble working the iPad, probably because his hands were sweaty. "We're going to need to go over each recipe, item by item, right, Josie?"

She ran her fingers through her long brown hair like she was posing for a photo shoot. "Yep."

"No problem. You two sit tight. Let me go get my notes and we can dive in."

As it turned out, Miller and Josie had a problem with everything, from the menu to the itinerary for their trip. I never imagined that campout cookie skillets could take up so much headspace and result in dozens of minor changes. Josie insisted on tasting twenty different varieties of chocolate chips until we finally landed on classic semi-sweet chips, my first suggestion. She sent Miller running all over Ashland for swatches of picnic tablecloths and miniature floral bouquets for her official seal of approval. It was as if we were hosting the President of the United States and the cabinet, not a high-tech company for a corporate retreat.

I quickly regretted my decision to take Bamboo on as a client. I spent the next three days trying to appease Miller and Josie and keep them out of the kitchen. By the time Friday finally rolled around my nerves were frayed, as were the nerves of the rest of the team. I couldn't wait to get out to the Rogue to give my staff some breathing room. Miller had made it a habit of popping downstairs every day to check on progress and request new tastings. He was worse than the handful of bridezillas we'd had over the years. Josie was less intrusive. She tended to camp out upstairs and make disparaging comments about the bakeshop and Ashland in general.

My team was usually pretty chill, but they had reached their breaking point as well.

"What is wrong with those two?" Sterling asked as he chopped fresh rosemary and thyme. "They've been lurking for days, and for no reason. Marty's threatening to break out his wooden spoon and swat them out of the kitchen. Steph might take it a step further and whip out her pastry knife. Miller and Josie are killing the vibe in here. Do they not understand this is a professional kitchen?"

"I've asked them at least a hundred times." I had sighed, and tossed my hands up. "I don't know what else to do. This is the first time in my career that I've regretted having an open kitchen design. I told Carlos last night that you guys might need to build a temporary barricade."

Sterling tossed a dish towel over his shoulder. "Don't sweat it. We can handle it. It's just annoying."

"One more day," I said, but that wasn't really true, at least not for me. Tonight was the team dinner and then I had two days on the river with the Bamboo executives. "Unless you want to trade? You can do the event and I'll stay and manage the bakeshop."

"Nope. No way. You couldn't pay me enough to spend two more days with those self-important . . ." Sterling trailed off as he tried to come up with a safe-for-work term to describe Josie and Miller. "You know what I mean."

If they had managed to get under Sterling's skin, then I knew the remainder of the weekend wasn't exactly going to feel like a vacation.

Somehow we had managed to get through the last three days without injury or violence. As long as tonight went smoothly, we should be out of the woods. Or maybe "into the woods" was the better phrase.

I glanced at the clock; it was nearing four. The kitchen smelled divine. Marty pulled loaves of herbed focaccia from the oven. Sterling finished chopping rosemary for the salmon, which we would grill right before serving. Bethany forked butter and sugar together for the base of the marionberry cobblers.

"We're still baking these in individual ramekins, right, Jules?" she asked as she added cinnamon to the crumbly mixture.

"Yes." One of the sticking points in our conversations with Miller and Josie had been on tonight's dessert. Neither of them had been convinced that cobbler was an "elevated" dessert. Then they had tasted our marionberry cobbler, served hot and bubbling with a hearty scoop of our vanilla bean concrete and fresh grated lemon zest.

Miller had acquiesced that the dessert was better than he had expected from a humble cobbler, but then he and Josie fought amongst themselves about how best to serve it.

I had done my best to ignore their bickering. Josie treated Miller like her personal lackey. Any idea he suggested she would immediately shoot down and often go so far as to belittle him in front of my staff and me. It wasn't my style. I believed in partnerships. Over my years running Torte I had learned as much from my team as I hoped they had learned from me.

"I thought so," Bethany replied, pulling me from my thoughts. "But then again, I feel like there were at least a thousand discussions about the cobbler."

"Yeah, that might be an understatement." I glanced toward the open door frame to make sure neither Miller nor Josie was in earshot. "If we never discuss cobbler again, I'm okay with that."

Bethany cracked up. "Hey, on that note, is there anything else we need to take care of over the weekend?"

"Not off the top of my head." I looked at the whiteboard where we kept track of custom orders, deliveries, and schedules. "You've got it all mapped out. I'm impressed as always."

Marty and Sterling would be in charge of the kitchen while we were at the river. Bethany and Steph would take the lead on cakes. Rosa was going to watch over the register and pastry cases and Andy and Sequoia would work the espresso bar. I was confident that Torte would run as smoothly with me gone as it did when I was here. Plus, the team had already helped prep the bulk of the food for the weekend event. I'd have Carlos and Ramiro with me, and Mom and the Professor were planning to come as well, which was a bonus. The Professor had paid his way through college as a rafting guide. He couldn't wait to introduce Ramiro to the Rogue's rapids.

"I'm going upstairs," I said to Bethany. On my way, I stopped in the storage area to get a box of red camping lanterns and twinkle lights that we would use to decorate the dining area for the private event.

We were closing early for the dinner party. Rosa was just flipping the sign on the front door to CLOSED.

"Time to decorate?" I asked, holding the box.

She nodded and pointed to flower arrangements waiting on the counter. "Janet delivered the flowers. She's coming back soon with the gift bags."

The flower arrangements were in the same camping theme. Janet had used ceramic retro camper vans in red and white for the vases. Each camper van was filled with poppies, succulents, and greenery.

We pushed tables together and covered them with

long white tablecloths. I set a vintage camper bouquet at each place while Rosa and Andy hung the lanterns and lights. A knock sounded on the door as I went to get a stack of plates.

It was Thomas, my high school friend and Ashland's soon-to-be lead detective.

"I come bearing gifts," he said as I let him in. "Mom needed a hand with these."

Thomas was dressed in his blue uniform, shorts, and hiking boots. He balanced armfuls of expensive camping totes. "How much money does this company have? Have you seen what's in these?"

"A lot." I took two of the totes from him.

Thomas followed me. "There are Pendleton blankets in here and every expensive piece of camping gear you can imagine. Mom says this is one of the biggest orders she's ever put together."

Janet, who owned A Rose by Any Other Name, had partnered with other businesses in the plaza for the elaborate camping tote bags for the Bamboo team. She had sourced camping totes, which were packed with items from the mountain shop, books from the bookstore, chocolates from the candy shop, and so much more. Bamboo's extravagant budget wasn't just a boon for Torte; it was great for our entire small business community. Every time I got irritated with Miller's outrageous requests, I tried to focus on the fact that Bamboo was pumping money into our economy.

"I heard they hired Lance to put on a campfire tales show tomorrow night," Thomas said, readjusting the totes. "I think I picked the wrong profession."

"Yeah, the campfire tales is a new addition this week.

But, trust me, you're in the right profession. You don't want any part of the cutthroat chaos of this group."

"Has it been that bad?" Thomas motioned to the totes. "Where should I put these?"

"Every seat gets one on the chair." I placed two totes and grabbed more from him. "And, yes. I've never seen my staff ready to stage a walkout. It's a good thing that Carlos and I are taking the lead at the river this weekend. I fear that if I brought Sterling or even Marty with me they might resort to violence."

"Geez." Thomas let out a low whistle as he began placing swag bags at each seat. "Marty is the most jovial guy I've ever met, and Sterling is the definition of chill. If these executives are getting under their skin, then I say watch your back. Tell Carlos he can borrow my badge if he needs to make a citizen's arrest while you're on the Rogue."

I laughed. "Don't give him any ideas; he just might go rogue."

Thomas set down the last bag. "That's round one. I'll go grab the rest."

"Sounds good. Where's Kerry, by the way?"

Thomas and his co-detective Kerry had recently wed at a gorgeous outdoor ceremony in Lithia Park. They had been inseparable since they returned home from their honeymoon on the *Amour of the Seas,* a wedding gift from Carlos and me.

"She and the Professor are meeting with the Chamber of Commerce to finalize the parade route for Halloween. He wants us to take charge of the event this year. We're excited, but it's a lot of pressure."

The Professor had been slowly easing his way out of

his role as Ashland's head detective. He had spent the past few years training Thomas and Kerry and shifting more and more duties their way. Mom was doing the same with the bakeshop. She was always willing to roll up her sleeves to knead bread dough or mix vats of cake batter for large orders and events, but otherwise I had encouraged her to come in as she felt like it, instead of keeping traditional hours. To my shock, she had actually listened to my advice. It was a treat for all of us when she came in to bake. She was like a second mother to everyone on the team. I noticed whenever she was in the kitchen that Andy would work his way downstairs with a latte and linger to tell her about his latest custom roast and his life plans.

"The parade is going to be even bigger this year," Thomas said as he opened the door. "You should probably start on those famous pumpkin sugar cookies as soon as you're back from the river."

"Great, add it to my list." I returned my attention to the décor. The dining room was completely transformed within the hour into camper chic. The red lanterns cast a warm glow on the dining table to highlight the rustic flowers and greenery. It was a good thing, since Miller and Josie showed up early.

I wondered if they had overheard my conversation with Thomas about the Halloween parade, because they both arrived in costume. It took me a minute to realize they had dressed for the event.

Josie wasn't wearing black for the first time in three days. Her brown hair was tied in two braids. She wore a pair of intentionally ripped jeans, hiking boots, a green flannel, and expensive tiered gold necklaces with dangling gold earrings. Miller's flannel matched hers. On closer inspection I noticed that their shirts had Bamboo's logo embroidered on the front pockets.

"Not bad. This looks pretty decent," Miller said with trepidation. His eyes didn't veer from Josie. I could almost feel his nervous energy as he waited for her reaction.

She ran a finger along the back of one of the chairs. "I'd call it quaint, but I guess it will do. We are in backwoods *Or-ee-gun*."

I would hardly call Ashland backwoods, but I let it slide.

"Can I get you a glass of wine?" I motioned to the espresso bar where bottles of our Uva wines and sparkling glasses awaited guests.

"Red." Josie took her seat at the head of the table.

"I'll take a red, too." Miller started to sit next to her, but she shooed him away.

"What do you think you're doing? You're my PA." Josie acted like Miller had assaulted her. "This seat is reserved for Gus and the other VPs. You're at the other end of the table, over there, got it."

He bobbed his head in agreement. "Right. Sorry. Sorry."

The rest of the team arrived together. They looked like they could be on a poster for team bonding in their matching flannels. They posed for pictures as I circulated with wine and Rosa brought up the appetizers.

We had decided that since I was going to be the key point person for the weekend it made sense for me to hang out upstairs and keep an eye on everything. My team would bring up the courses as needed; otherwise, they didn't need to interact much.

I tried to be discreet, staying at the far end of the pastry counter and reviewing paperwork while the Bamboo execs enjoyed the appetizers and wine.

This wasn't new territory for me, but I had a hard time keeping my face neutral as I overheard Josie's horrible treatment of her staff.

"Madeline Solars, a very interesting look you're going for tonight," Josie said with a snarl to the woman to her left. "Did you come to raid my closet, Maddy?"

Maddy tugged at a braid. "I thought we were supposed to dress alike." She bore an uncanny resemblance to Josie. The two women were about the same age with equal build and height and long brown hair. They could easily pass as sisters, if not twins.

"With our Bamboo flannels," Josie said through pressed lips. "I didn't think you would dye and cut your hair to match mine."

Gus, a short, balding guy in his late forties who was sitting next to Josie, pulled his reading glasses to the tip of his nose. "I thought you *were* Josie when you came in. I was worried that I was already seeing double and I'm only two glasses of wine in."

"Don't you mean two bottles?" Josie swirled her wineglass. "What other company has a lush for a CFO? It's a good thing you oversee our financials and not my private wine cellar. There would be nothing left."

Gus puffed out his chest. "Whatever, Josie. It's the job; you know that, and it takes a lush to know a lush."

She was about to respond when a younger woman with a short blond bob interjected, "I'm loving this look right now. Josie, can you hold your glass a bit higher, so it catches the light from the lanterns? Gus and Maddy, lean in. I want to capture this for the Gram."

"The Gram?" Gus flared one nostril. "Is that what the kids call it these days, Elisa?"

"Um, I just got promoted to marketing director, remember?" She tucked a strand of her white-blond hair behind one ear. "I'm hardly a kid. I'm an older millennial now."

"An older millennial." Josie rolled her eyes. "Isn't that precious?"

Elisa and Maddy shared a look of disdain. Josie plastered on a smile that reminded me of a wild animal baring its teeth.

Elisa snapped a few shots. She reminded me a bit of Bethany, as she stood on a chair to get a better angle and texted madly with her thumbs.

"Don't get that angle. You know better," Josie directed, posing with her chin pointed to the ceiling. "This is my good side."

The front door swung open just as Rosa and Sterling came upstairs with planks of Pacific Northwest salmon, luscious salads, and baskets of fresh-baked bread. A woman wearing her flannel belted as a minidress danced in. She raised her arms over her head and swayed like she was at a music fest. Her colorful, unruly hair spilled out in every direction as she shimmied to the table. It was dyed in rainbow streaks, which matched her candy-striped boots and knee-high rainbow socks.

"Hello, hello, you lovely, lovely people. The party can start now that I'm here." She twirled before she took the empty seat next to Gus.

"Kit, what in the world are you wearing?" Josie's tone was like ice. "We've been over this a million times. I'm done with you and your little escapades. That outfit is not suitable for work or this event."

"What, this?" Kit flipped her hair and ran her hand over her skimpy outfit. "Why, I'm simply making a statement with the Bamboo flannel you sent us, dearest. I read the brief. We're in full campout mode for the weekend. I get it. As creative director, I have to put my own spin on fashion; you know that, babe."

"Over my dead body will you wear that to our executive retreat." Josie shot her finger to the door. "Go put some pants on, or don't bother to come back."

"Whatever you say, babe." Kit gave the table a dramatic bow and flitted away on her tiptoes.

"We won't be waiting for you, Kit. The salmon is getting cold." Josie picked up a fork. "Eat, everyone."

Kit caught my eye. She pretended to hold an imaginary fork and stab it at Josie's head before she ducked out the door.

Maddy's phone rang. She took one look at her screen and silenced it immediately. "Sorry, I've got to step outside for a second and take this." As she moved to the door, Elisa looked at her questioningly. Maddy shook her head and hurried outside.

Josie snapped at Miller, "I told you to make it clear that this dinner was mandatory and phones are not allowed."

Miller gulped down a sip. "I did."

"Some team retreat this is. Two people are already missing, and our food is cold. If this continues, you're out of a job. Get your act together and get this team in line, or you're dead."

I refilled wine glasses and tried to ignore the mounting tension in the dining room. I had a sinking feeling that this was going to be a long weekend. A really long weekend.

Chapter Four

It was an early start the following day. Carlos and Ramiro were up with me shortly after seven to pack the supplies we would need for the weekend. Torte was already bustling as we loaded Tupperware full of prebaked cookies and bread and coolers with all of our perishable ingredients into the van.

My team had cleaned up last night's dinner and were already serving coffee and pastries to the Saturday morning crowd. It was good to see that things were running seamlessly. At least I didn't have to worry about the bakeshop.

"How far is the river?" Ramiro asked from the backseat after we had finished loading. A strand of his wavy dark hair fell over one eye. He had grown his hair out over the summer, wearing it long and floppy like the other soccer players on his high school team.

"I believe he is asking whether he has time for a morning nap," Carlos replied.

"Nap away," I said, pulling up the directions on my phone. "It will take us about forty-five minutes, maybe even an hour, to get there."

Ramiro didn't put up a fight. "Good. My only complaint about American school is why does it have to start so early?"

Carlos gave Ramiro a sideways look in the rearview mirror. "I have no sympathy for you. In my day we had to walk miles to school."

"And stop to milk cows along the way," Ramiro interrupted. "Nice try. I've heard that story too many times." He propped the pillow he'd brought along behind his neck, put in his AirPods, and closed his eyes.

The campsite was located outside Shady Cove on the banks of the Rogue River. Fortunately, we weren't responsible for any physical setup, except for organizing our temporary kitchen however we saw fit. Bamboo had hired an event company that specialized in glamping to construct each of the tents and shared areas at the campsite.

We headed north on I-5. The freeway cut through the organic valley land with pear orchards and vineyards stretching along the hillsides. The Siskiyou Mountains surrounded us. Any direction offered a panorama of their densely forested rolling peaks.

We drove through the city of Medford, taking in majestic views of RoxyAnn and Mount McLoughlin. Big box stores lined both sides of the highway for a few miles. As neighborhoods and businesses began to thin, the road narrowed and the landscape became more rugged. Farms with herds of goats and free-range chickens ran parallel along both sides of the two-lane highway. Trees stretched as far as my eye could see, intermixed with charred sections that wildfires had ravaged.

"I see why you are so drawn to this valley. Everywhere

your eye can travel, there is such beauty. The mountain passes to our north and south and Table Mountain's flat top," Carlos said, keeping his voice low so as not to disturb Ramiro, who had fallen asleep before we had even gotten on the freeway. "It nestles us in and is changing with every mile. I cannot wait to see the river."

"The river is spectacular, but this group that we're going to be serving is rife with issues." I filled him in on last's night's dinner.

"Sí, but we will be together. It cannot be that bad."

"I hope you're right." I didn't share his confidence.

We drove in quiet contemplation, enjoying the view and the winding road taking us farther from civilization as we turned onto Crater Lake Highway. Greenhouses, hemp fields, and grassy pastures with grazing cattle and horses reminded me of how easy it was to escape into nature in southern Oregon. Everything looked like it belonged in a painting—the family farms with bright white fencing and classic red barns, the oak groves with bunches of wild mistletoe clinging to the trees, and the redtail hawks that swooped above us. Water-resistant shrubbery mixed in with spindly pines and ponderosas made the variegated landscape appear to have been brushed in soft watercolors.

Little roadside stands offered baskets of fresh eggs and miniature bouquets of cut flowers. In exchange for the goods, customers simply needed to leave cash in mason jars.

As we got closer to Shady Cove, we hit a "traffic jam" of rafting vans and cars with kayaks and paddles strapped to the roofs. The town of Shady Cove boasted a population of just under three thousand permanent residents. Those numbers swelled in the summer when rafting companies packed the small town, bringing in thrill seekers from all over the globe to tackle the Rogue.

The Rogue River literally ran through town, making Shady Cove a recreational hub for water lovers. We slowed our speed as we came into town, passing the pink Frosty Queen—a favorite spot for locals and adventurers to stop for milkshakes and burgers after a long day on the river. There was a pizza shop, Mexican restaurant, pharmacy, and at least a half-dozen rafting and fishing guide companies. I caught flashes of primary-colored red, yellow, and blue rafts and bright orange life jackets stacked and waiting for a day on the river. Signs pointed to parks and trails.

"Bison jerky?" Carlos commented, pointing to a fly-fishing shop advertising bait, cold beer, and the jerky.

"You want to stop?"

He stole a glance at the backseat where Ramiro was still snoozing. "Maybe on the way back. I must try it, sí?"

"Absolutely." I grinned.

We followed the antique green lampposts with rainbow trout and Chinook salmon banners through town. Practically every other building in Shady Cove was a rafting company. Businesses here made their income for the year during the summer season. Everything revolved around the river, much like the way Ashland revolved around the Oregon Shakespeare Festival.

The two-lane road was precarious from this point on. Red rock volcanic cliffs extended to our left. Vast chunks of the rocky prominence had broken off, leaving a slew of debris in the form of everything from tiny pebbles all the way to boulders the size of our car. To the right, I caught glimpses of the river about fifty feet below. Fishing lodges and cabins dotted the banks of the Rogue, many with large decks perfect for casting a line out into the water.

We lost cell service as the native trees became denser. A single milepost marked our turnoff, which took us down a narrow Forest Service gravel road. The thick, red-barked pines shuttered out the sunlight as the car bumped along the remote highway. A tingly feeling made the tiny hairs on my arms stand at attention. Ancient wispy moss and a carpet of ferns gave off an equally magical and creepy vibe. There was something almost mystical about how the forest seemed to envelop us.

"This is like nothing I've seen," Carlos noted, keeping a firm grip on the steering wheel as he navigated around potholes and rocks on the road. "It's like the trees have closed in on us and we are no longer anywhere near civilization."

"It's pretty incredible, isn't it?"

The campsite was off the beaten path, without access to running water, electricity, or cell service. I wondered how the Bamboo team was going to deal with being cut off from the outside world and technology.

When we arrived at the campsite, Carlos let out a gasp. Giant white firs and incense cedars towered above us. Sunlight cut through the canopy, casting a sparkling glow on the ground, which was coated in a blanket of pine needles.

He steered into a parking area. "It is like something from a movie, no? It reminds me of the travel postcards I used to collect when I was growing up in Spain. I wanted to come to America and see the rugged West.

The national parks, the forests, the lakes, and the rivers. Now here we are."

I appreciated his enthusiasm for the space that was such a part of me. Seeing the Rogue Valley through his eyes brought me an even deeper appreciation for the region. And he wasn't wrong. The campsite was like a movie set. Large canvas yurts, each with their own small deck entrance complete with a shoe rack and Adirondack chairs, had been constructed in a semi-circle in the grassy clearing. The yurts appeared to have peekaboo views of the river from the backsides. Lanterns and string lights like the ones we had used to decorate the bakeshop last night hung from the interior of the structures and were also strung between the canopy of trees. There were outdoor showers, an inflatable hot tub, and benches with gingham pillows arranged around a giant fire pit.

Our tents and cooking station were adjacent to the fire pit. We would serve meals on the long picnic tables draped with matching gingham tablecloths and decorated with citronella candles and bouquets of wildflowers. The kitchen had its own yurt as well as a wash station with hot running water.

"This is camping?" Carlos sounded as incredulous as I felt.

"Uh, no. Don't get used to this. If we take Ramiro backpacking, we're going to be roughing it for real."

"Okay, I will enjoy this luxury camping while I can." Carlos parked the van.

Ramiro stirred. He stretched and yawned. "We're here?"

"Look around. That is your tent." Carlos pointed to

a smaller yurt next to the kitchen. It had been outfitted with lanterns and a cozy cot with pillows and extra blankets.

"The river. It's right down there." Ramiro grinned as he got out of the car, pointing to the path that led to the Rogue. "I can swim and raft. This is amazing."

The nap must have been what he needed, because he took no time unpacking his bags and peeling off his sweatshirt and stripping down to his swimsuit. He had tan lines from wearing a T-shirt to help Carlos in the vineyard. After he had put his things in his tent, he raced over to us. "Is it okay if I go down to the river?"

I rubbed my arms. "Aren't you cold in your swimsuit? It hasn't exactly warmed up yet."

"No. I cannot wait to swim." Ramiro tossed a beach towel over his slender shoulders.

"Okay, but fair warning—the water is probably pretty brisk," I cautioned.

"I'll test it with a toe first." There was a momentary flash of a younger boy as he raced off to check out the water.

"We may not see him again," Carlos said, opening the back to begin unloading.

"Let him explore. We've got this." I lifted a tub of muffins and cookies.

Prepping our temporary kitchen didn't take long. The camp stoves and barbeques were already in position; we just needed to arrange our supplies and figure out the best flow for meal prep. Once we had unpacked and established a system, Carlos brewed pots of French press.

"Coffee is a must, sí?"

"Yes." I could use a cup of his strong brew, and

given the amount of wine the team from Bamboo went through last night I had a feeling there were going to be some serious requests for coffee when they arrived.

"When do they come?" Carlos handed me a tin camp mug with a cute retro tent design.

"Miller said they should get here around nine. They need to do a safety training before their raft trip. Everything for lunch is pre-prepped. We just need to assemble the boxes."

"Show me what you need."

Carlos and I packed rafting lunches with our hazelnut chicken salad sandwiches, chips, apples and oranges, carrots and hummus, cookies, brownies, and bags of our house-made granola and trail mix.

"This is a hearty lunch," Carlos noted.

"I think they're going to work up an appetite on the river. Navigating the rapids takes some serious arm strength and teamwork, which might be an issue for this group." I couldn't imagine Josie following the rafting guide's commands, nor could I picture anyone on Bamboo's dysfunctional team paddling in synch.

We savored our coffee and the quiet of the forest while we packed lunches. The forest smelled of bark and pine needles warmed from the sun. The only sounds were the rushing of the river in the distance and the chirping of the birds in the trees. I was glad I had packed extra clothes for tonight, because there was a chill in the air that made me happy for hot coffee to warm my hands.

Two vans broke the silence as they rumbled over the gravel road, carting inflated rafts behind them.

"This must be the rafting company," Carlos said, standing to offer a hand. He and Ramiro helped the guides unload and carry wet suits, dry bags, and life vests down to the riverbank, while I fed them and made sure everyone was caffeinated for their day on the river.

The Bamboo executive team was supposed to have arrived by nine o'clock for their safety training, but they were late. It was nearly ten when a stretch limousine finally showed up.

Carlos couldn't contain his laughter. "Now that is as far from camping as I can imagine. How did the limos make those sharp turns?"

"Good question." I watched as the team unloaded. Well, actually Miller slogged their bags while everyone else posed for group photos and checked out their accommodations. Like last night, they were dressed in matching waterproof capri pants, Bamboo T-shirts, hats, and sunglasses. At least no one would get lost on the river in their twinning outfits.

Kit, Bamboo's creative director, had opted to tie her T-shirt like a bikini top and roll her pants above her knees. She wandered over to us. "Is that coffee I smell?" Her gaze lingered on Carlos. "My, aren't you a sight for sore eyes at this ungodly hour."

Carlos smiled and poured her a cup of coffee. "Cream? Sugar?"

She fanned her face. "Be still, my sexy heart. He has an accent, too? Forget the cream or sugar; I'll take you."

Carlos tapped his wedding band and put his arm around me. "I think my wife would not like that so much."

"It depends on who's on dish duty," I teased.

Kit twisted her rainbow hair. "How tragically adorable you two are. Please tell me you have a brother nearby. This weekend would be so much more enjoyable with some delightful eye candy."

"No. No brother," Carlos answered. "I can offer you a muffin."

She reached for a pumpkin chocolate chip muffin. "I'll have to settle for flirting with our rafting guides. Perhaps I'll have to take a tumble from the raft and see if they can rescue me. They're young and energetic." She winked before setting her sights on the guides.

Elisa, Maddy, Gus, and Miller came over for coffee. I noticed Josie was in a heated conversation with one of the guides.

"Is everything okay?" I asked.

"As long as that coffee is for us, it will be fine," Elisa answered. Her short bob was tucked beneath her Bamboo cap, making her heart-shaped face look like a pixie's. She reminded me of Peaseblossom from *Midsummer Night's Dream*. "I'm supposed to be documenting this for social, but Josie is in rare form at the moment."

"The coffee is all yours. Help yourself to the muffins, too." I turned to Miller. "The lunches are ready. Do you know where they go? Should we take them to the guides?"

He glanced over his shoulder and gave Elisa a nervous look. "Uh, I would give it a minute. Josie's um, uh . . . having a discussion with them."

Gus laughed. "That's a nice word for it. I'd hate to be on the receiving end of her 'discussions.'" His head was protected with a Bamboo baseball cap.

"Like you haven't already been. Dude, I would watch your back while we're on the water. Josie is out for blood, and I don't think she cares who she goes after. We're all in trouble." Maddy drowned her coffee in cream and sugar. "I mean, did you hear her last night? She accused me of fangirling her. She thinks I intentionally cut my hair to look like her. I mean, come on, how self-inflated is that? She told us to dress alike. I put my hair in braids; what's the big deal?"

Miller kicked a pinecone. "Everything with Josie Jones is a big deal. Guys, Maddy is right. We should all be on alert today. Josie's going to be on the rampage. I don't know if I should tell you this, but it's especially a big deal because she's flipping out over being on the water today."

"Why?" Maddy frowned.

"Because she can't swim," Miller muttered. He must have realized that he shouldn't have said anything because he threw his hands out. "Guys, listen, you did *not* hear that from me, okay? Please, please don't repeat that. Seriously, don't say a word about this to Josie. She will murder me. She's already super upset that I booked this trip."

"What?" Elisa's mouth hung open. "That is the best news I've heard in days. Josie can't swim, and she had you book a white-water rafting trip for our executive retreat. That's pure gold. I want to text like a thousand people right now. Can we put this on Bamboo's home page?"

"No. Please. No one can know, and she didn't exactly tell me to book it." Miller's hands shook as he tried to add cream to his coffee. "It was a misunderstanding, but by the time I figured it out it was too late to change anything and now it's a whole thing because she refuses to show any kind of weakness. She's over there reading the guides the riot act. She already had me direct them not to take us over any big rapids."

"What?" Gus rubbed his stomach. "I've been getting my dad bod in shape for the class-four rapids we were promised."

Miller's face had gone white. "Look, guys, you have got to keep this on the down low, okay? Josie can't know that I told you."

"I'm going to need so many more details." Maddy looked in Josie's direction. Josie was having the river guides check the fit of her hot pink life jacket. Kit was flirting with another guide. "I can't believe she didn't fire you on the spot, Miller."

Miller splashed cream on the table. Carlos helped him clean it up.

"Please don't let her know that you guys know." His voice trembled as he spoke. "She will kill me. I mean, seriously."

"We've got your back, man." Gus put a protective arm around him. "But that doesn't mean we can't have some fun with this information while we're out there on the water, now does it, team?"

Miller looked like he was going to throw up. Elisa and Maddy gave Gus a high five.

"You know what they say about payback," Maddy said with a cheeky grin. "I hope no one gets tossed off the raft when we go over the rapids."

Everyone laughed.

Miller shot me a nervous look.

Josie called them over. "Team, let's go. We're running late."

"Wish us luck," Elisa said to me, downing her coffee.

They gathered with the guides to go over safety procedures while Carlos and I cleaned up.

Another car arrived, one that was very familiar to me. Ramiro had returned from the river in time to listen in on safety talk. He waved with excitement as the Professor parked and got out of the car. I was used to seeing the Professor in tweed jackets and suits, so it was somewhat of a shock to see him decked out in his rafting gear.

"Ah, there's nothing like the smell of summer amongst the pines to greet the morning, is there?" he said as he approached us with a wet suit slung over one arm and a tube of sunscreen in the other. "It reminds me of one of my most favorite quotes from the Bard, 'One touch of nature makes the whole world kin.'"

"Speaking of kin, where's Mom?" I asked, greeting him with a hug.

"She's coming with Lance and Arlo, but this gentleman and I have a date with adventure, don't we?" He tossed Ramiro the sunscreen. "Are you ready to take on some class-four rapids?"

Ramiro practically buzzed with excitement. "Yes, the guides had me listen in on the safety training. I'm ready." He zipped and unzipped his life jacket.

"Most excellent." The Professor turned to Carlos and me. "If you two have no protest, we shall make our way to the rafts."

"Have fun." I watched them blend in with the Bamboo team.

"I do not like this at all." Carlos topped off my mug

with the last of the French press. "I have a very bad feeling about this."

"You mean about Ramiro? He'll be fine. The Professor won't let anything happen to him."

"No, no." Carlos's eyes were on Josie, who was snipping at one of the guides. "These people. I have a feeling something is going to go very wrong."

Chapter Five

While the Bamboo executive team and Ramiro and the Professor spent the afternoon on the river, Carlos and I prepped the campfire dinner. Working in an outdoor kitchen in the woods did have a certain rustic appeal. It was a far cry from the state-of-the-art commercial kitchens on the *Amour of the Seas.* Instead of navigating dozens of staff members and industrial equipment, we had to watch our footing so as not to trip over giant pinecones and keep a watchful eye on the fire so the flames didn't get too hot and burn our provincial meal.

Our cowboy beans were a favorite at the bakeshop. We started with a base of honey-cured bacon, garlic, and onions that we let sauté on low heat. Then we added kidney, black, and great Northern beans, fire-roasted tomatoes, chili powder, paprika, brown sugar, and salt and pepper. The beans would simmer over the campfire until we were ready to serve them with grilled sausages and a trio of salads later.

For the bulk of the day Carlos and I had the campsite to ourselves. Once we had finished meal prep, we took a short hike through the forest that dumped us out at the river. Patchy grass and rocks made up the bulk of the shoreline. The slow-moving water was about eighty to a hundred feet wide with a rocky island in the middle that created a channel. Farther down, a logjam formed, making ripples in the current.

This section of the Rogue was like glass. I was captivated by its mirror-like stillness, which reflected the surrounding basalt boulders, wispy aspens, and conifer canopy. It was extraordinarily quiet, short of the occasional call from the hawks and eagles circling overhead. And it was a bit like stepping back in time. Staring at the jagged wall of gray and rust-colored boulders on the far side of the river made me feel like we had time-traveled into the Jurassic period. I could almost picture the volcanic collapse that had carved out the incredible gorge. It was easy to imagine how years of erosion had formed the steep canyon. I half expected to see a prehistoric bird flying above us.

"This is magnificent." Carlos stopped in midstride as we reached the river's bank. "The water is so clear and the blue of a robin's egg here on the shore, before it drops off in the middle. Then it is like the teal of the sea."

"I know." I grinned as we took off our shoes and warmed our toes on the rocks. There was a slight stretch of open beach. Across the river the forest continued above the cliffs for as far as I could see. It was a strange juxtaposition to see the distinct red bark pines standing tall at least fifty feet overhead.

Someone had secured a rope swing into the side of one of the boulders. It would take a bit of skill to swim across the river and scramble up the rocks to get ahold of the rope, but I was fairly sure that Ramiro would test that out later.

"You can see every color of the pebbles in the water." Carlos made a beeline for the river, rolled up his sleeve, and plunged his hand in. He held up a smooth eggplant pebble. "It's like finding treasure."

I watched him explore, while I spread out a picnic blanket and unpacked our lunch. I had worked up an appetite on our hike. The chicken salad sandwiches smelled delicious, as did the oversized chocolate chip cookies.

Carlos joined me on the blanket with a handful of rocks smoothed by the clear blue waters of the Rogue. "So this area is very still. The rapids are higher, sí?"

"Yeah." I handed him a plate, watching a fleet of ducks skim the surface. "This is a great swimming hole. The rapids are pure white water. One of my favorite sections higher up the river is known as the Avenue of the Boulders. You see even more giant rocks, like on the cliffs across the water." I nodded my head in that direction. "Except higher up, the river cuts through churning, foamy white water and a literal avenue of boulders the size of our car. We'll have to come back soon and take a trip ourselves, especially if Ramiro has fun today."

"I am sure he will have a blast."

An aluminum fishing boat floated by, its motor off, as a fishing line bobbed in the water. We waved a silent hello, so as not to scare away any fish.

We enjoyed a leisurely lunch watching a heron fish as the river rushed past its spindly legs. I drifted off to sleep briefly in Carlos's arms, lulled by the sound of the gurgling river and the heat of the afternoon sun. It almost made dealing with Bamboo worth it. Emphasis on "almost."

After our siesta, we packed up our things and followed the pressed bark- and pine-needle path back through the trees to the campsite.

Mom showed up with Lance and Arlo shortly after four.

"Greetings, greetings." Lance posed and waited for a response. He was dressed like Puck from *Midsummer Night's Dream.*

"I had no idea that your campfire tales were going to come with costumes and all," I said.

Arlo rolled his eyes. "Please don't encourage him." Arlo appeared more prepared for an evening under the stars in his jeans, boots, and hoodie.

Mom's face broke out in a wide smile. "Remind me to always get a ride with these two. The trip out here felt like it took less than five minutes because they were like this the entire way."

"For real, though, I thought Miller hired you to do campfire stories, not a production of *Midsummer Night's Dream.*"

Arlo removed boxes of props from the car. Carlos went to help him.

Lance lifted one hand toward the treetops and the other to the ground. "No decent campfire show would be complete without a visit from a forest sprite."

As he was artistic director for OSF, it was rare for Lance to perform onstage, minus his welcome monologue before shows.

"He's in rare form," Arlo said, glancing at the fire pit. "I'm assuming that's our stage?"

"Yep."

Lance shook his head. "Oh no, no, no. That won't do. There isn't a stage. You can't expect me to perform on the dirt with those benches. How will I possibly get into character?"

"If left to his own devices, he would have brought along the fly equipment—ropes, pulleys, blocks, counterweights. All of the theatrical rigging to be able to fly from tree to tree. I said no to that." Arlo shot Lance a playful look.

"It's always about the bottom line for this one. As if borrowing the rigging system would have set us back."

"Or maybe it's because I'm committed to making sure your derriere doesn't end up on the dirt," Arlo countered. "Harnesses and ropes are dangerous enough under controlled circumstances on the stage. There was no way I was going to let him fly out here in the woods."

"Smart decision," Mom said.

"Dream crushers." Lance sighed.

"What's the plan for the campfire show?" I asked.

"Wouldn't you like to know?"

"Yeah, that's why I asked."

Arlo chucked and gave me a high five.

"Let's just say it will start with a spine-tingling tale from a friendly forest sprite. Our guests should consider it a warning, an omen, a cautionary tale of things to come. The forest might appear serene, but the sprite knows that these trees hold secrets so ghastly they make their own leaves shudder." Lance made his body quake for effect. "Tonight, secrets will be unearthed. Blood will be spilled. The forest will speak in screams. Be forewarned. Take cover and watch your back."

Carlos applauded. "Bravo! This is already wonderful."

Lance gave him a bow. "At least someone appreciates art when they see it."

Mom rubbed her hands together. "Campfire stories are so riveting. I'm already intrigued."

"Just wait until I have the glowing orange embers of the fire on my side. It's going to get spooky out here. Buckle up, my little buttercups." Lance smiled with evil delight. "That's why I brought Arlo along. He's the muscles if anyone freaks out."

"You've come to the right place for freaking out," I said. "The Bamboo team is a walking version of a campfire nightmare."

"Oh, do tell." Lance strummed his fingers on his chin.

I gave them a quick overview of the Bamboo team.

Mom frowned when I finished. "It sounds like a stressful place to work. It makes me appreciate our team at Torte even more."

"I totally agree."

As if on cue, the sound of voices interrupted us. We hurried down to the river. Bright yellow rafts pulled up to the shore.

"Let the games begin," Lance teased with his dazzling smile as he sashayed over to Miller.

I wish I shared his lighthearted attitude. These weren't the kind of games I wanted to be involved in, but it was too late to back out now.

With the Professor not far behind, Ramiro came bounding over to us. His lanky limbs and smile reminded me of a puppy. "That was amazing! The best experience of my life. The rapids were so cool and the guides are so chill." He rubbed his hair with his beach towel. "I think I want to drop out of school and become a river guide. That is a good idea, sí?"

Carlos's brow was crinkled.

"I solemnly swear I had no part in this," the Professor teased, greeting Mom with a hug. "Although he is a natural. He handled the rapids like a pro."

"I'm kidding." Ramiro kissed his dad's cheek. "But it was so amazing. We have to do it again. Maybe tomorrow, sí?"

"It sounds like you had a great time," I said, hugging him. His damp clothes and wet hair were proof that he'd gone into the river at least once.

"Thank you for inviting me. It was the best day ever. You are such a good teacher," he said to the Professor.

The Professor gave him a half bow. "The thanks are all mine. It was a delight to spend a day on the water with you."

Ramiro paused and stepped closer. "Except for those people. They are terrible to each other. Terrible."

"Was it bad?" I asked. "I'm sorry you got stuck with them."

"It's okay. I didn't have anything to do with them." He wrapped his towel around his shoulders for warmth. "It's just listening to how they talk to each other was terrible. You know Josie, the boss?"

I nodded.

"She can't swim. One of her staff, I think his name is Guy or Gus or something like that—"

"Gus," I said.

"Right, Gus. Well, we were in a very calm part of the river, and he started teasing her. I guess, I thought it was teasing, but now I don't know. He pushed her in." Ramiro sounded upset.

"What do you mean? Like actually pushed her in?" I caught the Professor's eye, who gave me a brief nod, confirming Ramiro's story.

"I mean he was sitting next to her on the raft and the next thing we know she is in the water and was screaming like she was going to die or something. It made me think she was scared of the water, but that doesn't make sense."

I waited for him to say more.

"Did she fall off the raft, maybe?" Carlos asked.

Ramiro shook his head. "I don't think so. I only saw a flash out of the corner of my eye, but I think that Gus pushed her in with his paddle. She was fine. She had her life jacket on and, like I said, the water was very calm. She wasn't in danger. The guides pulled her in right away, but she was very, very angry for the rest of the trip."

Gus had heard that Josie couldn't swim before they left. I hated to think the worst about someone, but was there a chance that his teasing had been more nefarious?

Ramiro turned toward the camp kitchen. "What do you need me to do? I'm ready to work."

"I think we're all set," I replied. "We will definitely need you for dishes later, but for now why don't you go take a warm shower or dry off in the sun?"

"Are you sure?" He glanced at Carlos for confirmation.

"She is the boss." Carlos winked.

"The boss says 'of course.'" I gave him a thumbs-up.

Ramiro's face brightened. "Okay, thank you. The guides told me they would take me out again to practice turns, if that is all right? I can be back in an hour or two?"

"Fine by me."

Carlos's tone turned serious. "Sí, but be careful and keep your life jacket on the entire time."

"I will." Ramiro hurried off before Carlos could change his mind.

After he was out of earshot, I looked at the Professor. "Do you really think someone pushed Josie off the raft?"

His lips pressed together in a frown. "I'm afraid so. It did not appear to be an accident. Although it turned out fine. Our river guides were consummate professionals. They recognized that someone had gone overboard immediately and acted swiftly to get her back in the boat. It was a good teaching opportunity for Ramiro."

Mom squeezed his arm. "Why don't you go get dry before you develop a chill?"

He nodded and left to change.

"Can I help you guys?" Arlo asked, joining us. "Miller is talking Lance's ear off about tonight's performance."

"If you don't mind helping Mom with place settings, that would be great," I said to Arlo. Mom had brought a box of flowers that Janet, from A Rose by Any Other Name, had arranged on the tables. These were new bouquets, not the camper van vases from last night. Miller hadn't been exaggerating when he had said that no expense should be spared for this event.

"I will finish the beans and then I can start grilling

the sausages," Carlos said, removing a block of Parmesan from the cooler. We topped the spicy beans with grated Parmesan and a sprinkling of fresh rosemary.

I began dishing up the salads that we had made at Torte into the blue speckled camp bowls that Miller had requested. Once those had been placed on the tables, along with the cast-iron pot of beans, Carlos began opening bottles of wine. I piled Marty's handmade buns on a platter and added an assortment of mustards, ketchup, and spicy dips to the tables.

According to Miller's detailed timeline of events, the team had half an hour to shower, change, and rest before dinner. That gave Carlos time to grill and me time to press our premade cookie dough into miniature cast-iron skillets. Time breezed by. As the team wandered to the picnic area and Mom poured them generous glasses of wine I had a neat row of chocolate chip, peanut butter, double chocolate, and snickerdoodle cookie skillets ready to go over the open flames. The cookies had taken thirty minutes to bake in our wood-fired oven at Torte, but since I couldn't control the heat from the open fire, I wanted to allow extra time in case they took a bit longer.

Everyone was seated around the long tables. The lanterns and twinkle lights cast a soft golden glow, giving the forest an even more charming ambiance. I breathed in the scent of the smoky fire and the pine needles.

Birds chirped overhead and voices of adventurers still on the water drifted from the river.

It was impossible not to be swept up in the serenity of the moment. Even the Bamboo team seemed subdued and calm. Maybe an afternoon on the water had been just what they needed.

The peaceful moment was shattered by a piercing scream. Everyone jumped to their feet and ran toward the sound of the screams.

They were coming from Josie's tent.

She emerged, still wearing her life jacket and holding a flashlight like a weapon. "Someone is trying to kill me!"

Chapter Six

Miller was to her tent first. "What's wrong?"

Josie waved the flashlight behind her. "My tent is crawling with spiders. Dozens of them."

"Spiders." Miller took a step backward. His voice went up in pitch. "Spiders?"

The women of the team—Maddy, Kit, and Elisa—all joined Miller at Josie's tent, but Gus noticeably stayed put at a picnic table, sipping his wine as if nothing had happened. I watched him lean back against one of the Adirondack chairs, take his baseball cap off, and flip it backward. Was it my imagination or was there a smirk on his face?

Arlo looked to Carlos and me. "Do we intervene or let them work this out on their own?"

"I mean, we are in the woods," Lance noted. "Josie left the flaps to her yurt wide open. It's no wonder there are spiders in there. It's the Rogue River and that's Camping 101. If you leave your tent open, you get bugs. I don't know what all the screaming is about. Spiders are nothing. Give me spiders any day."

"Really?" Arlo raised one brow. "Over what?"

"Over anything."

Arlo laughed.

"Please. Ye of such little faith." Lance pretended to be miffed. "I'll have you know that I went camping with my family every year as a child. I can hold my own in the wild."

"Did the wild involve costumes like this?" Arlo laughed harder, which only egged Lance on.

"I may have kept myself occupied creating flower crowns on our adventures, but that doesn't mean I can't pitch a tent or chop firewood." He flexed to show his muscles. "Growing up in a logging family has its advantages when it comes to surviving in nature."

"Are the spiders around here dangerous?" Carlos asked.

"Nah. Not unless she had a run-in with a colony of black widows, but they're very skittish. It's probably just a few zebra jumpers or maybe some crab spiders. I shall offer my spider assessment services."

No one had moved inside Josie's tent. She stomped her feet on the dirt. "Miller, you need to clean my tent out—now!"

"But I'm allergic to spiders." He made a circle in the dirt with his foot, while clenching and unclenching his fists. "I don't think it's a good idea for me to go in there."

"Stop being such a wimp." Josie yanked his arm. "I don't pay you to be allergic to anything. You're my PA. Get in there. I want every single item taken out and inspected."

"Uh." Miller didn't move.

The Professor emerged from our tent, with a fresh set of clothes. "Is there a problem?"

"We might need to be of service. Apparently, there's a spider issue." Lance gestured to the yurt. "I have experience with spiders. Let's just say I'm well versed with the flora, fauna, and insect populations in the valley."

Josie lifted one of the flaps to her tent as Lance and the Professor approached. "Be my guest." Then she shot her team a look of pure hatred. "Let's have everyone take a note that the artistic director who's dressed in costume is braver than every single one of you. And to think, I brought you out here to bond. You disgust me." She spit at Miller's feet.

He kept his head down to avoid making eye contact.

"Hey, you didn't even give us a chance to help," Maddy said.

"I know what you're plotting," Josie shot back. "First I get pushed off the raft. Now spiders. I'm going to have to keep one eye open tonight so that one of you doesn't kill me in my sleep."

"That's dark," Mom said.

I nodded. "I told you this group was intense."

"You weren't exaggerating."

"Josie, you're acting paranoid." Kit produced a shiny silver flask from her pocket. She took a long swig from it and then continued. "Bottoms up, babe. We're here to let loose, have a little fun, and bond. No one is trying to hurt you. If you want this team to get creative, you're gonna have to chill."

"No one is trying to hurt me? Please. Look at the evidence. Is this your little prank, Kit? Because I've already warned you that you are on thin, thin ice. One more mistake, and you're done. Got it?" Josie glared at her.

"Listen, let's all just take a beat, okay." Elisa jumped to Kit's rescue. "Josie, think about it for a minute; this could make for a great social media post. Our clients will love the authenticity, and we can spin it with your bravery." Elisa tried to de-escalate the situation. It made sense that as marketing director she was already thinking of how to leverage Josie's freak-out.

"Don't you dare take a picture of me right now." Josie threw a finger in Elisa's face.

"Chill." Elisa threw her hands up. "I'm trying to help."

"None of you are helping. Go back to your wine." Josie shooed them away.

Meanwhile Gus continued to lounge near the campfire. His casual smirk made me pretty convinced that he knew exactly how the spiders had gotten into Josie's tent.

The team followed her order, but not without plenty of comments under their breath. The Professor and Lance emerged from the tent a few minutes later.

"Helen, can you see if my phone has a connection?" the Professor asked.

"Okay, that's a lot of spiders." Lance caught my eye. "Jules, do you have a broom? Trash bags?"

"Sure." I grabbed both.

Josie stomped over to the tables. "Who did it? I want a name—now!"

I scooted past her and went to help Lance. "Is it bad?"

He grimaced. "How do you feel about creepy crawlers?"

"I don't usually have a problem with them."

"You might after you see this." He showed me into the yurt. The floor was moving like the river. There weren't just a couple of spiders inside Josie's tent; there were dozens of the arachnids.

I hadn't been lying when I said that spiders didn't bother me, but this was an infestation of epic proportions. "Lance, this is more than a few spiders crawling into a tent."

"I know. Strange things are afoot, darling."

"What do we do?"

He shrugged. "Burn it?"

Suddenly Josie's hysterics didn't seem so outrageous. There was no possibility of ridding the space of the spiders. The only solution was to have her move tents. Josie's bag sat on the bed, unpacked. That was a good thing. We could move her bag and find her another space for the night. I didn't envy the event company and whoever would be responsible for cleaning up the yurt.

The Professor returned with his phone.

"Any luck?" I asked.

He shook his head. "I doubted that we'd have service, but I thought it was worth at least checking."

"So you must agree with my assessment that something sinister is afoot?" Lance strummed his fingers on his chin.

"I can't say for certain, but in my line of work, I rarely find that these many coincidences end up being coincidences. First Josie was pushed from the raft. Now her tent is infested with spiders. I suspect that one of her staff is, if nothing else, trying to intimidate her. Perhaps send a message." He glanced at his phone again.

I wondered who he wanted to call.

"These aren't poisonous spiders, are they?" I asked.

"No. They're harmless. Upon first glance, I would assume that someone wants to scare her." The Professor sounded confident. "If you'll excuse me, I think I'll wander around a bit and see if there's a break in the trees where I might be able to get a connection."

He seemed intent on wanting to find a signal. Did he know more than he was saying? Was Josie in danger? Were we?

Lance picked up her suitcase and brushed a spider from his hand. "Riddle me this, who would come on an executive retreat and sabotage the boss's tent? This is like a scene from *The Parent Trap*. One of her staff is trying to send her a message or scare her away for good."

"Yeah." I thought about what Ramiro had witnessed on the raft. Was it Gus? He was the most likely suspect. The question was whether or not he was pulling a harmless prank, or if he had some kind of vendetta against Josie and was trying to hurt her.

Lance peered out of the tent. "And our culprit is sitting there leisurely gulping his wine. Did you say that he's the CFO?"

"Yeah." I nodded. "They got into a heated argument at dinner last night. She called him a lush and they fought about money."

"What if he's fed up with her excessive spending? Maybe this is his way of sending her a message to tighten her purse strings or else . . ." He trailed off.

"Or else what?"

"You know." He made a slicing motion across his neck. "Murder, Juliet, cold-blooded murder."

I shivered. Was it just my imagination or were spiders

crawling up my legs? A quick glance brought momentary relief that the spiders were still on the floor.

"Let's say it was Gus. How did he get the spiders in here?" I said out loud without even realizing it.

"Easy. Put them in a sealed box, poke a few air holes in the top, wait until Josie was out of sight, and dump the box in her tent." Lance pushed the broom around, not that it was going to do much good.

"Yeah, right." I thought for a moment. "I'm not fully convinced it was Gus, though. Her entire team hates her. It could have been any of them."

"Except for her lackey. What's his name?"

"Miller."

"Right, Miller. I was afraid the kid was going to hurl on my pointed shoes." Lance lifted a foot and proceeded to circle his toe. "I'm giving him a pass as our spider suspect. Unless he's a phenomenal actor, there's no chance he touched any of those spiders. If I'm wrong, then the kid is a genius and I'll hire him on the spot for the next starring role."

"Let's get her stuff out and figure out where to put her. I think the best idea is to give her Ramiro's tent. He can bunk up with Carlos and me tonight."

"But then you and that sexy, dark Spaniard can't cuddle up." Lance put his index finger to his eye to pretend like he was shedding a tear.

I shook my head and ignored his teasing. "I need to get back to the kitchen."

"Agreed." He motioned me closer. "But you realize, we have another case, darling. This evening just got much more fun."

Chapter Seven

Lance had telegraphed how the rest of the night was going to go. Things got worse after the spider incident. The bickering escalated while we served our cowboy cookout dinner.

"You realize I have the power to fire each and every one of you, and I won't hesitate. It is obvious that one or more of you is pranking me, and I'm done. That's not why we're here. We're here to focus on Bamboo. You are my executive team, and if you don't start acting like professional executives, I'll end each and every one of your careers. If you think I'm kidding, try me," Josie threatened. She cut her sausage into bite-size pieces instead of just eating it out of the bun. "We are here to map out our plans for total world domination in the next year. I want your heads in the game, and I want ideas on the table right now, or heads are going to start rolling. Understood?"

Everyone nodded and studied their food.

"I do not understand," Carlos said to me as he refilled a platter of perfectly charred sausages. "I thought this was a team-building weekend. Josie is destroying any hint of team."

"It's bizarre." I tested one of the skillet cookies with a long toothpick. The top of the cookie had baked to a golden crisp while the interior was soft and chewy. I removed it from the heat to let it cool before serving it with a scoop of our vanilla bean custard.

"She was like that all day on the water," Ramiro added. He had taken his job of running dishes seriously. "She kept screaming about money and how they were bleeding out. It seems like they are spending a lot though, yeah?"

"Yeah." I wrinkled my brow. "That's really odd. Bamboo is spending more than any client we've worked with in recent history. I'm shocked to hear that they're having cash flow issues."

Ramiro set a stack of dishes in a tub of warm, soapy water. "She and Gus were fighting about it all day. They bickered the entire time we were on the river. He kept telling her that it's her fault the company is in free fall—is that how you say it?"

I nodded and waited for him to continue.

"Gus said she's over budget and the company is in danger of going under. She was blaming everyone else. I tried not to listen, but they were so loud." Ramiro dried his hands with a dish towel and stuffed his hands in the front pocket of his sweatshirt. A cool breeze had kicked up from the river, sending wisps of smoke from the bonfire into the air where the faintest flicker of stars began to light up the indigo sky.

Carlos frowned and looked at me. "They did pay up-front, sí?"

I nodded. "We're good." With big events like our contract with Bamboo, we required half the payment up front and the remainder of the balance upon completion. Miller had already given me a check for the entire bill. "I guess I should probably deposit it, huh?"

"Yeah." Carlos glanced over to the team. "Tomorrow, as soon as we're back, we take that check to the bank."

"Agreed."

He delivered the platter of sausages.

I noticed that Maddy and Gus had moved away from the tables momentarily. Maddy had a thin stack of papers in her hands and was motioning with them. Gus had a desperate hold of a pine tree, like the trunk was the only thing keeping him upright. His eyes darted to the tables and then back to Maddy.

I couldn't hear what they were discussing, but it was obvious that Gus was uncomfortable. After a minute, Maddy stuffed the papers into the back pocket of her jeans. She appeared to give Gus some kind of warning, because she leaned in close, and whispered something in his ear. He, in turn, bobbed his head in agreement, before they both joined the rest of the group at the tables.

I finished dessert. Everyone moved to the fire pit for Lance's performance as more wine flowed. The sounds of their boisterous conversations carried through the quiet forest. I wasn't going to cut them off. No one was driving and we were in the middle of wild parklands. They were consenting adults. I certainly wouldn't have been guzzling wine nonstop like most of the Bamboo team, but it wasn't my job to parent them.

"There are going to be some serious hangovers

tomorrow," Mom noted, her eyes landing on Kit, who was guzzling from her flask.

Gus clutched a wine bottle and proceeded to chug straight from it.

"This is what they were like at dinner last night," I said.

Mom had stacked cartons of frozen custards for the cookie skillets on the prep table. "I think they've already made it through nearly two cases of wine and there are only six of them. That's more than a bottle per person so far."

Arlo had rolled up his sleeves to help Ramiro with the dishes. "I don't know, I might drink, too, if I had to deal with this level of corporate drama."

"How exactly did you work with Josie before?" I asked.

"I didn't have much interaction with her personally. It was always through her staff. Miller was my point of contact." Arlo swiveled his head toward the fire. "Miller is an anomaly. Josie has a reputation for going through admins every few months. I think he's been at Bamboo for over two years now, which is basically a lifetime working for her. He deserves a medal. I had no idea how awful she is." He gave me an apologetic smile as he handed Ramiro a clean plate to dry. "I thought it would be a good opportunity for you and some nice cash for the slower season, but now I feel terrible for connecting you with Bamboo."

"No, not at all. We so appreciate it." It wasn't Arlo's fault. I was grateful for the extra money going into the holidays, and this was temporary. I could handle Josie and Bamboo for a finite amount of time.

Carlos jumped in to back me up. "Sí, sí. It is wonderful. Ramiro got to go rafting. I get to see this beautiful forest and cook under the stars. We can handle their infighting. It doesn't affect us, as long as they don't start to complain about the food."

"As if that would ever happen." Arlo grinned.

We topped each of the skillet cookies with the frozen custard and sprinkled them with chopped nuts and extra chunks of chocolate. The snickerdoodles got a dusting of cinnamon. I was pleased with how the bakes had turned out. They had a rustic feel being served in the skillets and the melting scoops of ice cream and toppings elevated the cookies.

Everyone helped themselves to slices while Lance prepared for his campfire tales.

"Why don't you go listen?" I said to Ramiro. "It's not every day that you get to see the artistic director of one of the major theaters on the West Coast perform."

"But there are still some pots and pans to wash."

"It's okay. Your dad and I can finish. Go have a seat by Mom and the Professor." I pointed to the last row. To an untrained observer, the Professor appeared to be casually waiting for Lance's story hour to start with his long legs crossed in front of him and one arm draped around Mom's shoulder. But I could tell from how his eyes scanned the campfire that he was carefully observing each of the Bamboo execs.

"Thanks, Jules." Ramiro leaned in to kiss me on the cheek. "I feel like I am not working hard enough this weekend."

"You're good. We want you to have fun." I shooed him off. Ramiro had inherited Carlos's work ethic.

I appreciated his concern, but he was in high school and visiting for a year. Helping was fine. My goal was to allow him to fully immerse himself in American life, especially our unique Rogue Valley lifestyle. I didn't mind scrubbing a few pots while he got a front-row (or last-row) seat for Lance's one-person show.

Carlos must have had similar thoughts on his mind, because he came up next to me with a glass of Cab Franc. "Come have a seat. The dishes can wait."

"That's just what I said to Ramiro."

"Good, then you can take your own advice." He pointed out two Adirondack chairs that he had moved near the fire pit. "I reserved those for us. Let's sit, have some wine, and watch our friend."

He wasn't going to get an argument from me. I curled up in the chair under a Pendleton blanket and sipped my wine as Lance transformed into a forest sprite who had come to warn us of evil lurking in the dark woods.

Shockingly, there wasn't a peep from the Bamboo team, which was a testament to Lance's ability to hold his audience completely captive. Everyone was transfixed as Lance shifted into a throaty voice, sharing the secrets from the forest, of campers gone missing, of rivers that swallowed up entire rafts, of strange sounds in the night, of hauntings. Whether there was any truth to his campfire stories didn't matter. His performance sent shivers down my spine. I scooted closer to Carlos. Ramiro flinched twice after Lance had paused for effect and then followed the silence with a bloodcurdling scream.

"He's so good." Carlos rubbed my shoulder.

"I'm glad I'm not sleeping alone tonight." I leaned my head against his warm body.

Carlos laughed and squeezed me tighter. "I was counting on you for protection, mi querida."

"We're going to be a hopeless duo then."

Josie stood and applauded when the performance was over. "Bravo! Bravo!" She was visibly drunk. Her body swayed from side to side. She grabbed an open bottle of wine, not caring or maybe not aware that it sloshed everywhere as she addressed her team. "I'm going to bed. Tomorrow we are hitting it bright and early, and I don't care if you're hungover. I'll see you out here at eight A.M. sharp."

"Eight?" Maddy gasped. "Why?"

"Because I'm the boss." Josie unzipped her hot pink life vest, dropped it on the ground, and stumbled away. "What I say goes. I'm tired of you all slacking and lushing it up. We're here to work, people."

I was confused. Miller had made it clear that this was supposed to be a team-building retreat. The only thing I'd witnessed in the past two days was the Bamboo team imploding. None of it made sense. Why the lavish gift bags and big spending, especially if Bamboo was really in financial trouble?

No one moved until she had vanished into the darkness. Once they were sure she was out of earshot they began mimicking her behavior. Maddy grabbed Josie's life vest and took Lance's spot in front of the fire and pretended to be Josie. "Okay, team, I want you here bright and early." She paraded around the crackling flames in a life jacket.

"Shall we finish the dishes?" I asked Carlos.

"Sí." He looked as uncomfortable as I felt. Plus, if Josie was expecting her team to be ready to start the day at eight, we needed to be up much earlier to prepare breakfast.

The remainder of the cleanup didn't take long. Arlo and Lance came to say good-bye. "Thanks again for your help tonight, and Lance, you were brilliant."

He fanned his face with one hand. "You're making me blush. Don't stop, though."

"You are a phenomenal storyteller," Carlos added.

"Yeah, I almost fell off my seat a couple of times," Ramiro said. "There isn't really a killer loose in the woods?"

"No." Lance shook his head to assure him. "Those are merely tales passed down from generation to generation. These woods are perfectly safe."

"Exactly." Mom kissed Ramiro's cheek. "You're in good hands with your dad and Juliet, but remember Doug is a detective, so you're welcome to come sleep in our tent if it gets too spooky." She ruffled his hair.

I loved watching her get to tap into her grandmotherly instincts.

Ramiro squared his shoulders and placed his hands on his hips. "I will be brave. I must be able to tell my friends in Spain that I went to a real American campout."

"You're halfway to a cowboy," Arlo teased.

Ramiro laughed. "My friends will be impressed."

After we said good night, we packed up supplies in order to make sure no wildlife got into the kitchen, and then headed to bed.

"You're sure you don't mind bunking with us?" I asked Ramiro.

He shook his head. "I will only admit this to you, but I don't mind at all. I'm not sure if I could handle sleeping alone after Lance's stories."

Carlos laughed. "I agree."

I stopped at the entrance to our tent. A flash of motion caught my eye. Someone was inside Josie's new tent. There was a sound of a crash, followed by her nasal voice screaming.

"What now?" Carlos sounded incredulous.

Someone dressed in black came streaking from her tent and disappeared into the woods.

Josie ran to the entrance. "Don't you come back here!"

"Are you okay?" Carlos asked.

She waved the bottle of wine in her hand. "I'm fine. Another one of my staff is trying to play a prank."

Another prank?

The Professor emerged from his tent. He looked from Josie to us but didn't say anything.

After everything that had happened today, I was surprised she wasn't calling for the head of whoever had been in her tent. Then again, she was drunk. Maybe she wouldn't even remember the exchange in the morning.

She zipped her tent closed.

The Professor strolled over to our tent. "I have half a mind to put this entire group under house arrest. What now?"

I told him what we'd seen.

His cheeks creased with concern. "I'm not sure what to make of any of this. The Bard's words 'The path is smooth that leadeth on to danger' keep ringing through my head."

I didn't like the sound of that. I clutched Carlos's hand.

The Professor must have sensed my nervousness. "Don't listen to an old man rambling. I've seen too much dysfunction in my tenure. Rest easy and enjoy sleeping under the stars." With that he returned to his tent.

"I guess that is our cue," Carlos said, keeping his hand clasped over mine.

We got settled in our own cozy tent. I was glad that Ramiro was staying with us. He and Carlos told me stories about their adventures in Spain before we all eventually drifted off to sleep.

I was the first to wake up the next morning. The sounds of birds greeting the dawn tugged me from the warmth of the covers. Faint light cracked through the darkness.

I pulled on a pair of jeans, a hoodie, and boots and headed outside, leaving Carlos and Ramiro peacefully sleeping. There was no need to wake them yet. I could get the coffee started and light the fire. It would still be a couple of hours before the Bamboo crew began to stir.

The ground was damp with dew. Everything smelled fresh and clean like nature had bathed itself in the dew overnight. Sparkling droplets of moisture clung to the evergreen branches. I breathed in the cool air and paused in a moment of gratitude, taking in the sounds of scrub jays, chattering squirrels, and the rush of water nearby.

The fire had burned out overnight. I added more wood to the pile and stoked the embers to get it started again. Soon flames lapped at the wood, sending smoke like a signal into the air. With the fire burning, I could focus on the most critical task of the day—coffee.

I crept so as not to wake anyone as I gathered Andy's special campfire roast and the French presses we had brought. I poured bottled water into a pot to boil over the flames. While that boiled, I could go down to the river and fill a tub for washing dishes later. We had packed in gallons of drinking water for consumption and cooking.

The short walk to the river took me past the other tents. No one else was awake at this hour. It was just me and the expanse of the forest. I breathed in the thought as I made it to the riverbank. What a gift to greet the morning in solitude.

The narrow trail had been packed down by people and probably deer and other wild animals. It cut through the towering evergreens and forest floor thick with yellowing manzanitas and leafy ferns. A squirrel jumped from a low-hanging branch, startling me and making me nearly lose my footing.

It's just a squirrel, Jules. I chuckled as the trail wound to the left and then down toward the rocky shoreline.

I took a moment for a moving meditation, focusing on the sound of the rapids in the distance, the cool morning breeze on my skin, and the smell of pine and woodsmoke. How lucky was I to get to live here, and have adventures like this?

I emerged from the canopy of green onto the banks of the Rogue. Pebbles the color of sand and slate with touches of pink and blue mixed in stretched in both directions. The vibrant shrubbery growing out of the craggy cliff face made me think about resiliency and how the moss, ferns, and golden currents found their way toward the sun through the cracks in the historic boulders. I let my face arch toward the sky, breathing in the awe-inspiring views of the canyon.

It was cooler this close to the water. I could feel the breeze kiss my cheeks.

"It's so beautiful here," I said out loud to no one.

A path cut through the sandy beach, like something significant had been dragged up from the water.

It must be from the rafts, I thought.

As I approached the edge of the water and bent down to fill up the tub, I realized that I might be wrong about the rafts. My eyes focused on the center of the river where a body was floating facedown.

Chapter Eight

I blinked hard.

Was I seeing things?

Maybe it was a log floating downstream.

But logs don't wear bright pink life jackets, Jules.

It had to be Josie. She was the only person with a pink life jacket.

Everything snapped into focus. I screamed for help.

"Help! I need help!"

I yanked off my sweatshirt, pulled off my boots, and raced into the water.

"Help!" I yelled again as cold pierced through my thick wool socks. I splashed through the shallow banks until I was waist-deep in the water. The current wasn't strong in this section of the river, but the water was like ice. My jeans weighed me down as I trudged deeper.

It probably wasn't the smartest idea to go in after her, especially fully clothed, but I didn't have a choice. If there was even the slightest chance that Josie was still alive, I had to get to her.

"Julieta! What are you doing?" Carlos appeared on

the shore. His feet were bare. He tugged on a hoodie and rubbed his eyes.

"It's Josie!" I pointed to the lifeless body floating a few feet away.

"Can you reach her?"

"Yeah. I think so."

"Be careful. I will go get the Professor and more help." He took off toward the campsite.

The water had gotten too deep. I was going to have to swim. Thankfully, I had grown up spending my summer afternoons at Emigrant Lake. Swimming had come naturally to me. Water has always been a place of comfort. Maybe it's because I'm a Pisces—a water sign. Mom and Dad used to call me their little fish when I was young. My love of the water is one of the many reasons I felt drawn toward a life at sea in my early twenties.

Despite my being a strong swimmer, navigating the freezing water and current in jeans and a T-shirt wasn't exactly easy.

My lungs burned as I pulled my arms through the water to try to reach Josie.

When I finally made it to her, Carlos had returned with the Professor, Ramiro, and Gus.

"Do you have her?" he called, rolling up his pants.

The Professor held his phone, trying to get service.

"Yes." I clutched the pink life jacket. "I'm going to try and roll her over." During our training on the *Amour of the Seas* I had opted to take an advanced lifesaving course taught by the ship's lifeguards. I had learned how to properly hold a drowning victim in order to protect their head and neck. The technique was necessary for diving injuries. I didn't think that Josie had hit her head, but it was better to be safe.

I carefully cradled her neck in one hand and submerged myself entirely in order to roll her over.

The second I looked at her blueish, puffy face, which was almost unrecognizable, I knew she was dead.

Just swim, Jules.

I kicked hard as I dragged her body to shore. The Professor, Carlos, and Ramiro raced into the water to help me lift her out.

Gus hung back, kicking the dirt with his bare feet.

"She is not breathing." Carlos dropped to his knees. He paused for a minute and stared at me. "Julieta, go change. I don't want you to go into shock from the cold."

I hesitated.

The Professor concurred. "Yes, Carlos is right. You need to get dry immediately. We'll take it from here."

"It is okay." Carlos held my gaze. "We have this. Go get dry. This is your priority."

I nodded. Everything looked blurry. Maybe it was from having water in my eyes or maybe I was about to lose it.

Josie was dead.

I couldn't believe it.

Had she gone into the river last night?

Why?

She couldn't swim.

When she had left the fire, she'd been drunk, and she'd taken the rest of the wine bottle with her. Could she have been so intoxicated that she'd become disoriented? But, given her extreme phobia of the water and the fact that she hadn't taken off her life jacket the entire time we'd been here, it seemed odd that even under the influence she would have decided to go for a late-night swim.

Was there another explanation?

I thought back to the person Carlos and I had seen running from her tent.

Could one of the Bamboo executive team members have killed her?

She'd certainly given each of them plenty of motive.

The question was who and how?

Maybe Josie had left her tent at some point for more wine or a bathroom trip and someone had accosted her. They could have killed her and then dumped her body in the river. Or forced her into the river knowing she couldn't swim.

But she was wearing a life jacket. That would have kept her afloat.

My entire body broke out in uncontrollable shivers as I made it to our tent. I stripped out of my wet clothes and dried off with a towel. I couldn't stop replaying the scene. Josie had been floating facedown in the middle of the river.

That had to mean that she was killed or knocked out *prior* to going into the water. Or she could have drowned.

I hadn't heard any screams after falling asleep last night. If there had been a struggle, it seemed plausible that we would have heard it. Sound carried through the forest. Surely someone would have been woken up if Josie and her assailant had gotten into a physical altercation.

My skin was red from the cold. I rubbed my hands together to create friction and then found a pair of warm sweats and a fresh pair of cabin socks. I wrapped myself in a blanket and sat on the edge of the bed.

There hadn't been any visible signs of injury on her face, but then again, it wasn't as if I had studied her body either. I had taken a quick look. My singular goal had been to get us both back to shore safely.

I had done that, but obviously Carlos was right. I must be in some sort of mild shock.

Who wouldn't be under the same circumstances? It wasn't as if I expected to see a body with my morning coffee.

What about the rest of the Bamboo team?

Gus was the only person who had come to help with the Professor, Carlos, and Ramiro. Did that mean something? Was he trying to cover his tracks? Ramiro had been convinced that Gus had pushed Josie off the raft and he had definitely been acting weird when Josie discovered spiders in her tent.

Hadn't everyone else heard my screams for help?

Were they simply hungover? Or could it be that one of them already knew that Josie was dead?

Feeling was starting to return to my fingertips. I took that as a good sign. My heart rate was finally slowing to a more normal pace as well.

There was the sound of movement and voices outside the tent. I could hear people talking and a car pulling away. The Professor—or someone—must be going to get help.

We were at least thirty minutes away from Shady Cove, the nearest town. I wondered who would respond in a case like this. Was it the local police or someone from the Forest Service?

Question after question surged in my head.

I had warmed up enough that the shivering had subsided. I pulled on a dry sweatshirt and dried my hair with the towel. I twisted it in a ponytail and loosely laced my tennis shoes over the thick cabin socks. My hands felt like ice and my fingertips were blue. I wasn't sure if it was from the cold or the shock. I needed to get them by the fire.

As I stepped out of the tent, Mom was standing in front of it holding a cup of coffee.

"Mom, you scared me." I placed my hand on my chest.

"I'm sorry, honey. I was coming in to bring you this." She handed me the coffee. "Doug told me what happened. He's on his way to see if he can get a signal farther down the road. If he can't, he'll drive into town for help."

"Good." I clutched the coffee.

"You look pale. Let's go sit by the fire." She put her hand on my waist.

Everything still felt like a dream. We sat next to the flames. I took a long sip of the coffee, which warmed my throat.

Mom stoked the fire. "Do you want to talk about it?"

"It all happened so fast. It doesn't even feel real."

"Of course it doesn't." She patted my knee. "You're in shock."

"Am I?" I held the mug tighter like it was my personal life vest. "I don't get it. How could she have drowned in a life jacket?"

Mom shook her head. "I don't know."

"Do you think she was killed?"

"I don't know that either." Mom sighed. "That's what Doug will have to figure out."

I drank more coffee and watched the flames devour the stack of firewood. Time felt fuzzy. We could have been sitting there for five minutes or an hour. I wasn't sure. But before I knew it the Professor's car rumbled over the gravel.

The Professor got out of the car, closed the door, and zipped up his puffy vest. He walked over to join us. "How are you feeling, Juliet? You have a bit of color in your cheeks. That's a good sign."

I tried to smile. "Thank Mom and the coffee."

"Were you able to get service?" Mom asked.

"Yes. EMS is on their way."

Sirens in the distance punctuated his point.

"Do you think she drowned?" I asked the Professor, knowing full well that he probably didn't have answers yet, but I couldn't help it. Josie's death didn't make sense.

"It's too soon to say," he replied. "I'm going down to the beach."

"Can we come?" I asked.

"Are you feeling up to it?" Mom's walnut brown eyes clouded with concern.

"Yeah, I feel better," I assured her. It was true. Between the heat of the fire and the coffee the shivering had subsided completely.

We walked together on the path.

Carlos knelt next to Josie's lifeless body. Ramiro and Gus stood nearby. Elisa and Kit had also shown up. They were huddled together in a blanket. Miller was pacing in front of the river in his pajamas muttering to himself. I had completely forgotten about the rest of the team in the blur of everything that had happened. However, I realized that Maddy was noticeably absent. Could she have slept through all the commotion?

The Professor took control of the scene until the paramedics and police arrived. Once they did, everything sped up.

"Everyone, I need you to move away from the area," the Professor directed as the first responders surrounded Josie's body. "Please stay back, or feel free to head to camp. We're going to be taking statements soon, but we need space to assess the area."

"I kept trying to revive her, but there was no hope," Carlos said as we moved closer to the trail where Ramiro had found a large rock to plant himself on.

"It's not your fault," I assured Carlos. Then I turned my attention to Ramiro. "How are you holding up?"

He pulled on a sock. "I'm okay."

"Are you sure?"

He nodded. "I mean, it's awful, but I think I'm okay."

I sat down next to him and wrapped my arm around his shoulder. "It *is* awful."

I lost track of time as the paramedics attempted to revive Josie and then ultimately called time of death. The three of us watched in silence.

The Professor finally addressed everyone. "We're going to be removing the body, so I'd recommend that everyone return to camp. Please stay close," he said, taking out his Moleskine notebook. "You're welcome to get coffee or change clothes, but no one is to leave until I say so, understood?"

"Where would we go?" Kit asked. "We're in the middle of nowhere."

"Miller, when is the limo coming to take us back?" Gus asked.

Miller ran his fingers through his already-disheveled hair. "Uh, I don't know. I need to check the schedule. I think at eleven, but Josie had asked me to change our departure time last night."

"Why?" Elisa asked.

"You know Josie." Miller shrugged and glanced at the body. He threw his hand over his mouth, like he was trying to stop himself from throwing up.

"I could use a coffee," Gus said, starting to move away.

At that moment someone came down the pathway.

"What's all the commotion? I was trying to sleep." A shrill voice echoed through the trees.

Everyone turned toward the sound and gasped in unison.

It was Josie.

"Josie, you're alive!" Miller ran toward her with his arms outstretched.

She pushed him away. "Of course I'm alive. What are you doing?"

If Josie was alive then who had I pulled in from the river?

Chapter Nine

"Wait, I thought Josie was dead." Elisa tossed the blanket off her shoulders.

"Clearly, I'm not dead." Josie's tone was fierce. "I'm standing right here."

"Then who is that?" Elisa's finger shot toward the ground.

The Professor held out his hands to keep everyone back. "Let's all take a nice, long, slow breath." He modeled breathing in through his nose.

"Oh no! Oh no! Is that Maddy?" Elisa wailed.

"Maddy?" Kit repeated.

"Why does Maddy have my life vest on?" Josie asked.

"Some good it did her," Gus said under his breath.

The Professor flipped his notebook to a blank page. "I'm going to need the full name of the deceased. I presume you are Josie Jones?" He directed his question to Josie.

"Yes, for the third time, I'm Josie and I'm obviously alive." She scowled. "That is Madeline Solars, my VP, who for some unknown reason is wearing my life vest."

"Ah, I see." The Professor made a note.

Was this a case of mistaken identity? Had someone killed Maddy by accident? That made sense. It would have been dark last night. The killer probably spotted Josie's bright pink life vest and assumed it was her. Josie had already remarked on Maddy's haircut and style mimicking hers. The killer could have easily mistaken them for each other.

"How did she die?" Josie asked.

"It's too soon to say," the Professor answered. "We'll be conducting a full investigation. At this point, I'm not ruling anything out, which is why I'll need to take each of your statements." He caught Mom's eye. "Helen, could I beg a favor of you and Juliet?"

We moved closer to him.

"Would you be willing to serve coffee and breakfast? I'd like to keep this area clear for some one-on-one conversations. As the Bard said, 'Time shall unfold what plighted cunning hides, Who covers fault, at last shame them derides.'"

"Count on it." Mom leaned in to kiss him. "You do whatever needs to be done. Juliet and I will keep them fed and caffeinated."

"Many thanks." The Professor clasped his hands in gratitude. "Before you depart, is there anything else you witnessed that might be of importance?" he asked me.

I thought for a minute. "The thing that stands out the most is the life jacket. Josie didn't take it off. You saw that, too, right? Not even during dinner and Lance's performance last night. Apparently, she was terrified of the water and couldn't swim. I don't understand how Maddy ended up wearing it, and I know we shouldn't jump to conclusions, but it seems like there's a good chance that this could have been a case of mistaken identity."

"Mmm-hmm." The Professor made a note.

"Do you have any idea what the cause of death could be?"

He shook his head. "I have some suspicions, but as you stated, it's too soon to let them lead me in a solid direction. I have a strong sense that foul play was involved. Again, we'll have to wait for the coroner to confirm that."

"Right." I took a final glance at the riverbank where the paramedics were lifting Maddy's body onto a gurney. "We'll take care of breakfast. Just let us know if there's anything else you need."

Mom looped her arm through mine. "How is Ramiro holding up?"

"I don't know. I mean he seems okay, but what if he's bottling up all his feelings? I mean he just witnessed me pull a dead body from the river and his dad try to revive her." A wave of panic hit me. "How terrible is that? It was such a whirlwind. I came down to the river to get water and spotted Josie—Maddy—and I jumped in without really thinking about it. I called for help. Carlos and Ramiro came, but then once I got her body out, I was so cold that I went to dry off and change and just left him there."

Mom tightened her grip. "Don't worry, honey. I'm sure he's fine. He's a strong young man, just like his dad."

I felt terrible. What kind of mother would I be if, in the midst of an emergency, my first thought of concern wasn't for my child?

"He's a wise young man," Mom said, trying to reassure me. "I didn't mean to make you think you did something wrong in your response."

"No, it's not your fault. I should have been thinking more about Ramiro. Everything just happened so fast."

"That's normal. You were also in shock, honey."

A lump formed in my throat. "Yeah."

Her brow crinkled with concern. "Juliet Montague Capshaw, I know that face. I know that you have a tendency to put way too much pressure on yourself. You just went through a shocking, horrific experience. You responded to the emergency. And you were soaking wet. You took care of yourself, as Doug and Carlos recommended, which is one hundred percent the correct response. The last thing Doug and his team need is a second emergency situation. Had you gone into shock, we'd be in a very different position now. Look, there they are." She pointed to the fire pit where Carlos and Ramiro were sipping warm drinks. "You go sit down. I'll start the coffee."

I hurried over to them. "Ramiro, I have to apologize for leaving you in the middle of all of that. It just sort of dawned on me now, and I feel so bad."

His nose twitched. "What do you mean?"

"I deserted you in the midst of all of that chaos to come change. I feel terrible."

Ramiro and Carlos shook their heads in unison. "But why? I was not in danger."

"That had to be terrible for you to see a body like that."

"Sí, but you went into the river to try and save the

woman. I am fine." Ramiro patted the bench. "You should come sit. Padre, you will get her a coffee, sí?"

Carlos was already to his feet. "On my way."

"How are you really?" I put my hand on Ramiro's knee.

He cradled a camp mug. "I have a warm drink and a fire. I'm fine. It was not expected that I would see a body, but I'm okay, I promise."

"What is your mom going to think?" I couldn't imagine having to call Ramiro's mom to let her know that her only son had been on the scene of a potential murder.

"She will be okay, too." He patted my hand. "I promise, I'm okay. It is sad, but I do not feel like I'm in danger or anything."

"Good."

"Does Doug know what happened to her?"

"Not yet." I turned my attention to the kitchen area where Mom was setting out muffins and pastries and Carlos was pouring coffee. "This is between us, but he is fairly confident that it wasn't an accident."

"How could it be?" Ramiro stared at his mug. "Does he think she was poisoned?"

"What makes you say that?"

He nodded to Josie's tent. "See that smashed wine bottle? I saw two more like it."

"You did? Where?"

"There's one in front of the tent that Maddy was staying in and there was another near the river. It's like somebody went a little crazy and smashed wine bottles everywhere."

How had I missed that?

"We were talking about the smashed bottles while we were waiting for you and the others to come back from the river. Could it be that one of them contained something that the killer wanted to keep secret? Maybe that's why the bottles are all broken."

"You're thinking like a detective," I said. "Make sure you tell the Professor this when he interviews you."

"I will." Ramiro took a sip of his coffee. "I will also be sure to tell him what I saw last night."

"What did you see?"

"I don't know for sure if it means anything or is even connected to this, but I woke up at two and was thirsty, so I got up and came out to the kitchen. It was dark. I had my flashlight, of course, but it was still hard to see. I think also because I was half-asleep. When I got here to the fire pit I heard voices."

"You did?"

Ramiro nodded. "I snuck out quietly, so I didn't wake you guys. I thought it was Josie because I saw the reflectors on the life vest, but now maybe I realize it wasn't her. She was standing near the kitchen holding a bottle of wine and arguing about addiction."

"Addiction?"

"Sí. She was with a man, but I'm not sure if it was Miller or Gus. It was too dark to see him. He was standing in the shadows. They were fighting about drugs, I think."

"Drugs?" I knew I wasn't offering much to the conversation by repeating Ramiro's words, but I was surprised by his revelation.

"Drugs. Yes. Josie, or maybe it was Maddy, was

saying that she knew about the drugs and she wasn't going to keep quiet any longer."

"Really? Then what happened?"

"I think they must have heard me coming toward them, or maybe they saw my flashlight, because the man said, 'We have ears in the forest.' Then they broke apart and went in opposite directions. I got some water and came back to bed."

"This is essential information for the Professor."

"Do you think?"

I nodded. "Absolutely."

Carlos delivered a steaming mug of coffee. "Here you go. This will help warm you up."

I took it from him. "Ramiro was filling me in on what he heard last night."

"It is suspicious for sure."

"I just wish I knew who was arguing with her. Do you think that person could be the killer?" Ramiro asked.

"I don't know, but it's definitely a possibility." I savored a few sips of the coffee. Did someone on the executive team have a drug problem? If so, who? And could they have killed Maddy to keep that quiet?

Chapter Ten

After savoring more coffee, we went to help Mom. "Do you think we should go ahead and make the full breakfast we had planned?"

The police team from Shady Cove had spread out around the campsite. They were indicating spots that must have potential evidence with yellow numbered markers. The broken wine bottles Ramiro had mentioned were all being flagged.

"I don't see why not. I have a feeling that we'll be here for a while. It's going to take Doug some time to get through interviewing everyone and if nothing else it will give us something to focus on, don't you think?"

"It's like you read my mind." Nothing helped to center me like baking.

"What can I do?" Ramiro asked.

"Would you be willing to take Doug a cup of coffee and a pumpkin chocolate chip muffin?" Mom asked. "I know that he'll never eat otherwise."

"Sure." Ramiro was happy to help. "I will see if I can tell him about what I saw too."

"Well, how is he?" Mom asked after he left with breakfast reinforcements for the Professor.

"He's fine." I pointed to the Shady Cove police officers and told her about what Ramiro had seen last night and how he had noticed smashed wine bottles around the campsite.

"There was one here too, but someone must have cleaned it up."

"Where?"

She pointed to the ground near the camp stoves. "Over there. I noticed it when I first came to get a cup of coffee. In fact, Carlos told me to watch my footing because of the broken glass. But now it's gone."

"Maybe Ramiro is on to something with his theory." I opened the coolers and took out cartons of eggs and honey-cured bacon wrapped in butcher paper.

Carlos was heating the camp stoves and chatting with Kit, who had changed into a pair of faded bell-bottom jeans with flower patches and a flowy rainbow sweatshirt.

Miller, Elisa, and Josie took their coffees to the fire pit. Gus was nowhere to be seen.

"Have you seen Gus?" I asked Mom, handing her a package of bacon.

"He got a cup of coffee a few minutes ago. Maybe he's in his tent?"

"Yeah." I found a bowl and began cracking eggs. "Or he's making a break for it."

"Where would he go?" Mom glanced around us.

"True." The forest, which had seemed so calm and peaceful a few hours ago, now felt dark and sinister, despite sunlight spilling between the trees and drying the morning dew. Nature was none the wiser that a woman was dead. The birds continued their serenade; the river rushed on. Meanwhile my world felt like it had been turned upside down.

"If Doug was concerned about that, he would have stationed one of the officers here," Mom noted.

"You're right. I guess I'm more on edge than I realized."

"Do you want to sit by the fire? I can handle breakfast. Carlos will help."

"No, really, I think the best thing I can do right now is cook and try to let my mind concentrate on something else."

"Okay, you say the word, though if something changes . . ."

"I will." I took my own advice and whisked the eggs. I added spices, fire-roasted red peppers, sun-dried tomatoes, and feta cheese. Carlos would scramble the eggs with hash browns. Then we'd serve them with thick slabs of the bacon, the muffins and pastries that we'd brought from Torte, and pancakes. Our original breakfast menu had been for French toast casserole, but Miller had made a last-minute change, insisting that flapjacks "fit the brief" for their cowboy-themed cookout better than French toast.

With the eggs ready, I turned my attention to the pancake batter. There's nothing better or more classic than pancakes for a camping trip. We would offer three pancake options for our guests this morning. A classic buttermilk with maple syrup and fresh berries, lemon ricotta pancakes smothered with lemon curd and blueberry compote, and mocha chip pancakes with a coffee glaze.

The key to pancakes is not to overmix the batter and to

include the right amount of leavening agent to achieve light and fluffy, stackable cakes. I scooped flour, baking powder, and salt into another mixing bowl; then I incorporated eggs, buttermilk, vanilla, and a touch of oil for the buttermilk base. We would use the base to build the two specialty pancakes. I divided the batter into three bowls.

"What can I do?" Mom had finished layering the bacon on the griddle. "Carlos is going to oversee the bacon, so I'm free."

"Can you make the coffee glaze?"

"Sure."

I finished the mocha chip batter by adding coffee, chocolate sauce, and mini chocolate chips to one of the bowls. The lemon ricotta got an addition of fresh lemon juice and zest and ricotta cheese.

"Bacon is ready," Carlos called. "Pancake me."

I smiled for the first time all morning and handed him the buttermilk batter and a ladle. "Do you need help?"

"No, I'm good. If you can cover the bacon and then the eggs will be last."

Mom and I carried platters of bacon, fresh fruit, muffins, and pastries, along with coffee, tea, and hot chocolate, to the tables.

Josie raised her camp mug. "Uh, refill."

I forced my lips shut so as to not say something rude. I knew these were unusual circumstances, so I would give her more leeway, but still—talking to anyone in that kind of a tone was unacceptable in my book. I had made that clear to my staff. Yes, we wanted to make everyone who walked in Torte's front doors feel welcome and comfortable, but not at the expense of our well-being.

I'm a firm believer that what we put out into the world is reflected back upon us. I traded in kindness, and I had no tolerance for people who treated my staff or our customers disrespectfully.

"How long is this going to take?" Josie asked.

I assumed she was addressing the team. No one answered.

"I'm talking to you."

"Me?" I pointed to my chest.

"Yes, you're clearly connected to the detective. How long is this going to take? We have a full agenda for the rest of the weekend. We can't be stuck out here all day. We have serious business to take care of."

Josie had made a lasting impression on me since our first meeting. Let's just say not a good one, but this was a new low. Her colleague was dead, and her only concern was about making sure their agenda for the retreat didn't get altered.

"I have no idea," I answered truthfully. "You'll have to speak with the Professor."

"Surely there's something you can do. You must have influence. He simply needs to understand the importance of the work we're doing. There's absolutely no reason to detain my entire staff."

What important work were they doing? I hadn't seen the Bamboo team do anything other than bicker since they had arrived in Ashland. "This is an investigation into the death of your employee. I have no influence over that, and even if I did, I wouldn't feel comfortable getting in the middle of it."

She rolled her eyes. "This whole situation is ridiculous. I don't understand what's taking so long. We all know why Maddy is dead. We know the cause. Are the police that dumb?"

"You know the cause of death?" I stared at her, surprised that she was being so forthcoming and that she had an idea of how Maddy was killed.

"She was sauced. She obviously was drunk out of her mind and didn't realize she was in the water. It's a shame, but it's not a shock." She looked to her team for validation. Everyone stared at their coffee. "Fine, no one else wants to say it, I will. She had a problem. Am I disappointed that it had to come to this? Yes, but I'm also a realist. We can't sit around here and pretend to be distraught when we came here with a mission."

"Some of us are distraught," Kit said. Her eyes were bloodshot and puffy like she'd been crying. "Maddy's dead and you're acting like nothing even happened."

She gave Kit a threatening look. "I'd watch your tone if I were you. I saw you and Maddy last night."

Kit spilled her coffee. It splashed on the table and her outfit. "What? What are you talking about?"

Josie narrowed her eyes. "You know exactly what I'm talking about."

I handed Kit a stack of napkins. She dabbed coffee. I noticed her hands were as shaky as mine had been earlier.

"Kit's right." Miller spoke with a burst of confidence. "None of us have ever seen a dead body. Let alone the body of someone we know and adore."

"Adore?" Josie's voice was laced with anger. "Do you care to elaborate on that sentiment, Miller?"

He sputtered. "What I'm trying to say is that Maddy

just died. It doesn't feel right to pivot straight to planning and work discussions."

"I don't care how it *feels*," Josie snapped. "Bad things happen, but at the end of the day we have a company to run. On that note, Elisa, I need you to write a press release and get it out ASAP. We have to get out in front of this and there's a real opportunity here."

"An opportunity for what?" Elisa had been silent throughout the conversation. She nursed her coffee and kept her head tilted toward the river.

"Do you have a degree in marketing? Do I need to spell everything out? I would think it would be obvious. I'm talking about the tragic death of Bamboo's VP, Madeline Solars. You can't pay for this kind of publicity. Her tragic and untimely death will make headlines, which is good for the company."

Kit gasped. "How can you say that?"

"Any press is good press, right, Elisa?" Josie looked to her young PR specialist for confirmation.

Elisa shrugged. Her chin quivered like she was trying to fight off tears. She seemed dazed, like her attention was somewhere else.

"The story will put Bamboo in the forefront of customers' minds. We need to make sure we spin the sadness of the piece."

"You are beyond cruel." Kit stood up and dumped the rest of her coffee on the dirt. "This is low, even for you, Josie."

"What? I thought I was a boss babe." Josie's nostrils flared. "I do what I need to do to get things done. That's what it takes to survive in this corporate world, especially as a woman. You of all people should respect that."

Kit walked away without responding.

"Hey, has anyone seen Gus?" Miller changed the topic.

Elisa shook her head. Her complexion was pale and unhealthy—her cheeks were as white as her hair. She didn't look good. I wondered if she was on the edge of going into shock, too.

"He's probably crying in his coffee somewhere. He had a thing for Maddy, you know," Josie said.

"He did?" Elisa poured a refill. She tugged at her hair, like she was trying to hide.

"How did you not notice that?" Josie snarled. "He would hang on her every word. He followed her around the office like a lost puppy dog. It was embarrassing."

Mom arrived with a stack of pancakes. "I hope everyone is hungry. There are more on the way. Bacon and eggs are coming next."

"I don't think I can eat," Miller said, staring at the food like it was tainted. "I feel kind of sick."

"Me either," Elisa agreed.

Josie reached for a mocha chip pancake. "You need to eat. Whether we're stuck here today or if they let us go, we're getting this work done. I'm not going to return home without completing the task we came here to do."

"Even though Maddy is dead." Miller rubbed his temples.

"Like I said, the work doesn't stop. I suggest you two eat up and prepare yourself for a long day."

At that moment the sound of a loud crash reverberated through the forest.

I looked to see Gus lying on the ground in front of Maddy's tent, which had come tumbling down on him.

Chapter Eleven

Everyone hurried over to Gus.

"Gus, are you okay?" Miller bent over to help lift him from the rubble. The canopy had collapsed on one side.

Gus rubbed the base of his head. "I think I hit my head."

"What happened?" Miller supported Gus's back as he lifted him to a seated position.

"I don't know. The tent came crashing down on me." There was a dull quality to Gus's eyes.

"What were you doing in there?" Kit asked.

I wondered where she had come from.

Gus didn't answer. He blinked rapidly, like he was trying to get his bearings. "Is everyone else okay?"

Miller studied his face. "We're all fine. Why wouldn't we be?"

Gus massaged his neck. "Is my tent the only one that collapsed?"

"This isn't your tent, man. This is—was—Maddy's tent." Miller looked up at Kit with worry.

"No, no." Gus shook his head. "This is my tent."

"It's Maddy's tent," Kit seconded what Miller had

said. "Your tent is over there." She pointed across the pathway.

"No," Gus insisted. "We traded."

"You traded tents?" Kit asked. "When?"

"Last night. Maddy asked me if I would mind trading tents with her. I didn't care where I slept at that point. I hadn't unpacked my things yet, so it wasn't a big deal to lug my suitcase over here."

Miller stood up. "Why did she ask you to trade with her?"

Gus concentrated on a tree in front of him, like he was trying to remember. "Um, it's kind of fuzzy. I don't know if that's because I hit my head or if it's because we had a lot of wine last night. I know she had a reason, but I can't remember what it was."

Was it fuzzy, or was Gus intentionally being evasive?

"Wait, so you and Maddy were the last two up last night and she asked you to trade tents before you went to bed?" Kit sounded like she was trying to piece together the clues.

I was on the same track. Could the tent swap be connected to Maddy's death?

"Yeah, that's right. I think she said she wanted to keep an eye out for someone. Or something." Gus massaged the base of his skull.

That wasn't exactly a lot to go on. Someone or something was about as open-ended as you could get. But I was intrigued by the idea that Maddy had requested a tent change in order to keep watch on the camp. That had to mean something. Could she have witnessed something that put her in harm's way? Or did she know that a killer was after her? Maybe the idea to trade tents had nothing to do with keeping watch and everything to do with trying to stay safe. She could have asked Gus so that she could hide in his tent.

The thought made me even sadder for her. What if she had known that she was in danger the entire time?

"How did your tent crash?" Miller asked.

Gus slowly got to his feet. He turned to survey the damage. "I don't know. The yurt seemed stable, but it looks like the side supports were loosened."

Everyone moved toward the side and back of the structure.

Miller started to reach down to pick up one of the ropes that had clearly been severed.

"Don't touch that," I cautioned. "We need to get the Professor. The police will need to take a look at this."

"Why?" Gus sounded confused.

"Because it might be connected to Maddy's death. This could be a crime scene. We can't touch anything."

Carlos had come over to see what the commotion was.

"No one touch anything. Stay put. I'll go get the Professor." I turned to Carlos and whispered, "Don't let them move until I get back."

"I won't." His gaze was serious.

I headed for the water. I knew the path well now. It was brighter than it had been earlier. The bark and pine needles warmed from the sun. I couldn't believe that just a couple of hours ago I had discovered Maddy's body.

The memory sent a wave of dizziness through my head.

Maddy was dead.

I blew out a long breath and continued on, forcing my

thoughts and visions of her body floating on the river to the back of my mind.

Keep it together, Jules, I told myself as I made it to the shoreline.

From the looks of things, the police were finished documenting the scene. Two local Shady Cove officers snapped a few final pictures and the EMS team had departed, along with Maddy's body. The Professor picked up a crime scene marker.

"Juliet, how is it going? Have you been able to keep them calm with your beautiful pastries and coffee?"

"Until a few minutes ago yes, but there's been a development."

His eyes flooded with concern. "What kind of development?"

I told him about the tent collapse and how Maddy and Gus had traded places last night.

"Is that so?" He made another note. "This does indeed sound like it requires my attention. Let me touch base with the Shady Cove officers and I'll be right with you."

I waited while he checked in with the team responsible.

He returned a moment later. "Shall we?" He pointed to the trail, and I followed behind him.

"What do you think by now?" I asked as we moved away from the river. "Do you have any better sense of what happened to her, or is it going to come down to the autopsy?"

"I'm afraid confirmation will have to wait, but I don't have many doubts that she was murdered. This new development, as you put it, only confirms that."

"Do you think she knew that someone was watching her? Or maybe even that someone had threatened her? At first when Gus mentioned trading tents he said she was on the lookout, but after I thought about it more, I'm wondering if she changed sleeping arrangements on purpose. A way of hiding from her killer."

"It's a solid theory."

"Which makes it seem even more plausible that Gus's tent collapsing could have been because the killer didn't realize they'd swapped places."

The Professor put an arm around my shoulder. "One of the many reasons I appreciate your mind, dear Juliet. In circumstances like this I have found it most likely that two incidents are connected. To not find a connection would be the exception."

"There are so many twists in this case," I said as we navigated the path back to camp. "It could be that Maddy was mistaken for Josie, and now we've learned that she was in a different tent. If she wasn't the intended victim, then it was a really bad string of mistakes that led to her death."

"Agreed." His eyes drifted to the campsite as we rounded the final bend on the path. "As the Bard would say, 'O, that way madness lies.'"

I showed him Gus's collapsed tent.

As expected, he cleared everyone from the area. "Please go have a seat. I'll be with each of you shortly."

The group shuffled to the picnic tables. Everyone except for Elisa, who I noticed headed in the opposite direction.

On a whim I decided to follow her. I'm not entirely sure what prompted my decision. Maybe it was because she had checked to make sure none of the team were watching her, or the fact that she wasn't heading for the bathrooms or her tent, but she was on a direct route to Maddy's tent.

My breath caught in my chest as I watched her stop, and take a quick look at the picnic area and then Gus's tent, before she pulled back a flap and stepped inside.

What was she doing in Maddy's tent?

Part of me wanted to run in after her, but that would be too obvious.

Think, Jules.

I could barge in and tell her the Professor needed her, but we'd just left everyone. I could go in and tell her that the Professor sent me to look for something, but what?

I needed to do something fast.

If Elisa was the killer, she could be removing critical evidence from the tent. I didn't have time to waste.

My only play was the truth.

I peered through the tent flaps. "Hello, is someone in here?"

Elisa clutched a laptop bag to her chest. "Oh, it's you. You scared me to death."

"Sorry. I was heading to get some supplies and I thought I saw movement in here."

She kept the bag glued to her body. Her face turned ashen. "Right, yeah, that was me. I need to log in to Maddy's laptop to get her personal details for the press release. I can't believe Josie is making me send a press release today. It's gross, but I don't know what else to do. If I don't put something together and get it out to the press, I know she'll fire me. I'm in PR; this is what

I do—spin stories. It's just that the stories don't usually hit so close to home, you know?"

I thought she might break down. "It's been a rough morning, for sure."

She moved closer. "I'm trying to hold it together, but I can't believe Maddy is dead. I mean last night we were drinking and laughing around the fire and now she's gone. It doesn't even feel real." She glanced around the tent, which was neat and tidy. Maddy's bed didn't look like it had even been slept in.

"That's normal. I think we're all in shock."

"Which is why it's insane that Josie is making us work. She's the worst." Elisa tucked her white-blond hair behind her ear. "You know what I think? I think she did it."

"Did what?" I had a feeling I knew exactly what Elisa was going to say, but I wanted to hear it from her.

"Killed her. I think she killed Maddy." She held the laptop bag tighter, like she was cradling a stuffed animal or some sort of talisman to help calm her down. "She hated Maddy. She was constantly jealous of her. There wasn't a day when she didn't come to my office asking what people were saying about her."

"About who, Josie?" I asked.

"Yeah, she was paranoid that the staff was gossiping about her."

"Were they?"

She laughed. "You've met her, right? Yes, of course. Josie *is* the topic of conversation around the office. Everyone is terrified of her, except for Maddy." She sniffed. "Maddy was the only person who was ever willing to stand up against some of Josie's most outrageous requests. It infuriated Josie, but she tried not to let it show. She would put on a game face at team meetings and then come into my office and vent for hours about how annoying it was that everyone on staff adored Maddy and not her."

"Do you really think she could have killed her?"

Elisa nodded. "Without a doubt. She's been up to something." She peered toward the front of the tent, as if making sure no one was listening in. Then she spoke in almost a whisper. "Secret meetings. A strange dude was hanging around after work who I've seen her sneak off with."

"Maybe she's dating someone and doesn't want it to be the topic of office gossip."

"Trust me, this guy isn't a date. More like a hitman."

"A hitman?" I couldn't contain my skeptical tone. Was Elisa kidding? That sounded like something out of a movie.

"Like I said, I think she's been planning this for a while. I'm sure that Josie is a killer."

Chapter Twelve

Elisa kept a tight hold on Maddy's laptop bag. "I need to get to work on this ridiculous press release. My career is probably already over. I can't imagine having any creditability with the media after sending out a press release about a dead colleague, but I'm sure that's Josie's end goal. If you want a word of advice, watch your back around Josie Jones. That woman is a monster." With that she left the tent.

I didn't move for a minute. Elisa was convinced that not only had Josie killed Maddy, but also she'd been planning it in advance. That was a huge turn of events and something the Professor definitely needed to know about. Unless Elisa was lying. There was also the possibility that she had made the story up on the fly when I'd caught her taking Maddy's bag. She did work in PR, after all. Storytelling was her livelihood.

Could there be another reason that she had taken Maddy's laptop? Was she even allowed to go through Maddy's things? It wasn't as if the tent had been roped off by the police, but then again, maybe they just hadn't had time to get to it yet.

I went straight to the Professor to let him know what I had seen, and that Elisa had Maddy's laptop.

"Thank you very much, Juliet. I believe I'll put Elisa at the top of my interview list." He glanced at his watch. "I'm hoping not to have to detain you much longer. The police team from Shady Cove will be taking statements as well. I've agreed to help manage the investigation since I was already on the scene, but as is customary on the force, I need to defer to whatever my colleagues request."

"Should we go ahead and start packing up?"

"Absolutely. I don't see any problem with that."

Carlos, Mom, and Ramiro had finished cleaning up breakfast dishes.

"Looks like I showed up at the right time," I teased.

"What did Doug say?" Mom asked.

"He said that we have the green light to begin packing. It's fine to go ahead and tear down camp. We can't leave, of course, until they take our statements, but it sounds like we'll be able to return to Ashland in the next hour or two."

"That's a glimmer of good news in an otherwise sorrowful morning."

"Being home in Ashland has never sounded so good," I agreed.

We spent the next thirty minutes repacking supplies in tubs and loading the coolers in the van. In terms of the stoves, yurts, and tables, the event company would be responsible for that cleanup, which made things easy for us.

A young police officer came to take our statements. "I need exact times of where you were last night through this morning," she said to me as she took me over to a grouping of Adirondack chairs situated away from the rest of the camp for privacy.

I walked her through everything I remembered, from when we went to bed until I found Maddy's body in the river.

"Why were you up early?" she asked.

"I'm a baker. It's in my blood, and I wanted to get a head start on making coffee and starting breakfast before everyone woke up."

"No one else was around? You didn't see anyone else near the river? At camp?"

I explained that the forest had been quiet, serenely so, until I came upon Maddy's body.

The officer was professional and asked a litany of questions. I made a mental note to let the Professor know that she had done a great job of noting my whereabouts to establish a timeline for the murder while being kind and caring. It was a difficult balance to achieve.

Around noon he called everyone to the fire pit. "I'd like to thank you for your cooperation. You are all free to return to Ashland, but as we made clear, you are not to leave Jackson County until you check in with me. Is that understood?"

Everyone nodded.

"How long is that going to be?" Josie asked. "We have a chartered flight scheduled for midweek."

"Hopefully we'll have you on your way by then." He was noncommittal. "In the meantime, I may have some follow-up questions for you. I have your B and B contact information and your cell phones. Safe travels and I'll be in touch."

"Do you want to ride with us?" I asked Mom.

"Let me touch base with Doug."

"We'll finish getting our bags from the tent. No rush."

The limo arrived to transport the Bamboo team. Miller loaded their bags on his own and waited to get the last seat. As they drove off, I breathed a sigh of relief. At least we weren't going to have to be around them twenty-four seven. I knew we weren't done with the Bamboo execs, but having some breathing room from their dysfunction was most welcome.

Mom opted to come with us as the Professor would be spending the remainder of the day on-site and going over statements with the Shady Cove police.

Our return drive felt very different from the drive out to the campsite. For starters it felt like we'd been gone for a week, not a day. All of us were pretty quiet, sitting in our contemplation of Maddy's death as the rugged landscape shifted outside the car's windows.

When Mount A came into view, I let my shoulders sag. Thank goodness we were home.

The plaza seemed even more charming as we drove along Main Street. Maroon and gold Shakespearean banners hung from the antique lampposts, announcing the end of the season. The trees were just beginning to turn, like the tips of their leaves had been dipped in jewel tones.

Steph and Rosa had already swapped out Torte's front window, which was a relief after what had happened on the Rogue. Instead of the cozy camping scene, they had strung auburn fairy lights around the trim and dotted the display with cake stands showcasing three- and four-tiered cakes frosted in harvest colors.

My feet felt solid, like they were connected to the ground for the first time since finding Maddy's body, as I got out of the car and began the process of unloading.

Unpacking was even faster because Andy, Sterling, and Bethany came out to help.

"How was it, boss?" Andy asked. He was dressed in a pair of shorts and a retro T-shirt.

"You don't want to know."

"That bad?" He grabbed a box of heavy skillets and supplies and lifted it with ease.

"Worse, there was an accident."

"Accident?" Sterling's ice blue eyes narrowed with concern.

"Well, that's what the police are calling it for the moment. We aren't exactly sure. It might have been murder."

"Oh no. How are you all holding up?" Bethany placed her hand over her heart. "That must have put bad vibes on the trip."

"I knew that those people were trouble." Andy balanced one box in his left arm, and then picked up two more with his free hand. "Sorry you guys had to go through that."

"We're hanging in," I said with a smile. "And we're all very happy to be home."

"If it's any help, things have been running as smooth as butter," Sterling said. "We sold out of basically everything yesterday and this morning has been steady."

"Glad to hear it. We need all the good news we can get right now."

"You didn't doubt us, did you, boss?" Andy furrowed his brow.

"Not in the slightest, but you never know if Richard Lord might have decided to make an appearance while we were gone."

"Now that you mention it, he did stop by." Bethany frowned. "He wanted to make sure that I passed on a message that he needs to see you the second you returned. He said it's urgent."

"I bet he did." Richard was the owner of the ratty Merry Windsor Hotel across the plaza from Torte and was notorious for assigning unnecessary timelines to the most benign circumstances. An emergency in his mind would be not returning a call to discuss how we were violating one of the many imaginary rules he had created. "I'll get right on it."

"Don't worry. We took care of him. We sent him on his way with coffee and cupcakes." Bethany made a funny face. "Kill him with kindness."

Once the van had been unloaded, I sent Carlos and Ramiro home to shower. "I just want to check on a couple of things; then it's a long, hot bath for me."

"Helen, would you like a ride home?" Carlos offered.

"I'll gladly take you up on that offer," she said, turning to me. "As long as you don't need me here. A bath sounds wonderful."

"No. Honestly, I just want to take a few minutes to get everything settled and make sure we're ready for Monday. I'm not planning to stay."

"She says that now." Mom looked at Carlos. "Any bets on when you see her?"

Carlos tapped his wrist. "Midnight."

"Hey, I'm still here." I pretended to be upset.

They both hugged me.

"Don't stay too long, mi querida." Carlos kissed my cheek, letting his lips linger for a moment. "Call if you want a ride."

I promised that I would. I wasn't lying. I just needed an hour or so at the bakeshop to help center me.

That's exactly what I did. I went straight to the sink, washed up with our signature honey and rosemary soap, and tied on an apron.

Steph was hand-piping a fall leaf pattern onto a custom cake.

"What needs to be done?" I asked.

She glanced at the whiteboard where we kept a running tally of specialty cake orders and staff schedules. "We're pretty good. Marty just left to deliver a last-minute bread order. Sterling wrapped up lunch service. We don't need to restock the pastry case because we close in a few hours."

"What about the last few orders?" I studied the board. "Do you want me to do the cookies or the cupcakes?"

"Sure." She steadied the piping bag with her free hand. "Bethany already made the brownies for the cookie platters and baked the cupcakes, so if you want to do the designs for those that would be good."

I pulled the order sheet from the board. "Did they specify what kind of fall flowers they want?"

She shook her head. "Nope. It's your favorite kind of order—decorator's choice."

In my early days on the *Amour of the Seas,* I distinctly remember panicking when my boss gave me leeway on cake design. Culinary school had been about following precise techniques. The idea of having complete creative license over a design had almost been paralyzing.

What if I made something the customer didn't like? What if my vision didn't match the final product?

My boss was wise and pushed me out of my comfort zone. She taught me to trust my instincts. "Jules, culinary school is about giving bakers a foundation. Out here in the real world, in the middle of the Atlantic Ocean. It's about taking that solid base you've learned and putting your unique spin on pastry. Anyone can follow a recipe; the test of a real pastry chef is tapping in to your inner artist and transforming butter, sugar, and flour into your masterpiece."

Thankfully, I had taken her advice, and in the years since I have tried to impart that same philosophy to my staff.

When customers came in for cake consultations, we were always happy to design off a photo or a Pinterest page, but getting the green light to compose as our hearts desired was a gift.

I set out rows of cooled apple spice, pumpkin, and chocolate cupcakes. Then I filled piping bags with our French buttercream. We used plant-based gel food colorings to achieve rich, natural colors for our frosting.

For the chocolate cupcakes I colored one of the piping bags with a brilliant yellow, then a sage green, and a brown. I used a leaf-decorating tip to pipe yellow sunflowers around the edge of a chocolate cupcake. Once I had created a perfect ring of petals, I used an open star tip to fill in the center with chocolate buttercream that resembled sunflower seeds. I finished the effect by adding a few wispy vines of green.

Next, I added a dark burgundy gel to the buttercream and secured the bag with a rose-piping tip. I changed the angle of the tip as I went in order to open the flower up. The deep maroon flowers were a lovely accompaniment to the sunflowers.

I took a minute to think about what design to create for the apple spice cupcakes. Succulents were popular and a trio of greens should balance the yellow and wine colors. Along with the sage I had already colored for the sunflower vines, I made moss green, juniper, rust, and sky blue with a touch of gray. To give these cupcakes height, I piped a blooming cactus in the center of each of them. Then I filled the space with echeveria, two-toned leaves, aloe, and burro's tail dangling from the sides.

"Those are incredible, Jules," Bethany gushed. "Can I please take a couple of snaps before you box them up?"

"Of course. Do your thing."

I cleaned up my workstation. Focusing on the cupcakes had done the trick. I hadn't even thought about Maddy or the team at Bamboo for the last hour.

"You look better, Jules," Sterling said, passing by with a tray of dishes from upstairs.

"Did I look that bad before?"

"Not to the casual observer." His almost transparent-blue eyes held a sense of knowing.

I grinned. "You're beyond your years."

"Maybe. Or maybe I have just learned to observe from the best." He set the dishes in soapy water. "Are you taking off now?"

I knew I needed a shower or a long hot bath, and it was clear that Torte was in my team's capable hands. "Yeah, I should probably go home and unpack."

"But?"

"Was there a 'but'?"

He rolled up his sleeves and plunged his hands into the sink. "I don't know, was there?"

I sighed. "I don't know. I guess I can't stop thinking about finding Maddy's body this morning. It's strange because it happened at the river, so part of me feels like it wasn't even real. Like it was a bad dream."

"That makes sense."

"I wish there was more that I could do."

"Like what?" Sterling concentrated on the dishes, but I knew he was listening intently.

"I'd like to talk to each of them alone. I feel like there's more to the Bamboo story I'm missing." Talking it through helped me piece together what I was thinking.

"Didn't you say the Professor told them to stick around?" He rinsed a soup pot and loaded dishes into our industrial dishwasher.

"Yes, he made it very clear that no one should leave town until he tells them they can."

"I'm sure they'll all be here at some point, then. What else are they doing?"

"They're doing a private backstage tour of OSF tomorrow. After that they're heading to Jacksonville for wine tasting and dinner. Finally, they have a matinée and the evening show at OSF on Tuesday, and then they go back to LA, as long as the Professor allows them to leave."

"Sounds like you have a golden opportunity, then." Sterling paused and raised one brow.

I knew exactly what he was hinting at. "Good thinking. You know, I just might take a stroll up to the Bowmer on my way home. Thanks for the chat."

"Anytime." He returned to scrubbing dishes.

I said my goodbyes and left the bakeshop. I knew exactly what I needed to do—find Lance and get myself an invite to tomorrow's backstage tour.

Chapter Thirteen

The plaza was buzzing with activity. The high school acting troupe had taken over the center square, offering a preview of their fall show—*The Lion King*. I stopped for a moment to watch them perform "The Circle of Life." A crowd quickly formed around the young starlets who had the good fortune to have actors, directors, and choreographers from OSF as mentors. From costume design to staging, Ashland High School Theatre had a serious advantage over other regional schools, thanks to an ongoing partnership with OSF. Many of my classmates who got their start on the Mountain Avenue theater stage had gone on to star on Broadway and in major movies.

Once the song was finished, I joined in the applause and then continued on the sidewalk past the rafting kiosk where tourists queued up to book trips on the Rogue. I hoped their outings would be smoother than the one I had just experienced.

Next was A Rose by Any Other Name, where galvanized tins with vibrant sunflowers and variegated hydrangeas sat waiting to be made into bouquets. At Puck's Pub the keg barrel tables near the front were already occupied by a mix of locals and out-of-towners getting a head start on happy hour.

When I made it to Elevation, the outdoor store, I glanced up the stairwell that led to my old apartment, where I'd spent the first couple of years in Ashland. Again, I was struck by how much my life had changed since those early days of cocooning myself in.

I smiled at the thought as I started to cross the street toward the Shakespeare stairs, but a booming voice shook me out of my memories. "Capshaw, I need a word!"

My stomach sank. I knew that voice. It was Richard Lord.

He stood on the front porch of the Merry Windsor, supporting his weight on the precarious railing. His purple and white checkered golf cap hid the fact that the top of his head was starting to bald.

I exhaled and walked toward him. "What's up, Richard?" The Merry Windsor was in need of some serious TLC. The "r" on the end of "Windsor" had fallen off the sign on the second story of the fake Elizabethan façade. Richard loved to tout how authentically Shakespearean the hotel was, but the satellite dish protruding from the roof and the tacky mustard yellow booths in the lobby said otherwise.

"Don't take that tone with me, young lady." The railing sagged as he leaned farther down. He could have easily stepped off the porch, but I knew he wouldn't. His end goal was to maintain higher ground—literally and figuratively. Instead of his usual attire of gawdy golf shorts, he was wearing an electric purple sweatshirt that clashed with his ruddy complexion. The sweatshirt had Shakespeare's bust across the center, with one twist—the Bard had a quill stuck between his teeth.

"Look, Richard, I don't have time for this. Did you need something?"

"You know exactly what I need." He spewed spit as he spoke.

I took a step back. This was a common game with Mr. Lord. In his fantasy world our grudge rivaled that of the Capulets and Montagues. In reality, Richard was nothing more than an irritation for me. I spent very little time pondering what he might be up to next, even though I was sure in his mind he imagined that my every waking hour was consumed with thoughts of him.

"You stole my client again."

"What?"

He cleared his throat and pulled away from the railing, yanking up his tight white pants. "You heard me. You know what you did."

"Richard, I promise I have *no* idea what you're talking about. I've been gone at an event all weekend. How would I have stolen a client?"

"Exactly." He threw his index finger in the air. "Exactly what I'm talking about."

Any conversation with Richard made me wonder if I was secretly being filmed for a prank TV show. "What are you talking about?"

"The retreat. You stole that business right out from under my feet."

My eyes drifted to his feet. His shiny white leather shoes reminded me of something a clown might wear. "Your feet are pretty big, Richard." I tried to keep my tone nonchalant.

"Don't play games with me, Capshaw."

"Help me understand how I stole business from you. Bamboo reached out to us."

"Ha! A likely story. They came to me first, and you stole that business from me—typical Torte. You and your mom like to pretend like you're the sweetest thing in town. I know the truth. I know your dark side."

Torte's dark side. That was a new one.

"What do you mean Bamboo came to you first?" I asked, ignoring his dig.

"Miller, he came to see me. We had a great meeting. We wined and dined him at the Merry Windsor and then I took him to see Parchment and Quill—we're officially opening in a month, you know. My staff pulled out the red carpet for him. We had basically inked the deal and then he called and said they'd decided to go in another direction."

Suddenly the sweatshirt made sense. Upon closer inspection I noted the words PARCHMENT AND QUILL written beneath the Bard's bust. Richard and his second cousin, Ernest—a Shakespeare snob I had met while doing an event at the art museum at SOU last year—were partnering to open a new art gallery, Parchment and Quill. They had leased the building adjacent to the police station. The gallery had been slotted to open months ago. Richard had made it a point to stop by Torte on his way to oversee renovations and threaten our Sunday Supper concept. He claimed that once the gallery opened, he intended to host his own art dinners in direct competition with us. I had blown it off. For starters, it was hardly as if we had a copyright on the concept. I also learned over the years that Richard was prone to overselling his abilities. That seemed to be what was happening with Parchment and Quill. The gallery had hit dozens of snags (most of them self-inflicted) and had yet to open.

"That's not on me," I said to Richard. "I didn't steal him as a client. As I said, Bamboo contacted us. We put together a proposal, as we always do for potential clients. They agreed to our proposal and signed a contract. End of story."

"It's not the end of it for me." He puffed out his chest. "I'll have you know, young lady, that Bamboo has opted to dine at Parchment and Quill tomorrow evening."

I was used to his empty threats. "I thought they were booked for wine tasting and dinner in Jacksonville."

Richard made a tsking sound. "It's such a shame the vineyard had a water pipe burst. We were able to make special accommodations and book them for dinner tomorrow night."

"Good for you." What I wanted to tell him was good luck, but there was no way I was going to divulge anything about what happened at the river to Richard.

"I'm surprised you didn't hear. Everyone is coming. Thomas, Kerry, Lance, Doug. It's going to be the event of the year. I'm sorry I don't have an extra seat for you." Sarcasm poured from his lips. "It's a shame that Torte can't keep your clients satisfied."

"I'm happy to share the wealth." The truth was that I was relieved that Bamboo was having dinner at

Parchment and Quill tomorrow night, but why the late booking? Had there been other plans that were canceled because of Maddy's death? I couldn't imagine Josie being okay with dining at any establishment with the Lord name based on the décor and aesthetic alone. Had the Professor made the switch? Maybe he wanted them in town so that he could continue to observe them.

"You better get used to it. We're opening Parchment and Quill early for them. They're getting a sneak peek of what is soon to be the most talked-about venue in the Rogue Valley. If I were you, I would be quaking in my boots."

I glanced at my tennis shoes. "It's a good thing I'm not wearing boots." With that I waved. "Duty calls. Good luck tomorrow." I practically sprinted toward the Shakespeare stairs. It made much more sense that Bamboo booked a dinner at the new gallery. I was surprised to hear that Richard was ready to host a dinner, though. The last I had heard from Thomas and Kerry, construction had come to a halt when Richard and Ernest's third contractor walked off the job site. They had gone through two contractors, both of whom had quit partway through construction because they couldn't take the constant berating and change of direction from the cousins.

Ernest and Richard were polar opposites when it came to Shakespeare. The Merry Windsor delt in kitsch. Richard sold bobbleheads of the Bard, keychains, and cardboard ruffs in the hotel lobby. Ernest was a purist when it came to Shakespeare. His elitist attitude had alienated the Professor, which was saying a lot. Ernest believed in exclusivity when it came to access to the arts. During his tenure on the board at SOMA (the SOU art museum) he had attempted to slash all family and community programming. Fortunately, he hadn't succeeded and he and the museum had parted ways. Hence, opening Parchment and Quill. I just couldn't picture how Richard's tacky, cheap aesthetic would pair with his cousin's opulent taste.

I'd have to get the details from Lance after tomorrow's dinner.

As fate would have it, Lance was standing in front of the Elizabethan, better known as the Lizzie to locals, talking with a member of the company.

When he spotted me, he said his good-byes and came over to greet me with a kiss on both cheeks. "Do tell, to what do I owe the pleasure?"

"I'm guessing you already heard what happened this morning."

He patted his heart. "It's absolutely tragic, darling. And rumor has it you found the body?"

I nodded.

"Shall we sit?" He swept one arm toward the bricks, the sloped grassy area with built-in concrete slabs for seating and a brick courtyard where a variety of performers served as the opening act for the nightly shows at the other theaters on campus. Over the summer Carlos and I had made it a habit to pack a picnic and come take in the free show almost every night. The Green Show was a true community gathering. Guest musicians, dance troupes, poets, and actors entertained theatergoers and locals before the doors to the main performance halls opened every night. It was always fun to see familiar faces amongst the audience and enjoy world-class shows and dinner al fresco.

Lance dropped his affect as we sat. He wrapped an arm around me. "How are you, for real?"

"I'm okay." We had built a long-standing trust over the years. I poured out every detail, minute by minute. It felt good to unload everything that I had been holding in.

He tightened his grasp. "That was obviously quite an ordeal, but let's narrow our scope to the most important piece of this."

"Which is what?"

"The fact that you are a true hero. I've said it before, and I'll say it again and again. You, Juliet Capshaw, are the bravest person I know."

I blew off his compliment.

"No, no, no. Your little tricks of evasion are no good on me, darling. You jumped into a raging river, fully clothed, to try and rescue Maddy. That deserves a medal of bravery in my humble opinion."

"Your opinion is never humble," I teased.

Lance laughed. "Ah, there's the Juliet I know and love."

"It's hard to describe, but I guess I almost feel tethered to Maddy now, like I have to be part of the solution. If I could help figure out what happened and who killed her, maybe I'll be able to let that go."

"And that is where I come in." Lance rubbed his hands together. "It's been too long since we've had a legitimate case. You're absolutely on point with your theory. The universe is practically demanding that we insert ourselves into the investigation. It's the only way you'll be able to sleep peacefully again, and lord knows we can't have Juliet Capshaw missing out on your beauty sleep."

I punched him in the shoulder.

He pretended like it hurt, massaging the spot with his free hand. "If the game is afoot, what's our plan?"

"Well, funny you ask. I was actually hoping to see if I could snag an invite to the backstage tour tomorrow."

Lance dabbed the side of his eye and fought back imaginary tears. "I have trained you so well. The protégé has become the star."

"I'm serious, Lance."

"As am I, darling. As am I." He paused as a group of patrons passed and asked if they could take a picture.

Lance acquiesced to their request with little protest. I took pictures of them.

Once they were out of earshot, he continued. "Yes, consider yourself invited. We can observe their every move under the cover of the Bowmer and Lizzie."

"I just bumped into Richard, and he said you're attending dinner at Parchment and Quill."

He gagged. "Don't remind me. Although, in light of this, I suppose it is a golden opportunity."

"Yes, you have to go. I can't wait to hear what the gallery looks like inside."

"Oh, I already know. It's going to be tacky meets bougie, as in Richard Lord bougie. Didn't you say Bamboo absolutely abhors bougie?" He rubbed his hands together. "This is going to be so much fun."

I laughed.

"You know it's true. You don't even need to see it. How Richard and Ernest ever decided to team up is the real mystery here." He shuddered. "I digress, though. While I'm stuck with the Shakespeare twins, you can do some serious snooping."

"What do you mean?" I could hear the trepidation in my tone. Lance tended to take our sleuthing one, two, or three hundred times outside my comfort zone.

He motioned for me to walk with him. "I know where they're staying."

"Okay?" I didn't like the sound of this.

"We know they'll be occupied with dinner."

"And?"

"Don't play coy with me; you know exactly what I'm implying."

"You want me to snoop through their B and B?"

He clapped twice. "Exactly."

"No way," I protested.

"Hear me out," he said, holding his hands up to pacify me. "Bamboo is staying at Abigail's. You know Abby well. I'm simply suggesting you pop over to the B and B, check in on your dear friend, and bring a basket of Torte delicacies. I'll arrange the rest."

"What?"

He tapped his wrist. "Look at the time. Must scurry. See you here on the bricks at one o'clock sharp." His grin spread up to his cheeks. "More details to come, ta-ta."

I watched him vanish inside the Bowmer. I was happy to have secured an invite to the backstage tour tomorrow, but Lance was out of his mind if he thought I was going to snoop through Abigail's Inn.

Chapter Fourteen

Maybe it was the comfort of my bed or perhaps sheer exhaustion, but after a long shower and a dinner of soup and breadsticks with Carlos and Ramiro I crashed and slept through the night. I woke the next morning feeling refreshed and ready to take on a day of investigating, with a healthy dose of baking tossed in.

I slipped out of bed and tiptoed downstairs after getting dressed. There was no need to wake Carlos or Ramiro. They had debated how Ramiro would get to school. Ramiro had won the argument without much pushback from his dad. He wanted to walk to school so he could have more time with his friends. I took it as a positive sign that he was already acclimating to life in Ashland, but I knew that Carlos wanted to spend as much time as possible with him. Our first year of having Ramiro with us full-time happened to coincide with a stage in his development where it was normal and important for him to be pulling away and hanging out with his peers. I had reminded Carlos of that fact as we drifted off to sleep. He agreed, at least from a cognitive perspective. In terms of his heart, well, that was another story. It was also one of the reasons I had fallen for him—hard—from the moment our eyes locked across the galley kitchen on the *Amour of the Seas*.

Carlos has never been afraid of showing emotional vulnerability. He prides himself on being in touch with his feelings. That had been evident last night when his eyes misted as we talked about Ramiro's changing needs as he matured into his older teen years.

Our conversation had left me feeling confident that if we did decide to have a baby of our own Carlos would be fully invested.

I tugged on a lightweight coat on my way out the door.

The air smelled of early fall, dewy leaves, a crispness, and even a faint hint of smoke from a fireplace nearby. An inky sky, dotted with stars, filled my view as I descended the hill. Soon Grizzly Peak would be dusted with snow and the leaves clinging to the sturdy oaks and maples would put on a show of color.

One of the best parts of living in the Rogue Valley was getting to experience distinct seasons. I had missed that on the ship. There was something refreshing about following the rhythm of Mother Nature's clock. Fall encouraged me to adopt a slower pace. I was already dreaming about lazy afternoons spent reading in front of the fire, while Carlos cooked a Sunday stew, and hosted board game tournaments for Ramiro and his friends.

Halloween was right around the corner. I couldn't wait to start planning our costumes for the parade. Torte would be at the epicenter of the excitement. Our entire staff would dress up for the occasion. We would serve a variety of specialty pre- and post-parade treats and have plenty of candy on hand for trick-or-treaters.

It was one of my favorite days of the year. Every business on the plaza would be decorated for the parade where thousands of costumed ghosts and ghouls danced along Main Street to the beat of thumping drums. I made a mental note to start brainstorming our Halloween offerings with the team.

As I approached the bakeshop, I noticed the lights were on at the police station. Ashland's downtown station was more like a welcome center with its blue awnings and window boxes filled with bright yellow marigolds. Tourists often stopped to ask for directions or dinner recommendations and pick up a map of Lithia Park. The small station housed offices for the Professor, Thomas, and Kerry, along with a small temporary holding cell and a lobby.

I wondered who was working this early.

On a whim, I knocked on the door.

Kerry appeared in the door frame a minute later. She was dressed for fall in a pair of buttery brown leggings, knee-high boots, and an oversized green sweater that complemented her auburn hair and green eyes.

"Hi, Jules, what's going on?"

"I'm on my way to open Torte and noticed the lights on. I thought maybe the Professor was working on the case, but since I'm here, I'm about to fire up the ovens and make a pot of coffee. Come over if you need a morning caffeine hit."

She gave me a half grin. "You know me; caffeine and I are basically best friends."

"Did you pull a short straw for the morning shift?"

She shook her head. "No. I offered. Thomas has a call with a detective in LA who has some prior dealings with Bamboo, so I came in with him. We're trying to get Doug to scale back."

A call with a detective from LA? I was intrigued. I also knew Kerry probably couldn't tell me much, but it was worth trying, right? She and I had grown closer over the past few years, especially after her father had shown up unexpectedly and almost ruined her wedding. I had intervened and made it clear that I would do anything to support her. Ever since, something had shifted between us. "I doubt you can say, but what kind of dealings did the detective have with Bamboo?"

"Lance is a bad influence on you." Kerry pressed her lips together and gave her head a slight shake.

"I know." I shrugged. "But you have to cut me some slack. I did find the body."

She tilted her head from side to side like she was trying to decide what she could say. "Okay, I can't go into much detail, but we did discover that the police had been called to their headquarters on more than one occasion. Thomas is doing more digging. We'll see if he comes up with anything."

My interest was definitely piqued. I knew she couldn't divulge specific information related to the case. This was certainly a twist. Why had the LA police previously been called to Bamboo headquarters? Could it be connected to Maddy's death?

"How is the Professor doing?" I asked.

"He seems okay. I think this case has rattled him more than usual because he feels responsible. He had a sense that there was more than corporate drama at play. He told us yesterday that he should have followed that instinct further. He feels like he could have prevented the murder."

Murder? Kerry had used the "m" word. I wondered if that meant they had confirmed that foul play had been involved in Maddy's death. "It's not his fault," I said in his defense. "I was there. What could he have done?"

"Exactly." She gestured animatedly with her hands. "That's what Thomas and I told him, too, but you know Doug."

I nodded. "So has her death officially been ruled a murder?"

"Yes. The coroner's report came in late last night." She hesitated for a minute. "This stays between us, okay?"

"Of course." I glanced around us. The plaza sat in undisturbed slumber. A handful of businesses had lights on inside, but most were dark and would be for a while.

Kerry stalled for a moment. Her eyebrows squeezed together. She swallowed and tightened her jaw. "Maddy was drugged."

I gulped. "She was?"

"Cause of death wasn't drowning." Kerry's eyes drifted across the street as a delivery truck rumbled to a stop in front of Puck's.

My mind spun with possibilities. "Which means someone must have drugged her first and then dumped her body in the river?"

"It looks that way," Kerry confirmed. She unclenched her jaw. "Look, I'm serious; this stays with us."

"Absolutely. I will not say a word." I raised one hand

in a promise. "Do you think this is a case of mistaken identity? That Josie was the intended victim?"

"That is one of the many lines of inquiry we are currently following." A phone rang behind her. "I need to answer that."

"Come by for coffee and pastries anytime. The basement door will be open."

"Thanks." She left to answer the phone.

I continued to Torte. Maddy had been drugged, and there had been previous police activity at Bamboo. What did it mean?

The more I thought about the case, the more convinced I was becoming that killing Maddy must have been an accident. In the time I had spent with the executive team, Maddy had seemed to be the most respected member of the dysfunctional staff. She had been the voice of reason, and at least from my observations everyone had seemed to like her. I certainly couldn't say the same thing about Josie. So why kill Maddy?

No, it had to be that the killer made a mistake. They must have assumed that Maddy was Josie in the dark.

Although that didn't explain how she had been drugged.

I sighed as I removed my coat and went through the opening routine. I must be missing something, I thought as I lit the bundle of applewood in the pizza oven.

I started a pot of our custom Torte blend and gathered ingredients for caramel apple strudel.

The base of the strudel was our hand-rolled puff pastry dough. The dough was a labor of love, involving layering and rolling sheets of pastry with cold butter. We made it in large batches and froze sheets for our cherry turnovers and lemon puff tarts. There's no comparison with store-bought puff pastry. Our flaky, buttery puff pastry was one of our trade secrets. Laminating the dough took some time but resulted in a crispy golden pastry that elevated every dessert.

I poured myself a cup of coffee while I let the dough thaw.

When could Maddy have been poisoned? I thought back to dinner at the river. Could the killer have spiked her drink accidentally and then realized their mistake? What about the wine bottle Josie brought to her tent while everyone else stayed up sharing stories around the fire?

Could that have been tainted?

But how did Maddy end up drinking it?

It felt like the answer was right in front of me, but just out of my grasp.

Let it rest, Jules, I told myself.

Overthinking was rarely the solution to any problem. The better strategy was to bake. I found that when I was baking or jogging through Lithia Park or doing anything that brought me into the moment and out of my head was typically when I would experience a breakthrough or epiphany.

The scent of coffee and the applewood burning brought me back into the moment. It was hard not to feel centered in Torte's bright white kitchen with our distressed barn wood floors. When Mom and I had designed the basement kitchen, we had agreed that we wanted a space that first and foremost was functional, but also a delightful space to work in. We had achieved that with specific workstations, like Bethany and Steph's design area with built-in drawers for sprinkles and pastry tools and extra lighting for when they were doing detailed piping. The bread racks were situated near the wood-fired pizza oven for natural warming. The area near the stove had been organized for meal prep. There were sweet and savory stations so that we never ran the risk of chopping garlic and juicy pears together. I loved the flow of our kitchen, and I also loved the red and teal touches throughout, along with framed photos of the bakeshop on the first day that Mom and Dad opened the doors. It truly was a tribute to them and their legacy of serving this community with love.

With that sentiment in mind, I focused my attention on my strudel. I started by peeling apples and tossing them in lemon juice, so they didn't brown. Then I added them to a saucepan and turned the heat to medium-low. Next I covered them with a cup of our pressed apple cider. I let the apples simmer for a few minutes before adding sugar, cinnamon, nutmeg, allspice, and cloves.

Once the apples were tender and a thick sauce had formed, I removed them from the heat to let them cool.

I rolled out puff pastry sheets, set the pastry on greased baking sheets, and brushed the dough with an egg wash. I carefully spooned the caramel apple mixture evenly over the crust. Then I rolled it up like a jelly roll and pinched the ends so the apples wouldn't ooze out in the baking process.

The top of the puff pastry got another egg wash and a sprinkling of coarse sugar. I cut slats so the steam could escape, allowing the pastry to puff without getting soggy. Then I slid the trays into the oven to bake for twenty minutes or until the strudel turned a luscious golden brown.

Andy arrived as I was taking the trays out of the oven.

"Morning, boss." A stack of containers of freshly roasted beans precariously balanced between his arms.

"Looks like you've been busy."

"My grandma was teasing me that she's going to have to go cold turkey on coffee because I'm constantly offering up new roasts for her to try. Can you even imagine? That would be like giving up breathing, or worse, snowboarding." He winked and shifted the boxes.

"Um, is it weird that giving up snowboarding is worse than not *breathing* in your world?" I teased.

He arranged the boxes on an open section of the counter. "No way. I'm already starting the snow countdown."

"Andy, it's supposed to be in the mid-seventies later today."

"That's today, boss; who knows what next week will look like?" His eyes glowed as he rapidly nodded his head. "Remember we had that early snowstorm in November last year. I'm crossing my fingers for Halloween snow this year."

"You might have some chilly trick-or-treaters." I tried to wink.

"Hey, they're getting candy. Stop right there." Andy held his hand out. "They won't care if they have to wear snow boots with their costumes; trust me."

"I trust you implicitly." Andy had accurately predicted every snowfall we'd had in Ashland since I returned home. I wasn't about to start doubting him now.

"What new roasts do you have for us?"

He lifted the lid on the first container. Immediately the scent of brown sugar, cocoa, and sweet berries enveloped me.

"That's dreamy."

"Yeah? You think?" He couldn't contain a grin. "It's a new one I've been trying to perfect. I don't have a great name for it yet, but it's like the last of summer. Summer's final fling, or something like that. I feel like the roast captures straddling the seasons, you know?"

"If it smells this good, I can't wait to taste it."

"I've got you covered, boss. Let me get a brew started and I'll bring you a cup."

"That's music to my ears." I sliced the apple strudel into generous individual pieces. "It sounds like it will pair beautifully with this."

"I should probably take a slice upstairs with me, just to make sure I get the balance right, don't you think?"

"For sure." I handed him a slice. He went upstairs to prep the espresso bar. I returned my attention to baking. There was bread dough to start, cookie and brownie batter to mix, and our daily specials and custom orders to go through.

Kneading dough and having my hands coated in flour helped to center me. Baking had definitely gotten me out of my head. There was only one problem. I was no closer to coming up with a theory of who killed Maddy. Or why.

Chapter Fifteen

The morning breezed by. Andy's latest roast was a hit with customers, as was my caramel apple strudel. We sold out of both by late morning. The bakeshop saw a steady stream of customers coming in for spiced lattes, almond croissants, and Sterling's breakfast burritos on their way to work and school, along with the usual crowd that lingered at the coffee bar or on the comfy seating in front of the atomic fireplace in the basement with their laptops or a good old-fashioned paperback.

The leisurely early September vibe was a welcome relief from summer's rush. I had time to stop and linger, catching up with friends and familiar faces. It never ceased to amaze me that Mom had created a space where everyone felt like family. I loved that I got to continue that tradition and that our guests were comfortable lounging on the couch or chatting up Sequoia and Rosa at the counter upstairs.

I was delivering a tray of mason jar lasagnas for lunch when I spotted Miller, Kit, Gus, and Josie passing by the front windows. Elisa wasn't with them. I wondered if she had finally had enough. Or maybe Josie had sent her back to LA to hold a press conference about Maddy's untimely death at Bamboo's headquarters. That sounded about right for Josie Jones.

I glanced at my watch. It was nearly time for the backstage tour. This was my chance to observe them without needing to acquiesce to their every request. I hurried downstairs to change out of my apron and let the team know that I was going to be gone for an hour or so.

As I had predicted, the temperature had warmed with the afternoon sun. I let the heat warm my face. The Lithia bubblers gurgled, letting off a strong odor of sulfur. Posters for upcoming shows, theater performances, and a high alpine run around Mount A plastered the welcome kiosk. Otherwise, downtown was relatively quiet. There were the usual lunch goers and a handful of tourists, but with school back in session it was clear that we were entering the slow season again.

I was glad I had layered. On my short walk up the Shakespeare steps that led to the backside of the OSF campus, I peeled off my sweatshirt and tied it around my waist.

Lance was waiting for me by the ivy-covered doors that led to the Elizabethan. "Darling, there you are. I was worried we were going to have to proceed without you." He gave me a peck on each cheek.

"Sorry, I lost track of time."

"Don't give it a thought." Lance dismissed my apology with a flick of his hand. He wore slim black slacks and a white dress shirt with the sleeves rolled partway up. Even in casual attire (for Lance) he exuded an easy confidence. "I have them all down at the Black Swan anyway. One of my actors agreed to a monologue and then a quick private tour of the inner workings of our theater lab. They should be here soon. In the meantime, do tell? Any news? Or have you been connecting with your inner pastry muse?"

"I talked to Kerry briefly earlier this morning."

"Moi aussi." He pressed a hand to his chest. "Our lovely detective happened by my office an hour or two ago."

"She did?"

"Why do you sound dumbfounded?"

"I'm not. I'm just curious. What did she have to say?"

Lance cleared his throat. "It was quite rude, if you ask me."

"Wait, what? Kerry was rude?"

"She was hoping for a word with Arlo. When I offered my services, she was quite dismissive. Don't worry your pretty little head; I seized the opportunity to remind her that she was in the presence of greatness."

"I'm sure you did." I knew Lance was kidding. He and Kerry had gotten closer over the last couple of years as well. "What did she say about the case, though?"

"Oh, that." Lance checked our surroundings. Then he leaned so close that his lips were practically touching my ear. I could smell his expensive cologne and minty toothpaste. "She said they've confirmed it was *muuuurrr-der,* darling. Cold-blooded murder."

That solved my dilemma. I had been on the fence about whether to share what Kerry had told me. I had promised her I would keep that in confidence and didn't want to break her trust. If Kerry had confided in Lance, I figured I was in the clear to discuss it with him.

"I heard that, too." I readjusted my sweatshirt, tying it tighter. "Why did she want to talk to Arlo? Do you think it has something to do with his previous connection with Bamboo?"

"She didn't say." Lance squinted and moved closer to the rounded wooden doors to the Lizzie. Behind him timbered turrets peeked over the fencing and ivy that enclosed the outdoor theater. "I haven't had an opportunity to have a tête-à-tête with him. However, I assure you that as soon as I can track him down, I will charm every last detail out of him. Every single one."

That I didn't doubt.

I changed the direction of the conversation. "I've been thinking about it all morning. Suppose we can figure out *when* Maddy was drugged. That might narrow down our list of suspects. I've been replaying the dinner scene by scene. Everyone was at the tables and then at your performance. You would think if the killer slipped something in her drink that early it would have knocked her out sooner, so I keep going back to the wine bottle Josie took with her to her tent. What if that's the murder weapon? Maybe Josie gave it to Maddy? Or somehow Maddy ended up with the wine and drank it unknowingly."

Lance leaned one shoulder against the theater door. "Do you think Josie knew it was drugged?"

"I don't even know if it was poison," I admitted. "I just think it's more logical that the killer must have waited to strike."

"An excellent deduction, as always." He tapped one long, slender finger to his chin.

"But where does it leave us? I still can't figure out who did it, and if Maddy was the intended victim."

"Let's talk it through quickly. Review our list," Lance suggested. "There's Miller, who Josie treated like dirt. That gives him motive."

We waited momentarily as a crew unlocked the access doors to our left. OSF was dark on Mondays, but that didn't mean that campus was deserted. Staff used the time for general maintenance, touching up sets and costumes, meetings, and more. Lance gave them a nod of approval as they carted supplies across the street to the Thomas Theatre.

"Right," I said after the crew had continued on. "Josie treats everyone like dirt, though. It's such a dichotomy, because when I first met with Miller he was very clear about this being a team-bonding weekend and wanting to make sure every event and meal was lavish. He made it sound like they were coming to Ashland for a week of pampering. I mean, they must have spent thousands of dollars just on the swag bags alone, but now it sounds like Bamboo is in financial trouble."

Lance tilted his head to the side. "Hmm. Something doesn't add up."

"Right. I know Josie was upset with Gus about finances. It would be interesting to try and figure out what sort of financial shape the company is actually in. Is Bamboo about to declare bankruptcy? Then why the spending?" I paused for a second. "I'd also like to know about Kit. She and Josie have butted heads all weekend. Their personalities couldn't be more different. Kit is such a free spirit."

"Easy, easy," Lance cautioned, motioning with his hands. "Tread carefully. You're talking to an artistic director here, remember? Kit is my kind of free spirit. That's how she creates art."

"I'm not passing judgment. I'm simply noting that she and Josie are polar opposites. Josie seemed to single her out a lot. She made her change the night of their dinner at Torte. They were constantly bickering. It makes me wonder if maybe Kit finally had enough and snapped. Of course, that would mean Josie was the intended victim, not Maddy."

"What about Elisa, the PR maven?"

"She seemed pretty disgusted that Josie is using Maddy's death as a PR stunt, but not enough to not go along with putting out a press release and whatever Josie has tasked her with."

Lance cracked his knuckles. "It is quite macabre to leverage the death of an employee for free press. Maybe Elisa is worried about keeping her job and doesn't have a choice to not go along with it. My vote is on Josie. It's vile that she's taking advantage of the moment, but then again, I've seen worse."

"You have?" I wrinkled my brow.

"Don't even get me started, darling. But there's no time for that." He tapped his wrist. "Theater story hour will have to wait. Who else is on our list?"

"That's it. Well, except for Josie, obviously. Maybe she's the killer, and she intentionally made it look like a case of mistaken identity."

"It's a pretty brilliant plan if you think about it. Josie makes sure that everyone assumes that killing Maddy was a mistake. Perhaps she's not as awful as she appears to be. She could have intentionally been playing the role of Cruella de Vil in order to shift suspicion away from her. Then she waited for the perfect opportunity and pounced. It's a possibility."

I wasn't as convinced, but we were running out of suspects. "Unless it was one of the guides," I considered out loud. "But I don't see how that could have happened. They didn't stay the night and what possible motive could they have had to kill Maddy?"

"Touché." He snapped and pointed his index finger at me. "Not to mention that should one of the rafting guides have wanted to harm her they simply could have tossed her out of the raft."

That reminded me of what Ramiro had witnessed on the water. "Josie *did* get pushed off the raft."

"When?"

"Were you there for that conversation? I think you and Arlo were getting settled. It happened while they were on the river." I told him about Ramiro getting invited to tag along and how he had reported that the team fought for most of the trip and that Josie had gotten tossed off the raft at some point.

"Hmmm." Lance stared at the empty brick courtyard. "That does lend itself more to the theory that Josie was supposed to meet her maker, doesn't it?"

The sound of voices brought our conversation to a halt.

"We'll finish this later," Lance whispered as he shot his hand in the air to welcome the Bamboo executives.

They climbed the hill on Pioneer Street in a pack. I noticed Elisa still wasn't with them.

Lance waited for everyone to catch their breath. "It's

a bit of a trek to get from the Black Swan to the bricks. I always say the payoff is you burn enough calories to earn a second martini." He paused and waited for chuckles. "Ah, who am I kidding? Hill or no hill, a second martini is never a bad idea."

"I'll drink to that," Kit shouted. She removed her flask from her beaded purse and proceeded to take a drink of whatever was inside. I had noticed that she had been drinking out of the flask at the campsite, too.

Was she already drunk? Could it be a coping strategy or was she self-medicating as a way to ease her guilt?

I watched the group as Lance gave them his introductory speech. He was entirely in his element, explaining OSF's storied history and regaling them with insider tidbits of costume mishaps and theater lore. He held his small audience captive. Watching Lance work never failed to impress me. He spoke with such genuine love and enthusiasm about the company that it was impossible not to get swept up in his energy.

"A few rules and superstitions before we proceed," Lance said, lowering his voice for dramatic effect. "Never, never utter the word 'Macbeth' or whistle while we're backstage. This is the surest way to bring a curse upon the theater and yourselves."

Everyone chuckled.

"Do not mistake my tone. I am deadly serious." Lance narrowed his eyes. "Now, is anyone wearing blue shoes or do any of you happen to have a peacock feather upon your person? If so, I shall have to ask you to leave both at the door."

Elisa arrived as Lance was finishing his speech. Her splotchy red cheeks and breathlessness were a dead giveaway that she had sprinted up the hill. "Hey, did I miss anything?" she asked me, mopping her forehead with her shirt sleeve.

"Not really. Lance just finished giving some background on the theater and reminding everyone to keep an eye out for Thespis, the ancient Greek ghost. He's starting the official tour now."

"Okay." She studied me like she was trying to decide if I was teasing. Then she crouched over to catch her breath like she had finished running a marathon and was desperate for air. "Whew. I thought I was going to miss it."

"You weren't at the Black Swan earlier?" I asked.

She exhaled slowly, then fanned her cheeks. "No. I had a . . . a . . ." She stumbled as we moved to the entrance.

I caught her arm to steady her.

"Thanks." She stopped to tie her shoe. "No, I had to miss that because I had a meeting I couldn't get out of."

"I thought this was your meeting. Isn't the entire retreat a big meeting?"

She stood up. "Yeah, this wasn't a work meeting. I had to do something else." Her eyes drifted toward Main Street. "Anyway, glad I didn't miss the tour. I'm excited to get to see behind the curtain." She caught up with Miller.

I wondered what she meant by another meeting, but I didn't have time to dwell on it because at that moment Josie collapsed in front of me.

Chapter Sixteen

Josie landed on the cement with a thud, blocking the doors that Lance had just opened. She began screaming and clutching her back. "Help me! Someone stabbed me."

She rocked in pain. I noticed that everyone, except for Kit, was wearing matching Bamboo hoodies. Josie grabbed the side of her hoodie as she wailed on the ground.

Lance sprang into action. "Jules, call the police. Everyone else—back away."

The team from Bamboo did as he directed.

Josie yelped and curled into a ball. "It stings. It hurts so bad."

Lance caught my eye.

I called the Professor while Lance bent down to help Josie. I could tell he was trying to figure out where she had been stabbed. There wasn't any sign of blood.

The Professor answered on the first ring. "Juliet, to what do I owe the pleasure?"

"Actually, I'm calling for help. We're at the bricks. Are you downtown?"

"Yes."

Josie continued to rock on the ground like her stomach had been torn apart.

"Is that screaming I hear in the background?" the Professor asked, his voice filling with concern.

"It's Josie. She says she's been stabbed," I answered as Lance caught my eye and shook his head. "Well, she's hurt, anyway."

"Should I send an ambulance?" The Professor sounded concerned.

"Uh, can you hold on, one minute?" I checked with Lance. "Do we need an ambulance?"

"There's no blood. There's no sign of a wound," Lance said, studying Josie's face. "Do you think you could be having appendicitis or maybe you ate something that didn't agree with you?"

"No, I felt the stab," Josie wailed. She kept her left arm cinched around her waist and pointed to her back with the other.

"Juliet, is everything okay?" the Professor's voice cut through the chaos.

"I think you better come," I said to him. "I don't think we need an ambulance yet, but if that changes, I'll call 911 directly."

"Okay, on my way." He hung up.

Lance looked like he was managing to calm Josie down a bit. I turned to her staff. "Did anyone see anything?"

Miller shook his head. "No, she just stopped midstride and dropped to the ground."

Elisa nodded in agreement. "It's true. We were all right here. You were next to me."

That was true. It had happened so fast. Elisa and I had been talking. Lance had finished his speech and had started to open the door when out of nowhere Josie dropped to the ground and started screaming. I wished I had been paying more attention to everyone else.

Kit took another swig from the flask and shrugged. "I didn't see anything."

Gus appeared equally perplexed. "Neither did I. She was fine a minute ago and who would stab her in broad daylight? We were all right here."

"Any one of you could have done this," Josie yelled.

Lance had managed to get her to an upright position.

"I know one of you is out to get me. You're not going to succeed." Josie clutched her abdomen. "Someone is trying to kill me. How many times do I have to say it before someone believes me?"

The Professor and Thomas sprinted up the hill. Thomas was wearing his standard blue uniform with shorts and tennis shoes. The Professor wore a pair of jeans and a short-sleeve button-down shirt with a bluebird print.

"Can you give us some space?" The Professor took charge of the scene, motioning for everyone to move away, while Thomas dropped to his knees and checked Josie's pulse.

We moved to the benches at the top of the bricks while they determined whether Josie needed medical attention.

"Jules, she was not stabbed," Lance said, keeping one eye on Josie. "No way."

"Are you sure?"

"Please." He pursed his lips. "There wasn't a drop of

blood on her. Gus is right. Who could have stabbed her without any of us seeing it? Where's the weapon? How did a knife—or whatever—pierce through her sweatshirt? Nope. I'm not buying it."

"All good points." I watched as Josie lifted her hoodie partway for the Professor to get a better look at her side. "Do you think she's faking it?"

"It's either that or she has some sort of internal injury." Lance leaned closer. "She didn't break character once."

"What does that mean?"

"Breaking character?" Lance sounded miffed that I wasn't familiar with the acting terminology.

"No, I know what it means *literally.* What I'm asking is how was she staying in character?"

"I think it's one big charade." Lance absently rubbed his arm while he stared at Josie. "More fodder for her ruse. She's the killer and putting on a show for all of us." He clapped softly twice. "Props to her, it's not a bad performance, but it's not a good one either."

His theory made sense. If Josie had killed Maddy, continuing to play the role of the victim was an easy way to try to maintain her innocence. Had that been her plan all along? Was she conning us?

"I believe what we have here is some kind of an insect bite or sting," the Professor said, helping Josie to her feet.

Thomas had brought along a first-aid kit. He activated an instant cold pack and handed it to her.

"Do you have an allergy to beestings?" the Professor asked.

I stood up to get a better look. Sure enough, a large, red welt was on the left side of Josie's waist.

She pressed the cold pack on the sting. "No."

"Good." The Professor turned to Thomas. "Can you give her a package of anti-inflammatory medication?"

"Sure." Thomas dug through the first-aid kit until he found a packet of medication.

"If you develop a rash or trouble breathing, call 911 immediately," the Professor said to Josie. "Otherwise, a cold pack and some pain medication should do the trick."

"How do you explain a beesting?" Rage made her eyes look twice their normal size. "Do you see a hive around here? How did a bee get down my sweatshirt? This wasn't a bee sting. Someone stabbed me. Someone is trying to kill me. First the raft, then Maddy, now this. I suggest you do your job, officer; otherwise, you're going to have a lawsuit on your hands."

The Professor was unfazed by her threats.

I couldn't believe she was still insisting that she'd been stabbed. Could she have pinched herself to make it look like a bee sting?

"Were you sitting in the grass?" the Professor asked. He had removed his Moleskine notebook from his chest pocket and began taking notes.

"No." Josie shook her head. "I was standing right here." She pointed to the ground. "We were all crammed together, waiting to go inside, and someone stabbed me."

"Ah, I see." The Professor walked in that direction. He moved toward the cement benches built into the grassy hillside and picked a bunch of clover from the grass. "I do believe that our friendly pollinators are fast at work gathering the last of summer's nectar."

Josie glared at him. "Okay, if you're such a great detective, answer me this. How did a bee get from the patch of clover over there to underneath my hoodie?"

"Perhaps the bee was attracted to your green attire. Maybe it mistook you for a flower."

His theory made her fume more, but I had to agree. Her Bamboo hoodie did have a flowery vibe with its pale green color and wispy yellow stalks of bamboo.

"Some help you are. Classic. You already botched Maddy's murder. Now you're going to let a killer continue to run loose." She tossed the ice pack on the ground. "I'm watching all of you, got it? Anyone tries to hurt me again, and you're dead."

Her team stared at their feet.

"I don't believe threats are necessary," the Professor said in a severe tone. "And I can assure you that my team and I are doing everything we can to bring justice to Maddy and put her killer behind bars. I certainly don't want to place any blame on our dwindling bee population—we need them to save the planet—but I think that a sting is the most logical explanation. I suggest you continue on your tour and be sure to take that medication to help with the pain and swelling."

He caught my eye before he and Thomas left.

Lance clapped twice. "Shall we continue with our tour, everyone?"

Josie muttered under her breath as Lance led us into the Lizzie. Miller picked up her discarded ice pack.

Could someone have stabbed her? With what? Elisa and I had been right there and I hadn't seen anything.

If she was telling the truth, they hadn't caused any real damage. Could it have been a warning? Or maybe one of her team members was trying to mess with her?

Or, Jules, she was stung by a bee, like the Professor said.

The most likely explanation made the most sense. I tried to let it go as we stepped inside the doors to the Lizzie.

Backstage tours of the historic theater always brought back memories from my childhood. There was something magical about getting a peek behind the curtain. Growing up in Ashland meant that our school would take field trips to OSF every year. As kids we had the opportunity to experience set and costume changes, lighting and technical demos, and dozens of matinée performances of Shakespeare's canon along with modern productions. I hadn't realized at the time just how fortunate I had been to grow up surrounded by actors, writers, singers, dancers, and thespians who chose to make Ashland home.

Lance began the tour at the back of the open-air theater, touting the fact that there wasn't a bad seat in the house, regardless of whether you sat in the front row, the box seats, or all the way in the back.

"During the shoulder season we recommend you bring a coat and stop by the pillow booth to rent one of our luxurious blankets for the evening shows," he said to the group.

Miller interrupted. "I've already made arrangements for our own show bundle." He addressed Josie.

She brushed him off. "Fine. Don't interrupt. You're being rude."

That was ironic. Josie had been the textbook definition of rude to everyone and suddenly she was scolding Miller? I didn't wish ill on anyone, but I could certainly understand why her team was frustrated with her.

I noticed she kept a hand on the spot where she'd been stung as we proceeded through the rows of seats toward the stage.

Lance pointed out the tiered levels of the stage and gave us a brief walk-through of the variety of ways his acting company could navigate the space depending on the performance.

Elisa texted through his entire presentation. She tried to be subtle, but the blue glow on her face and the fact that she had her head glued to her stomach was a dead giveaway. Miller stuck next to Josie, and Gus and Kit kept chuckling and whispering to each other.

Josie shushed them twice. "Knock it off, you two. I've had enough of your inside jokes."

Kit tipped her flask and made a comment to Gus, completely ignoring Josie's warning.

Lance didn't bat so much as an eyelash. Ever the professional, he continued with his tour, ignoring any side comments and proceeding to lead everyone behind the stage where he turned things over to a dresser who demonstrated the incredible choreography and precise timing that goes into every costume change.

"Well, anything?" Lance moved next to me.

"Not really." I kept my voice low. "It's just more of the same. They're so dysfunctional, but I guess I was hoping that if one of them is the killer they would let something slip. I don't know. It's probably far-fetched."

"Oh, I wouldn't rule that out so quickly." Lance's gaze

traveled to Josie. "I believe we've already witnessed the killer putting on their own show for us, albeit an amateur production."

"How so?" The lighting behind the stage was dim. I tried to get my eyes to adjust. I wished that every theater patron had the opportunity to peek behind the curtain. It never ceased to amaze me how much work went into every scene the audience saw on the stage.

"The date, of course."

"I don't follow." We moved beneath a maze of ropes with heavy sandbags.

"I offered you a clue in my opening. We're in the shoulder season, yes?"

I nodded.

"Shoulder season—late September." He made a circle with his hand, trying to motion for me to catch up.

"Okay." I still didn't get what he was hinting at.

He sighed. "Must I spell it out for you? After our tour is done we must get you more caffeine; you're clearly not firing on all cylinders."

"I never turn down caffeine, but just tell me. What am I missing?"

"The bees, darling. The bees." He waited for me to clue in. "It's much too late in the season for bees. The Professor knows it as well. He gave me *the* look."

"The look?"

"Yes, *the* look. I don't know what game is afoot, but I know one thing for sure. Josie was not stung by a bee."

Chapter Seventeen

"You really don't think she was stung?" I asked as the dresser introduced a lighting technician, explaining the intricate and perfectly timed choreography that went into costume and set changes behind the scenes.

"No. I *know* she wasn't stung." Lance had a habit of emphasizing his speech whenever he wanted to make a point, which was most of the time. "Not a bee or any other flying insect. It's impossible."

"That means you think she's faking it, for sure?" I asked.

"For sure." Lance gave me a half nod.

A new thought formed in my mind. What if Josie wasn't faking? What if she was right about the killer being after her? We couldn't rule out the possibility. After all, the odds were good that Maddy's death had been a mistake. I had yet to come up with any motive for her murder, which lent credibility to Josie being afraid.

"What is it?" Lance wrinkled his brow. "Why are your beautiful cheekbones sucking in like that?"

"Let me play devil's advocate for a minute. What if she's not lying? What if the killer stuck her as a warning? We were all sort of bunched together, waiting to come inside. It's possible that someone could have bumped into her and stabbed her side. I'm still not ready to abandon the theory that Maddy's death was a mistake. What if the killer is just waiting to strike again?"

"Okay, okay, I'm listening," he said, warming to my theory. "I like the way you're thinking. Go on."

"Maybe she was stabbed as a warning. Or, I know this is out there, but what if whatever she was stabbed with had poison on the tip?" As I posed the question, it sounded like a scenario fit for the stage and much less plausible in real life.

"Yes, yes." Lance strummed his fingers together in excitement. "I love this theory. What's our weapon?"

I shrugged. "No idea. A pin? A needle?"

The lighting technician was demonstrating spotlights. Suddenly the top of Miller's head lit up like a star on a Christmas tree.

"What about a bamboo skewer?" Lance asked.

That was oddly specific. "Sure, I guess."

Lance raised his eyebrows. "A wooden bamboo skewer."

"Yeah. I said yes."

"Juliet, *look*." He tilted his head toward Miller.

I tried not to gape as I realized what Lance was trying to highlight. Tucked into the side pocket of Miller's satchel was a bamboo skewer. Its tip was razor-sharp, certainly sharp enough to poke through Josie's sweatshirt.

"Do you think he could have stabbed her?" I whispered.

The lighting demonstration had finally quieted the

group, as a kaleidoscope of reds, blues, and yellows flooded the stage.

"It's quite a coincidence, don't you think? One might say too much of a coincidence."

"What do we do?"

"We are going to the props department next. You distract him and I'll grab it."

I was about to protest, but Lance pushed me forward as everyone moved out of the dimly lit area toward the hallway. I bumped into Miller. He turned around and gave me a look of surprise.

"I'm so sorry. I lost my footing." An industrial cord held in place with blue electrical tape helped sell my story.

"No problem." Miller smiled as we followed the others out the side entrance that connected to the Bowmer.

"How are you liking the tour?"

"It's pretty interesting." His glasses had slipped down his nose. He pushed them up again. "I'm looking forward to seeing a play now. Not that I wasn't before, but it will be fun to know the inner workings of backstage when we're in the audience."

"I heard you're doing dinner at the new gallery tonight." I wanted to buy time for Lance to make his move. We moved in a pack toward the props department, a vast warehouse-like room on the left.

"Yeah, I hope that's not awkward for you." Miller stopped at the door and let me go in front of him.

"Not at all." I squeezed next to a wall of neatly organized fake swords.

"Good, yeah, we had to scramble a bit, but Richard came through for us." He inched closer to me as the props master removed an elegant sword from a production of *King Arthur* from the wall. From a distance you would never know that the sword was fake.

"I'm sure it will be great."

Miller frowned; he looked like he was going to say something more but hesitated. "Did you know I met with him earlier this summer?"

"Richard?"

"Yeah, he was pretty insistent that we *not* use you."

"That sounds like him." I watched as Lance snaked between Kit and Gus to get closer to us.

"I figured, but I just don't want it to be weird now." He snuck a glance at Josie. "We've already put you through enough."

"It's fine. Really."

Miller's shoulders softened a bit. "Is there any news on the investigation?"

"I'm not sure. Why do you ask?"

"You seem connected to the police. I've been wondering when they're going to release us to return home. I might need to reserve another meal or two at Torte if we end up being delayed longer."

I could feel Lance's presence behind me. Hopefully he had managed to get the skewer.

"For sure. Just let me know; I'm sure we can work something out or connect you with other restaurants in town."

"I hope it doesn't come to that." Miller's voice was thick with tension. "Josie already wants my head."

"Your head? That sounds scary." My gaze indistinctly drifted to a mannequin head on one of the worktables.

"She thinks this is my fault." Miller picked up a fake retractable knife and stabbed it into his palm repeatedly.

"Being stuck in Ashland?"

"All of it."

Josie snapped for his attention. "Stop chatting. Get over here. Are you not paying attention?"

He made a face and took off.

Lance slid next to me. "Success."

"You got it?"

He patted his breast pocket. "The item is secure."

The executive team moved to the back of the prop shop for a weapons demo. The last thing this group needed was a weapons demo.

Lance and I hung back. He pulled me into the hallway, waited to make sure that no one was watching, then proceeded to remove the skewer from his pocket. He had wrapped it in his silk handkerchief. "Take this to the Professor. I'm sure he can analyze it for any traces of chemicals."

I stuffed the skewer into my pocket.

"Don't dally, but do be in touch and let me know what the Professor has to say about our find. I do believe that it's highly likely that he'll end up awarding us some sort of medal for bravery."

I didn't bother to respond to that.

I left the tour and headed for the police station. It was probably a long shot that the skewer had traces of poison, but it was odd that Miller had it in his bag. And I wondered if there was a deeper meaning to his words. He had said that Josie blamed him for everything. Could that mean Maddy's murder, too?

If that was the case, maybe Josie knew that he was

the killer. He could have stabbed her as a warning, or maybe, just maybe, the pointy piece of wood in my pocket would point to who had killed Maddy once and for all.

I felt sheepish as I approached the main desk at the station. "Is the Professor here?"

The young park cadet on duty shook his head. "No, you just missed him."

"What about Thomas or Kerry?"

"Thomas is with the Professor," the cadet replied. "Kerry is over at Lithia Park. You might be able to catch her there."

"Great, thanks." I left and headed straight for the park. I practically jogged across Main Street, keeping my head down as I passed the bubblers and the Merry Windsor. The last thing I needed right now was another run-in with Richard Lord. Carrying around a potential piece of evidence that could be connected to murder wasn't on my agenda. I wanted to hand off the skewer and get back to work.

It didn't take long to find Kerry. She was giving an older couple directions to the Japanese gardens near the park entrance.

I waited until she finished. "Do you have a second?"

"Sure." She motioned around us. "Do you want to talk here, or should we go somewhere more private?"

"Am I that obvious?"

"I would hope that I'm that good. It is my job to read people, after all." Her smile conveyed that she knew me well.

"Fair enough." I didn't want to take any chances on being seen by Richard Lord, who had a tendency to hang out on the Merry Windsor's front porch to keep a watch over park activity. "Can we walk to the duck pond?"

Kerry fell in step with me. The pathway to the park took us past the backside of the Lizzie and through a tree-lined sidewalk. I knew I was biased, but there was no place on the planet as majestic as Lithia Park. Deemed the jewel of Ashland, the park consists of nearly one hundred acres of canyonland. The park started in the plaza and stretched all the way to Mount A, offering visitors the chance to lose themselves on the heavily forested trails or enjoy spending an afternoon in quiet contemplation on the banks of Ashland Creek.

"Does this bring back memories?" I asked. Thomas and Kerry had picked Lithia Park as the site of their spring wedding. Despite a few setbacks, like her dad showing up unannounced, the event had been nothing short of magical, a delightful evening of celebration at the bandshell.

"It's weird because in some ways the wedding feels like it was yesterday and in others it feels like Thomas and I have been married for much longer."

"I get that." Carlos and I had been together for nearly a decade, but sometimes I felt like we were still newlyweds. "Have you heard anything from your dad?" Kerry's dad had been released from prison shortly before their wedding. He and Kerry had had a strained relationship. In fact, his rocky relationship with the law was one of the reasons she'd been drawn into the profession. His time in prison had transformed him. He had come to Ashland to make amends and commit to trying to repair the damage that he had done.

"We've been talking once a week. He's in California again and apparently works a legitimate job at a greenhouse. Thomas thinks we should visit for Thanksgiving or Christmas, but I'm not sure I'm ready for that yet."

A group of joggers running in stride came toward us on the pathway. Kerry and I moved to give them space. "I'm sure Thomas will understand if you need more time."

She picked up a large branch that had fallen onto the pathway and moved it to the side. "He's great. He's not pressuring me. I guess it's more that I wish I were in a different space, but I'm not yet. I get that my dad is trying, but it's not like a few months can erase my entire childhood."

"Of course not." I couldn't imagine the struggles that Kerry had been through. I was acutely aware of how fortunate I'd been to be raised by two parents who loved and adored me and each other. We might not have had millions of dollars in the bank, but I knew with every cell in my body that I was safe, well cared for, and loved. You couldn't ask for more than that.

"I feel slightly silly telling you this," I said, sensing that it might be time to change the topic. "But I'm going to do it anyway because on the off chance that there's a connection to Maddy's murder, I'll feel even worse if I don't say anything."

"I'm a proponent of erring on the side of more information versus less," Kerry said in an encouraging tone.

"Did you see Thomas or the Professor after I called them?"

She shook her head. "No. I was following a lead."

Since she didn't expound on that, I figured that was all she was going to say on the subject. We made it to the duck pond. The turrets and timber framing of the Elizabethan Theatre reflected in the water. Japanese maples and leafy yellow oaks surrounded the tranquil pond.

"Can we sit?" I moved to a bench. A family of ducks swam over to greet us. Watching ducks and turtles in the pond was a favorite pastime for parkgoers of all ages. The only rule was not to feed the wildlife that inhabited the park, ducks included. Lithia was a natural habitat for deer, turkeys, an abundance of other birds, and even the occasional bear or cougar. Park staff and conservationists educated visitors that their good intentions of giving the ducks a snack would have the opposite effect. Feeding wild animals created food dependency and led to malnourishment and a disruption of their hunting and gathering skills.

I filled Kerry in on what had happened before the tour, including Josie collapsing in pain, and calling the Professor to get a handle on the situation. "At first, we assumed that she had been stung by a bee, but the Professor doesn't believe it was a bee sting. Lance, of course, raised the point that it's too late in the season for bees and it does seem odd that a bee would sting her in that spot."

"Let me guess, Lance has his own theory."

I nodded and reached into my pocket. "He does. It involves this."

Kerry unwrapped the skewer. "I'm going to need more to go on here."

"Lance thinks that Josie was stabbed by the killer,

either as a warning or maybe the killer was trying to strike again. Do you think there's a chance the tip of this skewer could be poisoned?"

Kerry shook her head and laughed. "Is Lance staging a Hercule Poirot play at OSF?"

"Not that I know of." A slight breeze fluttered through the Japanese maples on the far side of the pond. "Don't you think it's kind of weird that he was carrying around a skewer?"

"Maybe he had chicken satay for lunch," Kerry suggested.

"True, but I don't usually hang on to my skewers after I've finished lunch."

She shrugged. "I mean, I'll take this in as evidence, but the idea that the killer would stab Josie with a poisoned skewer in the middle of the afternoon with a handful of witnesses around is pretty implausible. Not impossible, but implausible." Kerry concentrated her attention on the ducks bobbing in the middle of the water.

"I figured you would say that, and I agree, but like I said, I had to at least give it to you and let you take it from here."

"I appreciate that." She waited for a group who had stopped to take a selfie with the pond and Lizzie in the background. "Doug didn't see any signs of a physical reaction, did he? Josie didn't have trouble breathing or complain of dizziness, nausea, that sort of thing?"

"No. She just complained about getting stabbed—that was the word she used. There was a red welt in the spot where she got stung. I was with her for at least another half hour, maybe forty-five minutes, and she was fine."

"That's good. If this were an attempted poisoning,

she would have begun to feel the effects within a short amount of time."

Unless the killer missed. Maybe the killer hadn't anticipated the thickness of her shirt, or perhaps they botched the attempt.

I didn't share that theory with Kerry.

"If that's it, I'll take this to the station." She patted the skewer and stood up.

"I'll walk that way with you." I felt a mix of relief and regret. It was good to know that Kerry had the skewer and she and Thomas could take it from here, but I also felt slightly silly for getting swept up into outlandish theories. What were the odds that Miller had stabbed his boss with a bamboo skewer, but then again, why was he carrying around the sharp object?

We fell into stride, passing the Lithia bubblers and a cellist offering a free afternoon concert to anyone willing to stop and listen.

"Did you notice any drug activity when you were at the river with them?" Kerry asked.

"Drug activity? No. They polished off a lot of wine both at Torte and at the campsite, but I didn't see any blatant drug use; why?"

"Our counterparts in LA have shared that they were called out on more than one occasion to Bamboo for incidents involving drug possession with intent to sell." Her voice was casual, as if she were telling me about the meal she had had last night.

I couldn't believe that she had dropped a bomb like that, and I was surprised she was sharing this piece of information with me.

As if reading my mind, she continued. "It's public

record. You could look it up, so I'm not telling you anything you couldn't find on your own."

"I'm guessing there's a reason you're telling me this."

"You know me; I just love to share," Kerry teased. "Actually, yes. We have the sense that there might be some dealing going down, and that Torte is a likely spot where you might observe said dealings."

"Why would someone do a drug deal at the bakeshop?"

"Because of that exact look on your face. It's the least likely place, which is the reason it becomes a potential site."

"Okay, what do you want me to do?"

"We want you to watch out for Kit."

"Kit?" I gulped. The creative director was certainly a free spirit, but a drug dealer—I hadn't seen that coming.

Kerry gave me a solemn nod. "Like I said, her arrest record is public. One of the other suspects confessed that they were aware that she was not only still using but dealing. It sounds like she's been active since she's been here in Ashland. Doug was planning to talk to you about this, but we're hoping you can keep an eye out if she happens into Torte. Call us immediately if you see anything suspicious."

"Forgive my naivety, but what would constitute suspicious with a drug deal at the bakeshop? I mean you don't think she'll be blatant about it, do you?"

"Depends on how desperate she is." Kerry thought for a minute. "If there's a way you can give your staff a heads-up to be on the lookout for her, without calling too much attention to the situation, that would be great.

You'll know what to do from there. Mainly it's watching her. Is she meeting with people? Who are those people? That sort of thing."

"Sure. No problem."

Kerry thanked me and continued across Main Street to the station. I stood on the corner for a minute to collect my thoughts. Kit was using and dealing drugs. Did that mean she was also a killer?

Chapter Eighteen

"You okay, boss?" Andy asked as I walked into the bakeshop. "You look a little out of it."

"No, I'm fine." I glanced around the cozy dining area. Customers lingered in the window booths savoring Sterling's lunch special and cups of our Oregon chai. A small line queued up for pastries and a family waited for their coffee drinks. A group of our youngest patrons was creating artful masterpieces on the bottom of the chalkboard menu. It's a space we reserve for our youngest guests, who are always welcome to doodle on the chalkboard or curl up with one of the books or board games we keep on hand, while their grown-ups savor a double espresso. Our kid's menu was another highlight that brought in return customers. For the non-caffeine crowd, we served hot chocolate with copious amounts of hand-whipped cream, sprinkles, and hot apple cider with a touch of caramel and cinnamon. Watching little ones devour warm chocolate chip cookies the size of their heads was one of the best parts of owning a bakeshop.

Fortunately, Kit wasn't anywhere in sight. That was good.

I scooted past the line and ducked behind the counter. Rosa was boxing up lemon curd cupcakes with fluffy meringue frosting and salted caramel chocolate bars. "Anything I can help with?" I asked.

She shook her head. "I'm fine. Check with Andy. Sequoia had to leave early for her massage class."

Sequoia had recently begun studying to become a massage therapist. Since many of our staff were college and high school students, we had made a concerted effort to ensure flexibility with scheduling. Sequoia had come to me with some trepidation about a month ago, explaining that she'd been considering the idea for a while but was finally ready to follow her dream. I'm a big believer in following dreams and I wasn't about to do anything that would get in the way of her pursuing her passion. When I explained that we would be happy to accommodate her hours so that she could attend afternoon classes a few days a week, she teared up and thanked me profusely.

The running joke at the bakeshop lately had been about who should volunteer to be one of Sequoia's practice massages.

"Do you need another set of hands?" I asked Andy.

He deftly poured dark espresso shots into a Torte mug. "I can't believe I'm going to say this, but yeah, I could use some beans ground for our drip. Can I trust you with getting the grind perfect?"

I winced. "Oh, Andy, I don't know. That's a lot of pressure."

He steamed vanilla almond milk. "Just don't touch the settings. I've MacGyvered them to perfection."

"I'll do my best." I tried to wink and then made a goofy face. After I had ground his home-roasted small-batch coffee and scooped it into our reusable coffee filters, I did another scan of the bakeshop.

"Do you know who Kit is?" I asked him, hitting the dark roast setting on the drip coffeemaker.

"Is she the one with the rainbow hair?" He swirled milk into the espresso shots, reserving the foam for the top of the cup. "The only nice one in that group."

"Yep, that's a fitting description."

"Can you hand me the chocolate shavings?" he asked, finishing the latte with a foam maple leaf. "I haven't seen her today."

"If you happen to see her, can you please let me know?" I handed him the chocolate shavings.

"No problem." He sprinkled the ribbons of chocolate on the latte and placed it on the bar for the waiting customer. After the customer had taken their drink, he moved closer to me. "You don't need to tell me details or anything, but is this connected to the murder investigation?"

I nodded.

He gave me a two-fingered salute. "You can count on me, boss. I'll keep a lookout and let you know, but I'll play it cool."

I grinned. "You always play it cool, right?"

"Except when it comes to my love life."

"Really, how so?" There was typically a long line at the espresso counter, not only for Andy's delectable coffee creations but for his charm and good looks. I had witnessed many teenage girls gushing over his witty coffee banter. Not that he was even aware of his adoring audience. That audience also included Bethany, who had been crushing on Andy for a while. I had thought that he reciprocated her feelings, but he'd been painfully slow about making a move.

"Did you hear about Bethany?"

I had to resist reacting like Lance. This was a juicy tidbit. Andy was bringing up Bethany in relation to his love life and confiding in me. I felt honored and didn't want to mess it up.

"No, what about her?" I leaned on the counter.

"Oh, uh, I thought you knew." He twisted the temperature gauge on the espresso machine.

"Knew what?" His face had gone pale. Was it bad news?

"I should probably let her tell you."

"Is something wrong?" I felt a lump form in my stomach. If Bethany had news, I had a bad feeling I knew what it might be.

"No." He sighed and busied himself with tamping grounds for the next shot. "I think she's downstairs. She'll tell you."

"Okay. I'm going to go find her. You're good here?"

"I'm in my element. The beans are in good hands." He flashed me his signature grin, but I could tell it wasn't as bright and carefree as usual. His smile didn't reach his eyes and the lightness in his tone was forced.

Why was he being cagey about Bethany? I went straight downstairs and nearly knocked her over. She was coming up the stairs with a tray of brownies. "You are just the person I'm looking for," I said.

She shifted the tray in her hands. "What's up?"

"Andy said you had something to tell me?"

"Let me take these upstairs and then we can chat for a minute if you have time?" She didn't meet my gaze. Instead, she hurried off with the tray.

Was she quitting? Bethany had become an essential part of our team; I didn't know what I would do without her. I had been trying to mentally prepare myself for the possibility of one—or more—of my staff leaving eventually. It was the nature of the restaurant biz. I just hadn't expected it to happen so soon.

"Sure," I said to her. "I'll grab a spot by the fireplace."

"BRB." She hurried upstairs with the tray.

It felt like it took her forever to deliver the brownies. When she returned, she sat across from me and fiddled with the strings on her apron. The retro atomic fireplace that we had installed in front of the collection of cozy chairs and couch in the basement wasn't turned on today, but I knew in a few weeks as the weather continued to cool this would be the most popular spot in the bakeshop.

"I've been meaning to talk to you about this for a while, but I wasn't sure it was going to come together and then the timing hasn't felt right. We were so busy with prepping for the Bamboo event and then you were gone for the weekend, and then the murder." She smashed her words together as she spoke. Clearly, she was nervous, which made me even more jittery.

She was definitely quitting. My stomach tightened. I waited for her to continue and braced myself.

"You know how much I love working here, right?" She wound a strand of her curly hair around her index finger.

That didn't sound good. "Yes, and we love having you on the team. I hope you know. I hope I've said that enough."

"Totally. You're the best boss, ever. Like, ever." She smiled, but it didn't reach her eyes. "That's why this is so hard."

My stomach sank. She was leaving.

"Ever since I started taking on social media for Torte, I've made a bunch of connections, which is awesome and so much fun." She trailed off and twisted her curl tighter. "I guess it's sort of because of social that an opportunity sort of arose."

"Okay." I swallowed hard. Was she going to quit on the spot? Of course, we could find a replacement for her position, but Bethany couldn't be replaced. Her baking and decorating skills were on par with professionals. She had taken full ownership of our social media and grown our following exponentially, but most importantly she was the heartbeat of our team. Bethany's positive attitude and genuine enthusiasm endeared her to customers and her co-workers. Not to mention she had a small share in the bakeshop. We would have to figure that out if she left.

"There's this guy who runs a roving kitchen. Jeremy DeSalt. You may have seen his stuff. He owns Pass DeSalt. Get it? Isn't that so clever? He's huge on social. Like, huge. He has close to a million followers and does tons of brand partnerships. He's liked a bunch of our stuff. That's how we got connected. It's pretty amazing if you think about it. He's based in Chicago and we're in southern Oregon." She had stopped playing with her hair and gnawed on her thumbnail.

I nodded, hoping secretly that she would get to the point. I had a feeling I knew what was coming and I wanted her to rip off the Band-Aid and put me out of my misery.

"He reached out a few weeks ago and wants to partner." She paused. "With me."

"That's great, Bethany. I'm seriously happy for you. I mean, I'm not going to lie, I'm going to be devastated to lose you, but no one deserves success as much as you."

Her dimple became more pronounced as she twisted her cheeks. "That's so sweet, Jules, I appreciate it, but I'm not leaving."

"You're not?" I unclenched my jaw.

"I mean, not permanently." She dragged her teeth over her bottom lip. "Unless you think it's best. That's what I wanted to talk to you about. I know it's not great timing. If I do this partnership, I'm going to have to commit to at least three, maybe four weeks of working with him. He's bringing Pass DeSalt his traveling kitchen here—to southern Oregon—and he wants me to be his social connection. Torte will be part of it, but the other issue, aside from taking time away from my work here, is that my role will be connecting him to other bakers and chefs in the valley. I don't want to put you in a weird position because I'll be promoting other businesses as part of this. That's kind of his thing. He's an amazing chef, but he passes the salt. To other chefs. He does a bunch of different features whenever he hits up a new city. He loves to show off regional flavors and talent. He does Bake-Offs, interviews, and recipe shares with local chefs. It's such a cool concept. Torte will definitely be part of it, but he's asked me to provide a list of other hot spots in the area for him to check out. I totally understand if you don't feel comfortable with that."

"That sounds amazing." I took a long breath and reached across the coffee table and squeezed her hand. "You have no idea how happy this makes me."

"Really?" Her cheeks were blotched with color. "I was so worried about talking to you. I don't want to do anything to jeopardize my role here, but this is a once-in-a-lifetime opportunity."

"It is. You have to do it." I exhaled slowly. "I can breathe again. I thought you were going to tell me you were quitting. I'm thrilled for you, and you know that our philosophy at Torte has always been about the community. I'm happy to have you promoting the Rogue Valley. It's great for all of us."

"Whew. I mean, I thought you would say that, but at the same time, I know it's kind of weird to have one of your staff formally promoting other bakeries and restaurants, but this is seriously such a huge deal, Jules, you have no idea." She reached for her phone. "Let me show you his social. You are going to lose your mind."

She leaned across the coffee table to show me pictures of Pass DeSalt's social profiles. She wasn't exaggerating that chef Jeremy DeSalt not only had a loyal and extensive following, but from the looks of the pictures he posted he had served celebrities, dignitaries, and politicians.

"Wow, this is incredible, Bethany, and so well deserved. I can't wait, and we will work around your schedule. I just had that same conversation with Sequoia. Mom and I want you all to spread your wings. I'm relieved you're spreading them and sticking around."

"You can't get rid of me that easy." Bethany grinned, tucking her phone back into her pocket.

"When will this start?" My mind went to scheduling.

"Two weeks. I know it's short notice."

"No, that timing is good. I'll see about hiring some extra help for Halloween prep, but otherwise October is typically much slower."

"You're the best, Jules. Thanks for being so understanding and supportive."

Andy called from the top of the stairs, "Hey, boss, can you come up here?"

I left Bethany with a hug. Everything I had said to her was true. She deserved this opportunity and it sounded like it would be good exposure for Torte, too. There was just one thing that hadn't been explained. Andy's statement about his love life. What did Bethany taking on this temporary role have to do with that?

Chapter Nineteen

Andy motioned with his head, raising his eyebrows twice. "Hey, boss. There's a special guest in one of the window booths."

I caught his drift right away. Kit was seated in the farthest booth from the door. She had her head pressed on the window like she was either taking a nap or waiting for someone. Given what I had learned from Kerry, I guessed it was the latter.

"She just came in." Andy held a drink ticket in his hand. "I'm making her order now if you want to deliver it."

"For sure." I waited for him to finish the Americano and then took it, along with a cinnamon honey scone, to Kit.

"Delivery," I said with a smile.

My voice must have startled her, because she bumped her head on the window and sat up with a jolt. "Oh, hi. Thank you."

I placed her coffee in front of her. "Can I get you anything else? Do you take cream or sugar in your coffee?"

"Ewww, no." Kit made a face. "Sugar in coffee is vile,

in my opinion. Do not ruin this nectar from the gods with sugary sweetness. This is good, thanks. Would you like to sit?"

On one hand, I wanted nothing more than to take a seat and see if she might confide in me, but on the other, I didn't want to interfere with Kerry's instructions, especially if Kit was waiting to make a deal.

"Are you meeting someone?"

She twisted her colorful hair. "No. I had to get away from the team. I'm so over Bamboo right now."

I hesitated before finally deciding to join her for a minute. If she wasn't meeting anyone then I shouldn't be jeopardizing anything.

"How are things going?"

She gulped her coffee. "You've been around us; what do *you* think?"

"That bad?"

"Worse. I'm still completely shook that Maddy is dead. She was the only thing keeping me at Bamboo. Now that she's gone, the first thing I'm going to do when we get back to LA is send my résumé to every agency in town. I have to get out of this dysfunction before it kills me, too." Her eyes were beady, and her movements were twitchy. Was she on something now? I thought about her drinking from the flask on the backstage tour.

Did she think she was in danger?

"Are you worried that there's going to be another murder?"

She ripped a chunk off her scone. "No. I mean who knows, but I'm not worried about getting killed if that's what you're asking."

"You said before it kills you, I guess you were speaking metaphorically."

"No, I was serious. If I stay at Bamboo, it is going to kill me." She took a bite of the scone.

For a second, I thought she was done talking and wasn't going to say more, but after she finished the bite, she met my eyes. There was a look of regret mixed with melancholy in her wide eyes. "I'm sure you've heard by now that I've had some issues."

I played naïve. "What kind of issues?"

"Substance abuse."

I tried to keep my face neutral. Kit was admitting that she had a drug problem—to me? I was basically a stranger. That didn't seem like a move a killer would make.

"It got awful about a year ago. It's the industry, you see. Client parties and dinners every night. Unbelievable pressure to perform as a creative director. At first it was fun. I would use in social situations, with friends. Or as a pick-me-up to give myself a creative boost. Then it turned into a habit. A daily habit. Sometimes more. Maddy found out. She caught me getting high in the bathroom at work. She tried to help me. She tried to get me to go to rehab, but I blew her off. I thought I could handle it. I really thought I could stop anytime."

"And you couldn't?" I offered.

She took a long sip of her coffee. "No. Everything fell apart. I needed more. I started dabbling in harder stuff and dealing. I was in a unique position; like I said, it's pretty common in the industry. Creatives, you know, and there's access to stuff everywhere. Plus the constant pressure to perform. I'm not the only one who's gone down this road."

I nodded, waiting for her to continue.

"Maddy called the police on me when she discovered that I'd been dealing at Bamboo." She strummed her fingers on the table nervously.

Now, that sounded like a motive for murder.

"They arrested me. It sounds terrible. I can see from your face that you think so, too, but honestly, it was the best thing anyone's ever done for me. She saved me. If she hadn't turned me in, I don't know where I would be now. Probably nowhere good. The arrest was my rock bottom. I went to rehab, did community service, and got my life together. I owe her my life."

"How does that translate to staying at Bamboo?" I wished I had grabbed a cup of coffee for myself. I could use an extra jolt of caffeine. My brain cells didn't seem to be firing fast enough. None of this made sense. Well, that wasn't entirely true. Her explanation made sense, but it didn't fit with the narrative of her being the killer.

"Maddy was my sober partner. She kept me on track and was always looking out for me. She was worried that I was going to start to slip. We were at a client party a week ago, where someone offered me a glass of wine. I took it—just to have something to hold in my hand. I didn't drink it, but she panicked when she saw me with it. She didn't even want me to come this weekend. She was too worried that I might have a relapse." She paused to sweep crumbs from her scone into her hand and then piled them on a napkin. "The night she died we had a long heart-to-heart, and she told me how worried she was about me. If I started drinking again, the next logical step was going to be to progress to harder stuff. She reminded me of how much work I've done and how horrible I felt. I promised her that I wasn't drinking. I'm not about to go back to that dark place, even if there are people trying to steer me down that path."

I couldn't believe that she was being so forthcoming with me. Kit and I hadn't spent much time together. Why would she confess all of this?

Unless she was lying. But then again, why lie to me?

I pushed the bombarding questions from my head. "Have you considered dealing again?"

She recoiled at the suggestion. "Dealing? No. Absolutely not. Like I said, I'm not falling down that rabbit hole again. In fact, that's why I'm here. Without Maddy, I don't trust myself right now. Not with anyone else from Bamboo. They don't care about me. They care about my work. Josie would gladly supply me with anything to keep me 'creating.' I wouldn't put it past her to 'accidentally' leave booze or drugs around. This morning, I put in an emergency call to my sobriety partner in LA. If the police let me leave, I'm going to turn in my resignation and get on the next flight out of here."

"I'm glad that you're taking care of yourself and being so thoughtful about your health and well-being." That was true, but it still didn't explain why she had come to me with this.

"Yeah." She sounded bitter. "It's taken a long time to get to this place. If it hadn't been for Maddy, I don't think I'd be here, and the irony is that she's dead." Kit broke down. Tears spilled down her cheeks. Her shoulders heaved as she sobbed.

I excused myself to get her some tissues. "Here you go," I said when I returned, handing her the box.

"Thanks," she said between sobs. "I'm sorry to be such a blubbering mess. I just can't believe that my only friend is gone. I've been trying to keep it together, but I can't handle this. I can't handle how cold and calculating everyone at Bamboo is. How can they keep going on with this ridiculous team retreat like nothing happened? Maddy is dead. She's dead."

I held space for her.

Once her tears had slowed, she gave me a pained smile. "Thank you for listening. I needed to talk to someone. I just sort of melted down and I didn't know where else to go. I know this is a lot to burden you with. I'm sorry. I've watched you with your staff and our messed-up group the last few days and you seem so calm and together."

"You don't need to apologize," I said with sincerity. "It's a terrible situation for you and it sounds like you and Maddy were close."

"She was the only person I trusted at Bamboo." She blinked back tears again.

"Can I ask you something?"

"Yeah, I'm an open book," she responded as she dabbed her eyes with a tissue.

"What about the flask you've been drinking from?"

"That?" She tossed her head back in laughter. Then she shifted position in order to remove the flask from her bag. She handed it to me. "Water. There's nothing more than fresh spring water in there. It's my crutch in social situations. People assume it's booze."

"Got it." I gave it back to her.

"You know what, the flask was Maddy's suggestion. She knew how much pressure there is to drink at events like this. She thought it would help if I had sort of a sober talisman. That's the thing; she wasn't jaded by this business. I don't know how. She managed to keep an open heart, which is saying a lot in our industry. I'm convinced that her open heart and kindness got her killed." She tore off another piece of the scone but didn't eat it.

I sat up straighter. "How?"

She tucked the flask back into her bag. "It wasn't just me; everyone confided in Maddy. She was like the office therapist. I don't know how she got any work done, because there was always someone in her office, pouring out their problems. She was such a good listener."

"And you think that got her killed?"

"I think she knew too much about all of us. I think that put her in danger, and I'm pretty sure I know who killed her."

My pulse sped up. I hadn't anticipated our conversation to take this kind of turn.

She leaned over her coffee. "I think Gus did it."

"Gus?"

"He's been interviewing with Bamboo's top competitor and Maddy found out about it."

"When?"

"The first night we were here. She's really connected—well, I guess I should say she *was* really connected in the industry. Everyone loved and adored her. The HR director at the company Gus was interviewing called her to give her a heads-up about it, out of courtesy to her. She confronted Gus at the river not out of spite, but she told him he needed to talk to Josie and be direct. That was part of her gift. She didn't try to sugarcoat difficult situations. She believed in transparency."

"What did Gus say?"

"He refused. They got in a fight about it. He was convinced that if he told Josie she would fire him on the spot and make sure that he never worked in the industry again."

"Do you think that's true?"

She moved her head from side to side. "Josie is vindictive. I wouldn't put it past her, that's for sure." She picked at the scone. "That's why I think he did it. I think he killed Maddy to silence her."

Chapter Twenty

I took a minute to let everything that Kit had told me sink in. Maddy had been her support system for her drug abuse and had tried to keep Kit on her path to recovery. Not only that, but if Kit was telling the truth about Maddy being the office therapist that certainly could have put her in harm's way.

Kit's phone rang. "This is my sponsor. I need to take this call." She got up from the booth and left.

I gathered her dishes. My head was spinning with possibilities. Could Gus be the killer? If he was desperate to leave Bamboo and Maddy was a threat to him leaving, it was certainly a possibility. I needed to find Detective Kerry and fill her in on everything I had learned. I had a feeling that she was going to be as surprised as me that Kit wasn't dealing drugs.

A quick trip across the street had me knocking on the police station door. No one answered. I left a voicemail for Kerry and returned to baking.

Ramiro had late soccer practice, so I decided to make a batch of our famous chicken pot pies. They would be ready to serve for lunch tomorrow and I could bring one home for dinner.

One thing that makes Torte pot pie special is the fact that we don't use a traditional pie crust, but rather puff pastry as a base. I buttered ramekins for individual servings as well as large pie tins. Whenever we made pot pie, we offered whole pies to go for family dinners. They typically sold out quickly, so I opted to make a double batch. The weather and misty fog rolling in over Grizzly Peak were perfect for curling up in front of the fire with a slice of pot pie and a glass of wine.

Once I had greased the tins, I rolled out puff pastry dough and cut it in circles to fit on the bottom of each pan, reserving additional circles for the top. I pressed the dough into the tins and poked holes in the bottom.

For the filling, I chopped white onions, carrots, celery, Yukon gold potatoes, and garlic. I sautéed the medley of vegetables until they were soft. Then I added diced chicken breast, fresh peas, corn, our homemade chicken stock, salt and pepper, and a healthy scoop of flour to form a roux. I let everything simmer on low for thirty minutes until the potatoes were tender.

Strong autumnal aromas filled the kitchen. As my team left for the evening, everyone commented on the delicious scents coming from the stove.

"I promise I'll have tasting samples ready first thing in the morning," I said as I waved good-bye to Steph and Sterling, who were the last to leave.

"I'm going to hold you to that promise, Jules." Sterling shot a finger at me. "And now the pressure is on to come up with a salad to accompany those beauties. Thanks a lot, there goes my sleep tonight."

Steph nudged his waist. "Yeah, right. He's a big talker. He's always sound asleep on the couch when we're only five minutes into one of my baking shows."

"Hey, what can I say? I find the cutthroat cake competitions incredibly relaxing."

I chuckled as they locked the basement door.

Knowing I had the bakeshop to myself, I poured a half glass of wine and blasted Gipsy Kings while I scooped filling into the ramekins and pie tins. I finished each pie with a top crust, brushed with an egg wash. For an added special touch, I used the remnants of the puffed pastry to cut out fall leaves and sunflowers that I painted with colored egg wash. I placed orange pumpkins and delicate green leaves on top of each crust. When they baked, the crust would puff in gorgeous golden layers with a bright touch of fall in the center.

I placed the pot pies in the walk-in fridge, reserving one for our dinner that I would bake at home. With that task complete, I finished the closing routine, checking to make sure that everything in the seating area downstairs and upstairs was ready to go for the morning rush.

My team had left the bakeshop in pristine condition. Darkness had already begun to invade outside. The antique streetlamps came on automatically as the sun vanished behind the mountains. The inky sky had an eerie glow from the wispy fog settling over the plaza.

A figure passed in front of the windows, making me nearly jump.

I looked up and locked eyes with Gus.

He motioned frantically to the front door.

I froze.

What did he want?

"We're closed," I mouthed, pointing to the sign on the door.

He knocked on it anyway, balling both of his hands into fists and pounding in a steady rhythm.

Clearly, he wasn't going to leave without talking to me. My pulse thudded in my neck. After my conversation with Kit, my theory on who had killed Maddy had shifted. What if it was Gus? What if Kit had told him about our chat?

I unlocked the door and peered out, making sure to only open it the width of my foot. "Can I help you? We're closed."

"Where is she?" He rubbed his fingers on the top of his shiny head. His eyes were like two tiny pinpricks.

"Who?"

"Kit." He stood on his toes, trying to get a look inside.

"I don't know. Why?"

"She was here a while ago. Where did she go?" His voice made me take a step back. Gus was a few inches shorter than me, and given his struggles on the raft and the fact that he was breathless now, I realized I could probably outrun him if necessary.

"I have no idea." I kept a solid grip on the door frame. "She was here, but that was a couple of hours ago. I haven't seen her since."

"Are you hiding her?" Gus bent to the left and right as if expecting she was hiding in one of the booths. Sweat poured from his brow.

"Hiding her? What?"

He grunted. "I know she's in there. I need to talk to

her." He stood taller and yelled over my shoulder, "Kit! Kit!"

I clutched the door handle, readying myself to slam it in his face. "There's no need to scream. Kit isn't here. I'm not hiding her. Why would I do that?"

"To protect her."

"What?"

"From Josie. She's on a rampage and I need to warn Kit. I have to warn Kit—now, she's in trouble."

Did that mean that Kit had followed through on our discussion? Had she quit? Was that why Josie was on a rampage? But how did Gus know, and why was he involved?

A barrage of questions threatened to take me out of the moment. I needed to stay alert. I couldn't take a chance that Gus wouldn't potentially hurt me.

Stop, Jules.

I wanted to slap myself on the cheek, to silence the questions bombarding my brain.

"What's going on with Josie?" I kept my tone as calm but stood firm. "Aren't you all supposed to be at the new Shakespeare gallery for dinner?"

Gus nodded. "Yes, that's why I have to find Kit before Josie gets to her first. I swear that Josie is going to physically harm her."

A cold gust of wind blew inside. I had to brace the door with my foot to keep it from swinging open.

"Why would Josie harm her?"

"Because Kit turned in her resignation and is threatening to go the press and air all of Bamboo's dirty secrets."

I was glad to hear that Kit had made the choice to leave Bamboo and focus on her health.

Gus craned his neck again. "She's not in there? Are you helping her? Because I'm telling you, I'm afraid for her."

"Is there something—or *someone*—she should be afraid of?" I gave him a hard stare.

He gulped. He shook his head from side to side in a rapid motion. "Wait, what? Are you talking about me? Why would she be afraid of me?"

I considered my options. If Kit had already quit then confronting Gus shouldn't impact her career, but would it put her in more danger?

Out of the corner of my eye, I noticed the lights come on at the police station. That was a relief. Gus wasn't going to hurt me. Not here. In the middle of the plaza. All I would need to do was scream loud enough and Kerry or Thomas would come running.

"I heard a rumor that you've been thinking about leaving Bamboo, too."

He forced another swallow like he was trying not to throw up. "You heard that?"

I nodded.

"From who? From Kit?"

"I'm not going to divulge my source, but it sounds like you might need to head over to the police station and have a chat with them."

"Look, I don't know what you think you know, but it's not like that. Yes, I've been applying for other positions, and I was trying to keep it on the down low. It's not a big deal. It happens all the time in this industry. Talent gets poached."

"Did Maddy know?"

His response left me speechless for a minute. "Yes. She knew."

"She did? I heard that you were keeping it quiet." It felt like a headache was coming on. Hopefully it was my brain trying to make sense of everything that I had learned in the last few hours. "You just said that yourself."

"Yeah, but Maddy knew everything." His shoulders crumpled. "She was one of a kind. She wasn't like the rest of us. Somehow she found a way not to let this industry get the better of her. She actually cared about us, unlike Josie, who would throw us to a pack of hungry wolves if given a chance. Maddy was helping me. She was going to be my reference. She offered to write me a glowing recommendation letter, and now she's dead."

None of this added up. Although his sentiment about Maddy's role at the company echoed what Kit had said.

"That's why I need to find Kit. Josie's imploding. I was leaving Bamboo because she's getting ready to sell the company. It was either jump ship or lose my job. Maddy was fully on my side. She was trying to salvage the company, which is why I'm sure that Josie killed her."

Chapter Twenty-One

Theories swirled in my head like the leaves kicking up in the wind.

Gus snapped his fingers. "Are you listening? Kit could be in danger."

"You think Josie is the killer?"

"It's the only logical explanation."

"Why are you here? You should be telling the police all of this."

"I tried. They were closed. I didn't want to call 911 because I didn't know if it was a true emergency. I think we should stick together right now—me, Kit, and Elisa." He glanced toward the station. "Oh wait, the lights are on now."

I followed his gaze across the street. Thankfully, the yellow glow still radiated from the police station. "You need to find Thomas, Kerry, or the Professor right now."

"Okay. You'll let me know if you see Kit, right?"

"Of course." I shut and locked the door after him and went downstairs to get the chicken pot pie and my things. Gus seemed sincere in his concern about Kit, but could it be an act? Maybe he had really come looking for her because he wanted to silence her before she shared her theories with the police.

I returned upstairs and checked outside to see if Gus was still hanging around. I kicked myself for not watching to make sure he had actually gone across the street to talk to the Professor or whoever was on duty at the moment, but before I had time to think it through a familiar face appeared.

"Darling, did you read my mind?" Lance strolled past A Rose by Any Other Name. He had changed since I'd seen him earlier. His navy suit with a red polka-dot tie and a single red rose tucked into his breast pocket was a sure sign that he was on his way to the dinner at Parchment and Quill.

"What? No." I was still reeling from my conversation with Gus.

"Why the long face?"

I gave him the condensed version.

"If this isn't a stroke of divine intervention, then I don't know what is." Lance leaned closer. I could smell his aftershave and minty breath. "I've been in touch with our dear friend Abby. She's waiting for you as we speak with a bottle of wine and some of her decadent delights. Scurry up there. Say hello for me, and don't forget to have a little look around while you're at it." He gave me an exaggerated wink.

"Lance, no. I already told you, I'm not going to snoop at Abby's."

"It's not snooping. You're merely having a happy hour drink with an old friend." He pushed me toward the corner. "I'll take on the crew at Parchment and Quill while you nosh it up with Abby. Ta-ta." He blew me a kiss and raced across the street before I could get another word out.

I hesitated for a moment; then I went back inside and checked the time. Carlos wouldn't be done at the vineyard for another hour or so and Ramiro had soccer practice. Maybe it wasn't the worst idea to go see Abby. Not that I had any intention of sneaking around her B and B, but I hadn't seen her for a while, and it wouldn't hurt to ask her how her experience with the Bamboo team had been.

I grabbed my coat, locked the front door, and headed outside again. Abigail's was located on the north end of town, not far from the hospital. The two-story white Victorian was an architectural beauty. Abby and her husband had created a welcoming retreat for guests with their lush front gardens with cozy collections of outdoor seating and a hammock strung up between two maple trees. Rocking chairs and pots filled with fresh herbs occupied the front porch. Abby waved to me from a rocker as I followed the redbrick pathway that cuts through pale pink cosmos and waxy begonias.

"Jules, so lovely to see you. Come sit." Abby patted the rocker next to her. On the side table there was a bottle of buttery chardonnay, two glasses, and an assortment of nibbles.

"Great to see you. I hope you didn't go to too much trouble."

"Never." Abby poured us each a glass of wine. "You know me. I always end up making something extra for our guests, especially since the theater is dark tonight. I set up appetizers and wine on the back patio for the

Bamboo team earlier. When I'm traveling it's nice to have a leisurely light snack before heading to dinner."

"One of many reasons why Abigail's is booked solid all season." I held out my wine in a toast. We clinked our glasses together.

"How's everything at Torte?"

"Good." I took a sip of the wine, which was crisp and light. It hit the spot. "We catered dinner and the rafting trip for Bamboo. I know you've had them staying here, and I'm guessing you've heard about everything that happened."

She swirled her wine. "It's terrible. I'm so sorry that you were there."

"It was a shock, to say the least."

Abby motioned to the platter of appetizers. "Please, help yourself."

I took a piece of bruschetta and tried to think of a casual way to approach asking her more specifics about Bamboo. Lance was much better at this than me.

"I shouldn't say this, but they've all left for Richard Lord's," Abby said, scooting her rocker closer. She wore a long silky wrap with a dainty butterfly pattern. "I'm not going to be sad to see them go. It's awful that Maddy was killed. Don't get me wrong. However, they are some of the worst guests we've ever had. Josie in particular. You know me, Jules; I'm usually fairly even-tempered. I've seen it all over the years of hosting guests from around the world, but this group exudes negativity. I wouldn't say this to anyone but you."

"Abby, trust me, I understand exactly what you mean, and I won't repeat it." I was glad she had opened the door.

"They've had some outrageous requests." She tightened her wrap around her shoulders. "They've been up at all hours of the night, like college students. I felt bad to hand them off to you, but I wasn't sad to see them leave for the Rogue. That first night was the worst. I think most of them were already tipsy when they came back from dinner at Torte. Then they took the wine out to the patio and stayed up until two or three in the morning."

"Really?" I bit into the bruschetta. Abby had grilled thin slices of crusty sourdough and brushed them with basil-infused olive oil. Then topped the bread with a melody of heirloom tomatoes, fresh basil, onions, garlic, and balsamic. It was pure bliss in my mouth.

Abby took a long drink of her wine. "I finally fell asleep around three thirty only to be woken up again at four. I heard a loud crash. At first, I thought it might have been a bear. It's that time of year, and I didn't go outside to get their dishes since they were up so late. I came down to scare it away, but it wasn't a bear."

"What was it?" I realized I was rocking fast—like a mother desperate to get her newborn to sleep.

"I know for sure it was Maddy. She was arguing with someone else. I couldn't see who it was, though. They had knocked over one of my patio chairs and taken off through the side pathway. Maddy was upset. I stayed with her for a good ten or fifteen minutes. She was crying and pretty shaken up."

"Did she say who she'd been fighting with?"

"No. I couldn't get anything out of her. She was basically inconsolable. I picked up the dishes in case a bear did wander down. She went to bed. That's the last I saw of her." Abby sighed.

"I'm assuming you told the Professor this?"

"Of course." She fiddled with the edge of her wrap. "Doug and Thomas have been here multiple times. I wish I had gotten a better look at whomever she was arguing with. What if that fight was the reason she was killed?"

"You're not responsible, Abby," I assured her.

She popped a piece of salami in her mouth. "I know; it's just terrible to think that a woman who had been staying with me was killed. Not to mention, I don't love the thought that the killer could be sleeping here tonight."

"I get that."

A group of kids on bikes zoomed past us on the sidewalk. They called out hello to Abby.

"Are there going to be cookies later, Ms. Abby?" a girl wearing a unicorn helmet asked.

"There are two batches of snickerdoodles ready to go in the oven," Abby replied. "Be sure to check with your parents first, though."

The kids promised they would get permission and return for hot-from-the-oven cookies later.

"I didn't know you were the cookie lady," I said to her after they had sped away.

"Only for our neighbors." Her eyes twinkled. "I tend to bake cookies for guests. I can't help myself. Technically, the only official meal that comes with a stay is breakfast, but there's nothing like a warm cookie and cup of tea to finish off the night. It started with our next-door neighbors. That's Alexa on the bike. I invited her mom over when I had extras and it caught on with neighbor kids. My only rule is they have to get the okay from their parents before they stop by."

"That's so sweet." And so Ashland, I thought. Abby embodied the community spirit. "Not to bring the mood down again, but do you have any sense of whether Maddy was arguing with a man or a woman?"

"No, I wish." Abby shook her head. "Doug asked the same thing. I was half-asleep. Earlier I know for sure there were men and women talking, but like I said, I had drifted off. The crash is what woke me. By the time I put on a robe and slippers and came outside Maddy was alone."

"Right." I wondered who Maddy had been fighting with. Could that argument have been the root cause of her murder?

"Shall I top you off?" Abby offered me more wine.

I placed my hand over my glass. "No, thank you. I'd love to, but I should probably start heading back to Torte. Carlos is going to pick me up on his way home from Uva."

Abby refreshed her glass. "Are you going to be ready for harvest soon? Let us know if you need extra hands."

"That would be wonderful. We'll repay you with wine."

"Say no more." She held the wine bottle like a trophy. "Wine or pastries is the only payment I ever need."

I thanked her for the drink and snack, promising that I would reach out as soon as the grapes were ready to harvest. On the way back to Torte, my mind latched onto what I had learned. Maddy had fought with one of her colleagues until the early morning hours the night before she was killed. If I could figure out who had been on Abby's patio with Maddy, then maybe I'd be one step closer to solving the crime.

Chapter Twenty-Two

On my way back from Abby's, I texted Carlos to let him know I was ready. He was going to swing by to pick me up at Torte, and then we'd grab Ramiro from practice. Instead of waiting inside, I opted to wait on the corner in hopes that I might be able to get a glimpse of any nefarious action going down on the plaza.

The evening air held the faintest hint of fall. I tugged on my coat and stuffed my hands in my pockets. There was definitely someone inside the station, but I couldn't make out who it was. I'd been at Abby's for at least an hour. Could Gus still be talking to the police? I considered wandering over, but that seemed too obvious. Plus, if Gus was really sharing his insight, I didn't want to interfere.

By the time Carlos arrived I had gone inside to get the pie and do one last sweep of the bakeshop. "Julieta, you have pie?"

"Chicken pot pie." I placed the pie box in the backseat. "Dinner and lunch are prepped for tomorrow."

"You have been busy."

I shot a final glance at the station as he steered through the turnaround. "You have no idea."

"That sounds bad. Is everything okay?" He reached for my hand.

"It's the investigation." I gave him a brief recap of what I had learned.

"How do you know so much?" His eyes veered away from the road. "I swear, Julieta, you are not telling me the whole story. Did Doug hire you as a secret agent?" While Carlos was trying to keep the conversation light and playful, I knew he had reservations about me being involved with anything connected to the murder.

I tried to laugh it off. "Ashland's secret detective, that's me."

"Do not laugh, mi querida." Carlos returned his focus to Main Street, where diners were enjoying the last of the temperate evenings at candlelit bistro tables in front of Ashland Springs Hotel. "You have a gift. People open up to you, but this can also put you in danger, sí?"

"It doesn't feel like a gift at the moment," I admitted. "I'm totally overwhelmed. I feel like I'm missing something major. None of it fits together."

"Maybe that's your answer."

"How so?"

"Maybe the killer is hoping that none of the pieces will fit together to keep everyone guessing."

"It's possible." I sighed and changed the subject. "Let's talk about something else. I have to give my brain a break. How was Uva? Do you think we'll be ready for harvest this week?"

"Good. It's looking very good, and I have a feeling we will have a high yield this year. I think we will only have three or four days left and the vines will be ready. It is exciting. I cannot wait to begin making wine. It is almost impossible to believe that at this time last year I was on the ship and now I'm here and I will be producing our own blends."

His enthusiasm helped lighten my mood.

"You will come and be part of it, sí? And Lance. We must invite him, too. We need a crush party. I am thinking maybe it's a special end-of-the-season dinner in the vines and we have our friends come and help with the crush. Like the way old-world wines were made."

"That sounds incredible. Let's do it."

"Sí? Maybe this Sunday? After we finish with the harvest. It does not need to be a full dinner. We can do cheese and fruit boards, small plates, dessert, and wine. Always wine."

I laughed. "We can't very well have a crush party without wine."

"I remember my grandparents making small batches of wine. They would bring out a half barrel and the kids and adults would take off our shoes, roll up our pants, and stomp for hours. I have so many happy memories of this time. It would be good to create those memories here with you."

"You're not thinking of trying to crush all of the grapes manually, are you?"

Carlos threw his head back and laughed. "No. That would take too long. It is more for the festivities and the ritual of the crush. Although we could try to take what our friends stomp and make a few special bottles to share."

"Sounds perfect."

We made it to the high school. Ramiro jumped in the back with my pot pie and immediately started chattering about soccer practice and his politics and literature class. I let thoughts of Maddy's murder drift away. It was easy to do with Ramiro's enthusiasm for soccer practice and his school day.

At home, I heated the pot pie in the oven while Carlos opened a bottle of wine and made salad. Ramiro took a quick shower before dinner. I was setting the table when my phone rang.

Thomas's face flashed on the screen.

"What's going on?"

"That was quick." Thomas sounded taken aback that I had answered on the first ring.

"Eager fingers." I laughed. "I guess I'm anxious for news on the case. Did Gus come to the station?"

"He did." Thomas didn't expand.

"Is that why you're calling?"

"Not exactly, but in a way, I guess."

I waited for him to say more.

"I'm calling on behalf of the Professor. He's at the Bamboo dinner at Richard's new place. He's planning on a press conference in the plaza tomorrow morning and wondered if you would be willing to set up coffee and muffins for the press."

"A press conference?" In all my years of knowing the Professor I had never seen him host a press conference.

"Yeah. I can't really say more at the moment, but do you think bringing out some coffee and muffins will work? He said to go ahead and bill the station like usual."

"That's not a problem at all. We can bring over a folding table. When should we have everything ready to go?" Carlos came over to hand me a glass of wine. His eyes searched my face for a hint of what I was talking about.

"Eight thirty or eight forty-five would be great. That will allow the press time to get seats and settle before we begin."

I took a sip of the wine. "Does this mean there's going to be an announcement about an arrest?"

Thomas cleared his throat. "I can't say. Sorry."

"No worries. We'll have hot coffee and warm muffins ready and waiting for you."

"Thanks, Jules. I appreciate it."

When we hung up, Carlos motioned for me to take a seat. He had finished setting the table. "What is it, Julieta?"

"They're holding a press conference in the plaza tomorrow morning."

"Who?"

"The Professor and Thomas and Kerry. It has to be connected to the case."

"And how does this involve you?" He sounded worried.

"It doesn't. They want us to make coffee and muffins."

"Okay." The wrinkles on his forehead vanished. "Are you ready to eat? I'll tell Ramiro to come down."

"Sure." I held my wineglass. "Thanks for this."

He went to get Ramiro and I settled in with my drink. There was no point in trying to imagine what the press conference was going to reveal. I would know soon enough. This evening was a chance to spend time with the two men I loved. I couldn't believe how easily we had all fallen into a domestic routine. I also couldn't believe how much having Ramiro with us had shifted the energy in the house. It made me even more grateful that his mom had been gracious enough to share him with us this year. When she arrived for a visit in a few weeks, I was going to have to make sure I went out of my way to let her know how much I appreciated it.

The conversation around the same table that I had grown up eating at reminded me of my youth. It was a delight to listen to Ramiro's comparison of the school day in Spain with that of America. "Did you know that almost everyone walks to Safeway for lunch? They eat chips and donuts and big sodas. There is no siesta and no long lunch. I'm going to have to start getting chicken and jojos at the grocery store."

"You wouldn't dare," Carlos teased. Then he turned to me. "Also what is a jojo? Do I want to know?"

"They're actually delicious," I replied. "A Northwest classic—potato wedges that are breaded, liberally spiced, and pressure fried. Not deep fried. That's an important distinction," I said to Ramiro, holding up my index finger. "If anyone offers you a greasy jojo, run. Jojos should be crisp and airy."

Ramiro responded with a solemn nod, as if I had imparted critical knowledge. "No, soggy jojos. Got it. If I am going to school in America, I have to live like an American student, sí? I think from now on you don't need to pack me lunch. I'll have a box of Pop-Tarts instead."

Carlos gasped. "You're stabbing my heart. At least let Julieta make you her handmade Pop-Tarts."

"I don't think those are cool," I said, catching Ramiro's eye. "Don't worry, I've got your back. If you want boxed Pop-Tarts, go for it."

"There is only one remedy for this. We must send you back to Spain. I cannot let my only son eat a grocery store lunch." He winked.

The conversation shifted to homework and the upcoming homecoming parade and dance. I sipped my wine and drank in the moment, feeling a deep sense of gratitude for our little family, despite the horrific events of the past week. Maybe tomorrow we would finally have answers about who killed Maddy.

I slept through the night, dreaming of harvest and grape crush dinners in the vines. When I woke the following day, a nervous hum of energy pulsed through my body. Maybe the press conference was nothing, but I had a feeling there was more to it.

As was typical, I snuck off to the bakeshop while Carlos and Ramiro were still fast asleep. I wanted to get a head start on baking and give myself extra time to prep for the press conference. Not that it would require an inordinate amount of time to make a few batches of muffins and pots of coffee, but the truth was that I was very curious about what the Professor intended to share with the press. Providing breakfast was the perfect excuse to listen in.

At Torte, I began with muffins. Not only would I take them to the press conference, but they could serve a dual purpose as our daily breakfast special. I felt especially glad that I had stayed later last night and prepped the pot pies for lunch. Sterling would simply need to bake them and come up with an accompanying salad.

I wanted to make a trio of muffins, so I started with the base. One easy "cheat" that I had learned in culinary school was to use the same batter as a base for cookies and muffins and then divide the batter into equal portions to add unique fillings and flavor combinations. It saved an enormous amount of time and allowed us to offer various options without having to do double or triple the work.

For the muffin base I combined melted butter, sugar, eggs, and milk. Then I sifted in flour, baking powder, and a touch of salt. Once a thick batter had formed, I scooped portions into large mixing bowls. I folded in whole blueberries, lemon juice, and zest to the first batch. Lemon blueberry is always a popular combination.

I used an ice cream scoop to fill muffin tins and then finished off the lemon blueberry muffins with lemon-infused sparkling sugar on the top. Once those were in the oven to bake, I moved on to the next batch. These would be triple chocolate muffins with cocoa powder, dark and milk chocolate chips, and a scattering of mini chocolate chips on the top.

For the last round of muffins, I decided to go with a fall favorite—pumpkin cranberry. I mixed pumpkin purée and our trio of fall spices into the batter along with dried cranberries. After scooping them into the tins, I sprinkled them with cinnamon and sugar, which would form a crackly texture for the top.

With the muffins baking, I switched gears to pastry. Daily croissants were a must at Torte. We always served a plain croissant, almond filled, and a savory bacon and cheddar. When time allowed, or when we were feeling inspired, we would add to the rotation. Today I decided to offer a special croissant—Nutella filled, with a dark chocolate drizzle.

Andy, Marty, Steph, and Sterling arrived for the morning shift as I took the buttery chocolate croissants from the oven.

"I'll take a dozen of those." Marty leaned over the tray to get a better whiff. "You know that Nutella is my kryptonite, don't you?"

"Marty is the man! Throwing down with a Superman reference. I like it." Andy shot him a thumbs-up.

"I'll have you know, young man, that I read every single one of the original DC comics when I was a kid. Long before you were even born." He pretended to be upset, but I knew this was part of their banter.

"What's on the agenda for the day?" Sterling asked.

I filled them in on the press conference, as well as the fact that there were dozens of chicken pot pies waiting in the fridge. "Before everyone scatters, I also wanted to touch base about doing a Sunday Supper at Uva this weekend." I told them about Carlos's idea for a grape stomp.

"Bethany will be all over that," Steph started to say, but stopped. "Oh wait, will she be around?"

Andy made a grunting sound under his breath.

"Where's Bethany going?" Marty asked.

"Didn't you hear her gushing yesterday?" Andy sounded irritated.

"She *should* gush," Steph defended her friend and decorating partner in crime. "It's an amazing opportunity for her."

"I wasn't saying that it's not a good opportunity."

Andy folded his arms across his chest in a defensive position.

"Did I imply that?" Steph didn't back down.

He huffed. "I need to go fire up the espresso machine. I'm thinking of a chocolate hazelnut mocha to go with your Nutella croissants, Jules."

"Sounds good." I smiled at him. Usually, I left the Shakespeare quotes to the Professor, but the line "The lady doth protest too much, methinks" kept running through my head.

"Someone's touchy this morning," Steph noted as she tied on an apron and reviewed the cake orders. "I wonder if he's finally going to make a move."

"Our sweet Andy is a slower mover. I think we might need to stage an intervention." Marty stacked applewood in the pizza oven.

"I'm not above that." A look of devious inspiration flashed across Steph's violet eyes.

"Don't give her any ideas," Sterling said. "You know Steph likes to play aloof, but she's basically a walking Jane Austen novel."

"How dare you!" She gave Sterling a playful glare before heading to the walk-in.

We talked through lunch specials while Marty lit the fire and Steph stacked a tiered cake she had crumb-coated last night.

"I already made the pot pies, like I said. Do you want to do a salad with them?"

"Sure. Maybe a shaved Brussels sprout salad with toasted pecans and cranberries. I can do a cranberry vinaigrette. That should be light with the hearty pot pie. Should I do a soup special, too?"

"Soup is always a good idea."

"How about an Italian wedding with mini meatballs and fall veggies?"

"Is that a nod to Marty's plan to stage an intervention?" I glanced at the bread station where Marty and Steph were deep in conversation, which was slightly unusual. Steph tended to put her AirPods in and blast music while she concentrated on highly detailed decorating techniques. Her skill set, like everyone else's on my staff, had only improved with time and practice. She didn't simply frost cakes with buttercream. She created edible art pieces. Not only had she meticulously studied Mom and me when we demonstrated how to hold a pipping bag or crumb coat a cake, but she also consumed hours of baking shows. As of late, she would often show up for her shift with sketches and notes from designs she'd seen on TV.

The latest trend she was working to perfect was bas-relief carving. It was a process used in sculpting that cake artists had adopted. Basically it involved creating slightly raised designs out of buttercream, giving tiered cakes an old-world elegance.

"No, I saw a recipe on one of Steph's cooking shows last night; it sounded good."

"It does. Go for it." I surveyed the kitchen. Things were already running smoothly. Sequoia, Rosa, and Bethany would be in shortly. "I'm going to set up for the press conference. Let's plan to go over some easy snacking plates for the grape stomp this weekend once I'm back."

"You got it."

I went to get a folding table and tablecloth. Setting

up a small table with muffins and coffee was nothing in comparison with the work that had gone into the private catering events we had hosted for Bamboo.

Hopefully the press conference would bring closure to Maddy's death.

Thomas had been noncommittal last night, but I had every intention of securing a spot and hearing whatever the Professor had to share firsthand.

Chapter Twenty-Three

Lance paced in front of the Lithia bubblers. "There you are, darling. I've been waiting forever."

"Really?" I set the table down. "I didn't know we were meeting."

He tapped his temple with his finger. "You obviously weren't using your telepathic powers."

"Obviously. It's weird, too, because I wasn't aware that I possess telepathic powers. That's very good to know."

"Don't toy with me before I'm fully awake. You are well aware of the fact that I don't function without my beauty sleep. It's not even nine. Shudder." He made his entire body quake.

"What are you doing up so early?"

"Waiting for you."

"Lance, seriously. Also, can you help me with this?" I motioned for him to take one side of the table.

"Oh, I'm deadly serious." Lance steadied his end of the table. "It's only serious business that would drag me from my bed at this ungodly hour, especially after what I had to sit through last night."

"That's right; I almost forgot. How was the Richard Lord dinner?" I unfolded the tablecloth and draped it across the table.

"Let's just say that my stomach is never going to forgive me. Is there such a thing as grease meat?"

"Grease meat?" I stuck out my tongue.

"Imagine a tough cut of meat drowned in greasy, unflavored fat. That would have been a Michelin star dinner compared with what we were served last night."

"Gross."

"You don't even know the half of it." He gagged. "But I digress. We shouldn't dally. The press will be arriving soon, and we have much to discuss."

"You know about the press conference?"

"Please." He tilted his head and gave me a look of disappointment. "How long have we been besties? There is nothing that gets past yours truly in the valley. Nothing."

He had a fair point.

"I happened to have a chat with the Professor at last night's Tums-inducing dinner and he let it slip that the press has been summoned to the plaza for a late-breaking news conference."

There was no chance the Professor had let anything "slip." If he had told Lance about the press conference, I was sure he had a reason.

"Do you think they've made a formal arrest?" I asked.

"Perhaps. Or ponder this. I have another theory." He lifted his index finger and tapped it on the side of his ear. "I used my oh-so-subtle sleuthing abilities to eavesdrop on conversations last night."

Nothing Lance did was subtle. I decided now was not

the time to point that out, though. "Did you learn anything?"

"Other than confirming that Richard Lord's latest venture is sure to go up in flames? The Bard must be rolling over in his grave at the sight of so much tacky Shakespeare in one place. Parchment and Quill is basically a glorified gift shop, at least when you first walk in. You're greeted by eye-piercing purple walls, purple carpet, purple, purple, putrid purple. I have no idea where Lord managed to procure so much purple. He's selling Shakespeare socks, gum, candles, and a Chia Pet. Shudder." Lance's body revolted at the thought.

"What about Ernest? I thought it was also an art gallery."

"Oh, it is." Lance made a gagging motion. "You have to weave your way through the plastic bobbleheads and cheap T-shirts. The rest of the space is a bizarre collection of classic art mixed with curios from the Elizabethan era."

"Do I even want to ask what sort of curios?"

"Not unless you're interested in a visual display of the sewers and public latrines of the time." He recoiled and placed his hand on his stomach, like he was trying to keep its contents in.

"Gross."

"Would we expect anything less from Richard Lord?" Lance brushed his hands. "Again, I digress. As I circulated, I learned a few tidbits that may be of interest. The first is that Elisa offered her PR services to Richard and Ernest."

"She what?" My eyes traveled to the Merry Windsor. The dingy half-timbered exterior with its mismatched stone foundation was in desperate need of a good cleaning and a fresh coat of paint. I couldn't imagine Elisa wanting to manage PR for Richard. She must be desperate herself.

"She was giving him quite the pitch. Big visions for a national launch campaign for Parchment and Quill—the works. You tell me why an up-and-coming young marketing maven would have any interest in uprooting her career in LA to come work for Richard and Ernest."

"It seems odd," I concurred.

"You know, the other thing that seems odd is why Miller puts up with so much abuse from Josie. He can't be making the kind of salary that would translate to golden handcuffs as a PA. She treats him like he's her personal lackey and he trots around after her, waiting to fulfill her every wish and command. Something isn't right there."

I agreed with his assessment of Josie and Miller's professional relationship as well.

"What about you, darling? Did you uncover anything at Abigail's?"

"Not really." I motioned for him to move the table closer to the information kiosk with me. "Maddy was up until four in the morning fighting with someone the night before she died, but Abby didn't see who it was."

"Intéressante." Lance slipped into a French accent.

Across the street at the police station, Thomas, Kerry, and two of the park cadets were stacking folding chairs. I guessed they were bringing them our way to set up for the press conference.

Lance noticed, too. "Here's my theory on this morning's press junket. What if it's a trap?"

"A trap?" We were in the middle of the plaza. It wasn't as if the area were tightly enclosed with nowhere for the killer to escape.

"Yes! A game of cat and mouse could be afoot. What if the Professor is baiting the killer to reveal themselves?" Lance flashed his signature Cheshire grin.

"I guess, but how?"

"That's what we're here to observe, isn't it?" He swept his arms across the plaza.

"On that note, can you watch the table? I need to bring coffee and muffins over."

He gave me a two-fingered salute. "I shall stand guard until you return."

By the time I had loaded up boxes of muffins, napkins, and coffee cups, Thomas, Kerry, and the cadets had arrived and recruited Lance to help them set up folding chairs and the podium.

"This looks like something from a movie set," I said as I began arranging baskets of muffins on the table.

Thomas tested the mic with his finger. "Test, test. Can you hear me okay?"

We nodded.

"I've seen the Professor belt out sonnets at the Black Swan," Lance said, measuring the space between each chair with his forearm. "The man commands the stage and innately understands projection. He would likely be fine without a mic."

"Standard procedure." Thomas turned the mic off temporarily.

I took another couple of trips to bring out pots of our regular and decaf house blends as well as cream and sugar and stir sticks. The press trickled in and made a beeline for coffee. Everyone thanked me profusely for providing a morning pick-me-up.

It didn't come as a surprise to see Miller, Gus, Josie, and Elisa take up the last row of seats. Kit was notably absent.

Could that mean that Gus's prediction that she was in danger had been correct?

Lance sidled up next to me and helped himself to a lemon blueberry muffin. "The gang's all here, *interesting*."

"Not Kit."

The Professor's voice coming over the mic made us both go quiet. "Good morning, everyone. I appreciate you taking the time out of your hectic schedules to join us on such short notice." He took his notebook from the breast pocket of his tweed jacket. "Before we begin, I would like to thank Torte for providing us with coffee and muffins."

Light applause broke out amongst the chairs.

I acknowledged their appreciation with a half wave.

"As you may have noted from the press release that my team sent out, I'd like to give you an update on the investigation into the death of Madeline Solars. We have been working in partnership with our colleagues in Shady Cove and we have a formal statement that we would like to read you this morning."

Hands shot in the air.

The Professor motioned for everyone to stop. "We will be taking questions, but not yet. I'd politely ask you to hold your questions until we've had a chance to read the statement."

I expected him to read the statement, but instead he stepped away from the mic and signaled to his left.

Lance gasped audibly.

I'm sure my face must have reflected the same response because I blinked twice and tried to make sense of what was happening.

Kit appeared from behind the team of police officers from Shady Cove.

She stepped forward and spoke directly into the microphone. "I'm the creative director at Bamboo. I'm here to read a statement."

Miller let out an audible gasp. Josie, who was seated next to him, punched him in the shoulder. Gus's face was narrowed in on Kit, like a hunter ready to pounce on his prey. Elisa stopped texting and stared at Kit in disbelief.

One of the members of the press asked Kit to spell her name.

While she did, Lance leaned in. "What an unexpected and delicious twist. Are you having a Miss Marple moment?"

"A Miss Marple moment?"

"Agatha Christie, darling."

"I know who Miss Marple is. I'm asking what you mean by 'a Miss Marple moment.'"

"I believe all is about to be revealed. This is the payoff moment on the stage. The crescendo. The climax. This is the very moment we've been waiting for. The audience is literally on the edge of their seats." He nodded toward the press.

"Technically speaking, I don't think journalists count as an audience."

"For us they do." He pressed a finger to his lips. "Now, shush, darling, the fun is about to begin."

Chapter Twenty-Four

Kit proceeded to read from her prepared statement. Only it quickly became apparent the statement hadn't been written by her.

"'For immediate release, dated . . . ,'" she began, inserting a date from the week before Maddy was killed.

"Is that a mistake?" Lance whispered. "Isn't Kit the creative director?"

"Yeah. I don't know," I replied, looking at Elisa. She had dropped her phone in her lap and looked as surprised as I felt.

Kit continued. "'Bamboo announces it will merge with the international holding company New Wave, effective immediately. Bamboo staff will be provided severance packages, aside from three members of the team who will continue with New Wave in the transition. Bamboo's stock has dropped dramatically, crashing into a free fall for the last two years. The buyout from New Wave will save the company from bankruptcy. Management issues have been documented internally, under the abysmal leadership of Josie Jones. For more information contact Elisa Haug, marketing director.'"

She finished by including Elisa's phone number and email address.

Murmurs broke out amongst the reporters, who appeared to be baffled by what was going on. Hands flew in the air. Cameras flashed.

"I don't get it," I said to Lance.

He shrugged. "I'm as in the dark as you, darling."

Josie jumped to her feet. "Where did you get that?" She thrust her finger at Kit, who was clutching the podium so tight that the tips of her fingers turned white.

"You know where." Kit stared her down.

I watched the Professor study both women.

A member of the press moved closer to Josie and aimed his camera at her face. Another held a notepad and pencil at the ready. "Do you care to comment? Is Bamboo being bought out?"

"I have no idea what you're talking about. Who wrote that? Who would do something so blatant to sabotage the merger?" She practically ripped a pencil from a reporter's hand. "Stop writing. Don't write that down. This is not an approved press release. I have no idea who wrote that or who is making up these lies."

Hands flew up again.

The Professor nodded to Kit, who handed him the statement she had read and stepped away from the microphone.

Josie screeched at her team. "Who did this? Maddy? Was this her final revenge?"

No one moved.

"I believe the writer of this release identified themselves quite clearly," the Professor said.

Realization dawned on me as I followed his line of

sight to Elisa. She had sunk in her seat, trying to make herself small.

Josie stood frozen for a moment before her violent gaze landed on Elisa. "You! You did this?"

Elisa's face turned ghostly white. She clutched her stomach and began rocking back and forth, like she was attempting to soothe herself.

"You wrote this press release? You little witch!" Josie looked like she was about to tackle Elisa. "You were going to sabotage the company? Me? After everything that Bamboo has done for you."

The throng of reporters pushed closer. A wave of dizziness came over me as chaos erupted. The press fought for position, shouting over the top of one another. Miller and Gus had both jumped to their feet, too. They had Elisa surrounded.

The Professor stood next to Kit at the podium, watching with a hawk-like eye. He didn't attempt to pull Elisa away or make an arrest. He seemed content to let the scene play out.

"This is so juicy." Lance bounced with excitement. "I didn't see that coming."

"What has Bamboo done for me?" Elisa finally broke her silence. She sat taller and spat at Jose, "You've done nothing for any of us. Nothing. Other than making our lives absolutely miserable. You know what you've given me? An ulcer at thirty." She stabbed her at her stomach. "Thanks, thanks a lot for that."

Miller threw his hand over his mouth. "Oh my God, did you kill Maddy?"

Elisa continued to rock as she spoke. "I didn't plan it. I sent her the press release because I thought she was on my side. I thought she was on all of our sides, but she wasn't. Her talk about creating a healthy work environment—none of it was true. The minute she read the release she threatened to tell Josie. I begged her not to. I thought we were friends. I thought she had all of our backs, but it turns out that was all an act. She didn't care about us. She was just trying to bide her time and keep things from imploding so she could get her massive payout. Guess what the rest of us are getting in this deal? Nothing. Three months of severance. After everything I've given Bamboo. You have, too, dude. You think you're getting a dime? Nope. It's all going to Josie Jones."

"Maddy didn't need to die." Miller's voice cracked.

"You think she cared about you? That was a lie. An act. She pretended like she was on our side, but she's been working with Josie to finalize the deal with New Wave this entire time. I found out by mistake. They called for a statement, not realizing that the staff didn't know the deal had been finalized. I went straight to Maddy. She admitted everything. She wasn't even sorry about it. She said that's just the way business works and that I should get over it. I should feel grateful that I was getting a crummy severance package and that she would write me a stellar letter of recommendation."

A reporter in the row in front of her turned around and began snapping pictures of her. Another had his camera zoomed in on her face. Every other journalist had their phone out recording Elisa's live confession.

Had the Professor known this was going to happen? If so, he had orchestrated the press conference to perfection.

"This is pure gold," Lance said with a devilish smile. "I couldn't have scripted it better myself."

"Maddy might have pretended like she was one of us," Elisa said to Miller. "She wasn't. She was Josie's lackey. They played the good cop/bad cop role beautifully. She had me convinced for a while, but then it all became clear. She was going to throw each and every one of us under the bus for her million-dollar-plus payout while the rest of us got nothing." She turned to Gus. "Remember when we were hired and promised that if Bamboo ever sold we would be rewarded for being the first in the company? Yeah, that's not happening. Josie and Maddy weren't about to share the wealth. They were keeping it all for themselves."

"So you killed her?" Gus sounded disgusted.

"She deserved to die. You know what she said to me that night? She said I should have seen it coming. Well, guess what? She should have, too." Elisa's voice didn't hold even a faint hint of remorse.

A shiver ran down my arms.

"That's cold," Lance said, mimicking my body language. "Ice cold."

Thomas and Kerry had moved to either side of the row that Elisa was seated in, blocking any way for her to escape.

She didn't put up a fight. Instead, she stood and held her arms in surrender. "Arrest me. I don't care. I did what had to be done. I did what any of you would have done in the same circumstance."

I doubted that.

Thomas escorted her across the street to the police

station with Kerry following, I supposed as backup on the off chance Elisa tried to bolt.

The Professor called for questions and was instantly bombarded by dozens of hands in the air. He methodically went row by row, allowing time for every reporter to ask what they needed to complete their stories.

Lance and I listened with rapt attention as the Professor explained that they had indeed called the press conference in an attempt to draw a confession from Elisa. "We had some doubts as to whether the accused would come forward, but I feel confident in making an arrest. Now we'll turn the case over to the prosecutor's office to take it from here."

There were several questions that he refused to answer based on not wanting to divulge anything that may be used against Elisa in the trial. The gist of what he was able to share was that they had identified the substance used to kill Maddy and discovered it in their search. Additionally, the Shady Cove team had searched Elisa's financial records and learned that she was in debt to the tune of nearly a half-million dollars.

"She must have been counting on getting a large payout when the company sold," Lance surmised as he chomped on a second muffin. "Money is always a motive."

"Yeah, it's just so sad, and I wonder if it's true."

"What part?"

"That Maddy was really that cold and working directly with Josie. She struck me as so genuine."

"Again, cash changes things."

"True." I just had a hard time believing that her personality could have been so radically different. Maybe

Elisa's perspective was tainted by her desperation. Maybe Maddy really had everyone's best interest at heart and was simply trying to do her job. Either way, it didn't justify Elisa's crime. Even if Maddy had planned to cut the rest of the Bamboo team loose without compensation. Gus was right. She didn't deserve to die.

As the press conference wound down, I began to pick things up. I would send the extra muffins back to the station with the Professor. Both coffee pots had been drained and there were only a handful of muffins left.

While I boxed them up, a realization dawned on me. My original theory about Maddy's death had been wrong. Very wrong. It wasn't a case of misidentification. Maddy had been the intended victim all along.

"Well, that's another case in the books." Lance brushed his hands. "We've solved yet another one, darling."

"Did we, though?"

"Of course. Without our help the police would obviously still be out searching the riverbanks for clues."

I chuckled. "Right. You tell the Professor that."

"Oh, look at the time." Lance tapped his watch. "Must scurry. People to see. Fans to adore me. You know the drill."

"You wouldn't want to leave your adoring public waiting," I said with a half grin.

"Never." He kissed my cheeks. "Drinks soon? A murderous recap, perhaps?"

"Anytime. You know where to find me."

He strolled away, with a casual aloofness.

I took the first load of supplies back to the bakeshop. I knew my staff was going to want a report, too.

I was relieved to be able to share the news that Elisa had been arrested. If nothing else, at least there was closure in the case. I just wished that it hadn't had to come to murder.

Chapter Twenty-Five

By the next day, news of Elisa's arrest had spread faster than butter on a slice of hot sourdough. Josie had flown to LA within hours of the press conference, in an attempt to try and salvage the deal with New Wave. Miller, Gus, and Kit had all stopped in to say good-bye and thank us for everything.

I joined them at a window booth with a platter of white cheddar and sun-dried tomato biscuits and cherry almond hand pies.

Kit stood to give me a long hug. "Thanks again for listening, Jules. I was at such a low point, having someone just hold space for me was such a gift. I'll never forget it. If you ever need creative work, I'm here for you."

"What will you all do now?" I asked, sitting next to her and helping myself to a hand pie.

"We made a pact to do something to honor Maddy's memory," Miller said, catching his colleagues' eyes to make sure it was okay to continue. When they both nodded, he went on. "We've given Josie our notice. It's time. Elisa was right about one thing. Bamboo was a toxic work environment and the three of us decided we're done. We're starting our own firm. We're going to call it Solars Creative, in Maddy's memory."

"That's a lovely tribute." I took a bite of the flaky pie. It was slightly sweet and tangy with notes of almond.

I still had so many lingering questions left unanswered. "And Josie left for LA already?"

Gus took a hand pie and a biscuit. "Yep. It's a classic move. It just goes to prove that the only thing that woman cares about is herself. She was on a plane last night to try and convince New Wave to proceed with the buyout. One of her staff is dead. The other is a killer. You would think it might be enough to pull her out of her self-absorbed head, but apparently not."

"It's never happening. Josie Jones is the textbook definition of a narcissist," Miller agreed. "Do you know she wanted me to leave a case of wine in your tent, Kit?"

"What?" Kit covered her mouth as she chewed. "Why?"

Miller cleaned a smudge on his glasses on the edge of his sleeve. "At the time, I had no idea, but now I think it's because she knew you were clean and she wanted to sabotage your recovery."

"That is low, even for Josie," Gus said with disgust.

I couldn't agree more. The mention of wine brought another question that had been nagging me to the surface. "Hey, speaking of wine. Do any of you know what happened to the wine bottles at the campsite?"

Kit raised a finger and bit the side of her cheek. "That was me."

Miller put his glasses back on. "Man, I'm so sorry. I had no idea. I never would have left the case in your tent, had I known."

"It's cool. You didn't know. I blame Josie. I kind of panicked. I thought I could handle being around so much alcohol, but I couldn't. I was worried that I was going to drink, and I knew if I started, I wasn't going to be able to stop, so I ended up dumping out a bunch of wine and shattering the bottles."

Gus put his arm around her shoulder in a show of solidarity. "You don't have to worry about boozy executive retreats from here on out, okay?"

Miller adopted a soft tone. "Gus is right. I hate these things anyway. They're so contrived and who wants to be hungover at work? We're making a pact right here, right now, that Solars Creative is going to be different. We're going to be committed to creating a company that cares about its people and we are going to embrace a culture of work/life balance instead of burning ourselves out."

"You guys are the best." Kit fanned her face to stave off tears.

My eyes misted, too. It was good to see them supporting each other and carving out a new path forward.

"I have a couple more questions, and this one is for you." I looked across the table at Miller. "Did you stab Josie before the backstage tour?"

He choked on a bite of biscuit. It took him a minute to recover. "How did you know?"

"Well, let's just say we spotted the instrument you used."

"Who's 'we'?" Miller squinted behind his thick frames.

"Lance. We noticed a skewer in your bag."

Miller pounded his forehead with his palm. "Oh man,

I thought it fell out on the tour. I can't believe you noticed."

"Why did you stab her?"

"This is going to sound juvenile, but I reached my breaking point. I was so irritated with her. She complained about everything I did. It was a moment of stupidity. She had bent over to grab something, and I had been fiddling with the skewer—it was left over from lunch. I don't know what came over me, but I saw her skin exposed and without even thinking about it I stabbed her." He hung his head. "I'm not proud of it. I know she's terrible, but I shouldn't have resorted to physical violence."

"I'm not so sure I wouldn't have done the same," Gus said. "Especially after everything we've learned about Josie. Giving Kit wine. Cutting all of us out of the buyout packages we deserved. Using Maddy's death as an opportunity for free press. The woman is vile. Yeah, I would stick it to her, too."

Kit cracked up. "Remind me never to order anything skewered for our future corporate lunches."

Miller's posture relaxed. It was probably a relief to tell his new business partners about what he'd done, and I was glad to have answers.

"I have one last question that has been bugging me," I said to Gus. "Did you put spiders in Josie's tent?"

"She's good," Gus said to his colleagues. "Are you sure you don't work for the police?"

"It didn't take much deduction to figure that one out. You were pretty obvious."

Gus's mouth dropped open. "Was I? I thought I was

very casual. I made sure to hang out by the fire when she discovered that her tent was infested."

"That's what made it obvious," I said.

Miller punched him in the arm. "Seriously, man."

Gus shrugged. "So much for being sneaky. I had that planned since the day I got the email invite. It's the ultimate camp prank, but then after Maddy was killed, I couldn't admit it or tell anyone because I thought for sure the police would think it was connected to her death. It wasn't. It was a stupid prank." He cleared his throat. "The perfect prank to play on someone like Josie Jones. Here's the thing I still don't get—why did she have you book a rafting trip?"

Miller pounded his forehead. "Don't even get me started. She told me we needed an adventure trip for team bonding. Her vision was that if we went through a physically taxing experience together it would be good for morale, but she failed to mention that she hates the outdoors and can't swim."

Everyone cracked up.

"That's what I call karma," Kit said.

We chatted more about their future plans for the company while polishing off breakfast. They had promised to stay in touch and offered to do pro bono marketing work for Torte if we ever needed it.

It was nice knowing they were moving forward and finding a way to honor Maddy in the process. I could only imagine what kind of rant Josie must have gone on when she heard that her entire executive team was leaving.

I didn't dwell on it, though, because I had happier

things to concentrate on, like preparing for harvest and our grape stomp supper. I took our dishes downstairs and checked in on the team.

Bethany had constructed stencils out of cardstock, which she used to make pretty powdered sugar designs on the top of brownies.

"Those are so sweet," I noted, leaning over her shoulder to get a better look at the outlines of birds and roses topping each chocolate square.

"Don't mind me. I'm just over here blinging out my brownies." She dusted the bright white sugar on top of another.

"I've never seen that technique. It's brilliant."

"Thank Steph." Bethany motioned with her head. "She saw it on a baking show. I want to have an impressive collection of new trends for this social collaboration. Torte is going to be seen by millions of new people. I'm hoping that we get a lot of followers and engagement, but I want to make sure everything I share is super fresh."

"These are super fresh. I love them." My team's talent and ability to take initiative and push themselves outside their comfort zone never ceased to amaze me. "When do we lose you to the powers of social?"

"A week from tomorrow." Bethany positioned a maple leaf stencil in the center of a brownie. "Remember you're not fully losing me. I'll be popping in with a camera crew. They're going to want to take a lot of photos of the bakeshop and the team and our products. They said they might even want to do some mini-interviews with our regulars, and I'm hoping we can do a live baking demo."

"Live on social media?"

"Yeah." Her curls bobbed as she nodded. "I'll set it all up. You just need to show off your superior baking skills. I need to talk through logistics, but maybe it's a class, maybe it's a Bake-Off, or maybe something simple like a recipe share and then you and Steph can demo some piping techniques."

"It all sounds great." It was true. I appreciated that Bethany was pushing me out of my comfort zone, too. "Tell me what you need from me, and I'll be ready."

"You're the best, Jules."

"The feeling is mutual." I left her to her design and checked in with Sterling. He was reducing gravy on the stove. "How's it going? That smells amazing."

He offered me a tasting spoon.

I took a bite of the sauce. It was thick and creamy, like a gravy should be, with herbal notes of rosemary, thyme, and sage. "Perfection."

A smile tugged on his chiseled jawline. "Thanks. I'm doing a biscuits and gravy special. Marty was also thinking of doing a smothered turkey and gravy panini. Start to get customers in the mood for fall. What do you think?"

"Count me in." I glanced to the whiteboard where we kept track of custom orders and staff schedules. "I wanted to touch base about the Sunday Supper this weekend. Carlos confirmed that the harvest is on, so I'm going to have Steph design some flyers to post. We're thinking casual since we'll be working in the vines all day. Can you take the lead on this? Maybe charcuterie platters, house-made hummus, that sort of thing."

"Is this just for the people who come help with the

harvest?" Sterling whisked the bubbling gravy as he spoke.

"No. We'll open it up to the community. We're hoping for ten to twelve people for the harvest and then maybe an additional twenty-five to thirty for the grape stomp and dinner."

"Cool." He made a mental note. "Do you want me to take care of everything? Ordering product, the menu?"

"As long as you're up for it, that would be great. My plan is to be gone most mornings to help with the harvest. I'll be in each afternoon, but I'll probably have a lot of catch-up to do." That was true, but I also wanted to keep giving Sterling more autonomy. Running a professional kitchen involved much more than being a good chef. He was ready to start learning the next phases of kitchen management, like vendor relations, inventory, and staffing. Even though I hated the idea of eventually losing him to his own kitchen, when he did move on I wanted him to be fully prepared to handle any issue that came his way. It was one of the biggest challenges for recent culinary school graduates. New chefs emerged from the classroom with bright eyes and bright visions for spending their days baking chocolate eclairs or hand-pressing pot stickers. The harsh reality was that over 60 percent of new restaurants failed in their first three years in business. I wanted my staff to not only have exquisite culinary skills but also have a solid understanding of the business of running a kitchen.

He gave me a one-fingered salute. "I'm on it."

I knew he was. I knew my entire team was capable and growing. The thought brought a smile to my face. After a week with the Bamboo executives, it was very obvious that the vibe at Torte was one of collaboration and creativity. I felt incredibly grateful to be surrounded by people who loved this space as much as me, and who went out of their way to make our time together at Torte never feel like work. I wasn't sure how I had gotten so lucky, but I did know that I would never take my staff for granted and I would do anything and everything in my power to make sure each of them followed their dreams, too.

Chapter Twenty-Six

The next morning Carlos was up and awake with me before the stars had made their exit from the sky. "Are you excited?" He tugged on an Uva hoodie and laced his boots. "I cannot believe it's finally time. I feel like a little kid. I do not think I slept more than an hour or maybe two last night. The grapes are waiting for us."

I grinned, watching his knee bounce as he struggled with his laces. "Do you need me to tie your boots, buddy?"

"I am not a kid," he bantered back. "I said I *feel* like a kid."

"It's pretty exciting. At least for the first hour or two of picking grapes. Then you start to realize how much work harvest is, but it's going to be worth it when you have overflowing tubs of grapes waiting to be transformed into glorious wine." I had memories of joining my parents at harvest parties when I was young. The entire town would show up with garden sheers, sun hats, and bottles of water to help local vintners with their yield.

Carlos had endeared himself to the wine community.

There was a true sense of comradery amongst growers in the valley. Everyone shared their knowledge and expertise and muscle power. For the next few days our fields would be filled with friends and fellow winemakers, and then that same group would rotate to a new vineyard until every last grape had been plucked from the vine. Watching the grapes turn during this time of year was almost like a sporting event. Friendly wagers, in the form of a case of wine, would be placed on which vineyard was likely to be the first to be picked.

Uva had earned that honor this year. Carlos had been taking meticulous notes, studying the grapes and waiting for them to reveal the telltale signs that they were ready for harvest. The first and most obvious clue was color. Grapes would begin their chameleon-like change from green to red in August, but seasoned wine producers knew it could still take weeks for the grapes to reach their full potential. Carlos had learned to pay attention to the color of the stem and seeds. Once both turned brown, the grapes were more likely to be ripe. The grape seeds should also be chewable and the grapes juicy and plump. Lastly, and perhaps most importantly, professional vintners would judge a grape's readiness by taste. Fully matured grapes were sweet without a hint of bitterness.

Carlos was well on his way to becoming a serious contender in the Rogue Valley's wine industry with his discerning palate. His training as a chef allowed him to be able to pull the varietal flavors of the grapes from each taste, giving an early clue into how the finished product would ultimately taste.

"Sí, that is the spirit." He won the battle with his lace

and reached for me. "Kiss me for good luck on our first harvest together."

He wasn't about to get any resistance from me. Our lips touched. His kiss was tender and slow. I wouldn't have minded lingering a bit longer, but the grapes wouldn't wait. We were meeting a team of temporary workers and volunteers at Uva to kick off the harvest. I had prepped at Torte by baking chocolate, almond, and ham and cheese croissants, which were packed in bakery boxes and waiting downstairs. Fortunately, Uva had its own kitchen. Once we got to the vineyard, I would make pots of coffee to accompany the pastries while Carlos went over how to pick the clusters of grapes and hand out sharp cutting shears.

"It is too bad the grapes are ready." Carlos was breathless when he finally released me. "I could stay like this all day."

"Me too." I gave him another kiss and stood up. "But now we need coffee."

The drive to the vineyard was yet another reminder of how lucky we were to live in southern Oregon. Grizzly Peak was backlit in tangerines and glowing reds, like the embers from a slow-burning fire. We breezed past organic orchards and family farms, until the single-lane road turned to gravel.

While Carlos prepped the gear for picking, I went inside to make coffee. Uva's previous owners had lived on the vineyard. That meant that in addition to the outdoor tasting area we used in the summer there was a house on the property that we had transformed into a tasting room and event space. It was perfect for weddings and small parties.

The kitchen was stocked with wineglasses and state-of-the-art equipment. I brewed a regular pot and one of decaf—just in case. As I was loading coffee carafes and cream and sugar on a rolling cart, Mom peered into the kitchen.

"Good morning." She was dressed to work in jeans and a thick flannel shirt.

"Hey, what are you doing here?" I stacked recycled paper cups on the cart.

"Doug and I wouldn't miss the first harvest." She wiggled her fingers. "We're here to work. Tell me what you need."

"I could use a hand wheeling this outside," I said, carefully gliding the cart over the hardwood floors.

"It looks like there's a good turnout," Mom said as we navigated the ramp on the front side of the house. "We should have the fields picked in no time."

"Carlos is so excited. He didn't sleep last night. In fact, don't let him near the coffee. He's already buzzing."

Mom chuckled. "I can't blame him. I know how much of himself he's poured into the vineyard this last year."

"He really has." The thought brought warmth to my chest. It was still hard to believe that Carlos hadn't just moved to Ashland for me. He'd made this place his own, rooting himself to this land, these fields, these friends and family that surrounded us.

I watched as he spoke in quick sentences with exaggerated hand motions, welcoming everyone who had shown up to pick with us and explaining the process for anyone new. Mom and I set up coffee, croissants, and bottles of water. I made sure to bring extra bottles of sunscreen. We didn't need it yet as the sun was slowly making its ascent, but later in the morning when it was directly overhead I knew I would want to make sure that my fair skin didn't burn.

The Professor fell in step with me as I took a pair of shears and a bucket to one of the rows. "Ah, what a morning to spend in Mother Nature's playground."

"It's so nice of you and Mom to come help."

"The pleasure is all ours." He nodded to Pilot Rock in the distance. Its rocky prominence was bathed in soft light. "The view alone is worth it."

"Any updates on Elisa's trial?" I asked, stopping at the top of the row. We would work methodically from the top to the bottom of each row of vines.

The Professor set his bucket on the dirt. "There's not much to report as of yet. She had her initial arraignment, but the case will go to trial for sure."

"I still can't believe that she killed Maddy and that Maddy was the intended victim. I was so sure that the killer had made a mistake and had been trying to kill Josie."

He clipped a bundle of grapes and set them in the bottom of the bucket. "It certainly appeared that way to us as well."

"What about the cause of death? Were you able to determine how she managed to drag Maddy out into the water?"

"Sleeping pills," the Professor answered, snipping another bunch of grapes. "She and Maddy went down to the river for a midnight drink. She slipped sleeping pills into Maddy's wine, waited for them to do the job, and then dragged her body into the water."

A shiver ran down my spine. The murder had been

well thought out and executed. "And it was just a coincidence that Maddy was still wearing Josie's life jacket? I remember she'd been making fun of Josie at the campfire."

"Yes, it seems so. Elisa has been tight-lipped. She's not saying much, per her lawyer's direction, but our best guess is that she didn't intentionally try to make it appear that Josie was the victim. Although that ended up being a benefit to her. Like you, our initial take on the case was that Josie had been the target. It wasn't until we began looking into Bamboo's financial records and personal histories of each employee that it became apparent we were on the wrong track."

One of the sails Carlos had constructed over the outdoor tasting area for shade flapped in the window. It brought a memory of the day of Maddy's murder to the forefront of my mind. "The wind in the sails over there reminds me. What about the tent? Do you remember how that morning, after we had found her body, Gus's tent crashed? Was that connected to the case at all?"

"Ah, yes. The tent. It's my understanding that Elisa was frantically searching for Maddy's laptop. The press release was on her laptop and she was desperate to get her hands on it. She was successful in convincing Maddy to have that fateful drink with her at the river and then she thought she could simply sneak back into camp, take the laptop, destroy the evidence, and no one would be the wiser."

"But Maddy and Gus swapped tents," I interrupted.

"Indeed." The Professor gently handled another bunch of grapes. "She hadn't counted on finding the tent occupied. I believe she didn't want to risk waking Gus, especially since she had just ended an innocent life. She also couldn't risk not being seen at the beach that morning. It would have been too obvious, so my guess is that once everyone returned to camp, she created a distraction by loosening the supports on the tent, and the rest is history, as they say."

I sat with my thoughts for a minute. "It's so sad and so senseless. Maddy didn't deserve to die."

"She did not." The Professor's voice was rich with emotion. I watched his gaze travel toward Mount Ashland. "As Rabbi Jack Reimer says, 'At the blueness of the skies and in the warmth of summer, we remember them.'"

"That's beautiful," I said, feeling tears building. He was right. I would remember. We would remember. Maddy's death had impacted all of us, but it had also brought us closer together. Her loss was a reminder for me to live fully in this moment, to drink in the vistas, to ground myself to the earth, and to hold tight to everyone I loved. We weren't promised tomorrow, so I intended to embrace today and all my future todays.

Chapter Twenty-Seven

We spent the next three days in the vineyard, picking until our fingers were numb, our hands were sore, and Uva's tubs were overflowing with bunches and bunches of plump grapes. The interesting thing about harvesting grapes was that the process wasn't messy. Volunteers were always surprised to find that when they finished a shift their clothes weren't stained purple. The color of grapes originates from their skins, not their juicy centers. In fact, most wine grapes don't yield much liquid. It's the crushing of the fresh grapes, stems and all, that creates the lovely juices that ferment into wine. And winemaking required a lot of grapes.

It took about six hundred to eight hundred grapes to produce one bottle of wine. Carlos was hoping that the vines would produce ten tons per acre this year, which would give us six hundred cases of each varietal. That was a drop in the bucket compared with some of the big vineyards but would set us up to be able to distribute regionally and have plenty of wine on hand for our wine club members and the tasting room.

It had been grueling work, but it felt great to have

the harvest behind us and to see the vines picked clean. When Sunday finally arrived, the weather cooperated, casting an autumnal glow on the vineyard when I arrived to set up late in the afternoon.

Carlos, Andy, and Sterling had gotten a head start. They had set up stomping barrels amongst the vines with towels and buckets of warm water for guests to wash their feet after pressing the grapes.

Mom, Steph, and Marty were covering picnic tables with white linen tablecloths and placing bottles of wine, candles, mason jars with bunches of wild sunflowers, and platters of meat and cheese. The vineyard's beauty stood out without any décor, but a few special touches made it even more magical.

"This looks amazing," I said, unloading boxes of our sugar cookies that we had cut out and frosted with burgundy buttercream to resemble bunches of grapes. Bethany had also made wine-infused brownies and miniature cupcakes piped with the same deep purple buttercream. Sterling had outdone himself with the charcuterie platters. Trios of bright yellow, red, and orange peppers had been cut and rolled to resemble roses. There were black and green olives, cherry tomatoes, artichoke hearts, and carrots. Platters of salami, deli meats, and cheeses were interspersed with baskets of breads and bowls of creamy dips. From pesto to yellow curry and hummus to garden ranch, there was something for everyone.

I like the idea of having bites for our guests to munch on instead of a formal sit-down dinner. Hopefully it would encourage mingling and get everyone to roll up their pants and join in the crush.

Andy was in charge of the music. I wandered over to check in with him. "What do you think about some Rosemary Clooney? Big band seems right for a grape stomp."

"Rosemary Clooney? Wow, that's a throwback." A vision of my parents dancing in Torte's original kitchen flashed in my mind. "My dad used to blast her stuff when he was in the kitchen."

"My grandma loves the Rat Pack. She's had me listening to Frank Sinatra since before I could talk."

"No wonder you're such a Renaissance man," I teased.

He blushed. "Hardly. I can't even talk to anyone I'm interested in without turning the color of a tomato."

"It gets easier, trust me."

"Ya think?" His lip curled. "I think I sort of blew it."

"You mean with Bethany?"

"I don't know." He ran his fingers through his shaggy hair. "I never officially asked her out. I invited her to ski, you know, like casual hangouts, but I guess I should have been direct. I should have told her that I like her. Now it's too late."

"How is it too late?" I made a face. "It's not too late."

"That celebrity chef is already here. Have you seen him? Jeremy DeSalt. He's the only thing Bethany and Steph have been talking about for days. They act like he's a god or something just because he has millions of fans." Andy's face blanched. "Steph is actually telling Bethany to go for it. To flirt with him. I can't believe it. It's not like he's going to stick around. She's just totally into him because he's a rich and famous celebrity chef."

"Really?" I frowned. "I don't know, I could be wrong, but Bethany doesn't strike me as the celebrity type."

"Yeah?" Andy didn't sound convinced. "I hope you're right, because she's going to be with him nonstop for the next few weeks. I know she's already crushing on him from his pictures on social. Pass DeSalt did this big intro video showing the truck rolling in past Mount A and then Bethany and Jeremy at all of the spots they're going to feature on social. I can't imagine what it will be like for her to hang out with him in real life. I blew my shot."

"Oh, I don't know about that. It's never too late to tell someone how you feel about them." I stole a glance at Carlos.

"We'll see." He adjusted the volume on the speakers.

"Andy, can I give you one piece of advice?" I tilted my head toward him.

"Sure, boss."

"I've learned this the hard way. Don't cheat yourself when it comes to love. Don't settle for the crumbs, just because you're worried it might not turn out the way you want. I spent years doing that. And here's the thing, maybe if you tell Bethany how you feel, she won't reciprocate, but living with the regret of never putting yourself out there is going to be so much worse."

"You're right, Jules. Thanks." He gave me a strong, decisive nod. "Plus, this Jeremy DeSalt guy has nothing on my coffee. Maybe I need to make Bethany her own roast."

My jaw dropped. "Um, Andy, yes, yes, you do." I stabbed my heart. "That's the most romantic thing I've ever heard of."

"Did someone say romance?" Mom came over to join us.

"Jules is giving me some good advice, Mrs. The Professor. What do you think of making Bethany her own custom coffee blend?"

Mom's face mimicked mine. She pressed her hands together. "You might need to go give Doug some advice. I've always considered him to be quite the romantic, but he has yet to make me my own coffee blend."

Andy's cheeks reddened. "I should probably get back to the music."

"Keep us posted. We'll happily sample the Bethany blend for you." She winked.

"You got it." Andy returned his attention to the speakers, which were working perfectly.

"Everything looks lovely, doesn't it?" Mom and I moved toward the food tables.

"So pretty." I looped my arm through hers. "How are you? How are things now that Elisa's been arrested?"

"Good. Doug seems more relaxed. He's already making plans to take off a nice chunk of time during the holidays. It's hard to believe that it's almost Halloween." She wrapped a beige shawl around her slender shoulders.

"I know. Ramiro's mom and the rest of the family are coming. I have so much to do to get ready." I took in the vineyard. Vintage strings of Edison-style lights zigzagged between the oak trees. Tables with simple white linens and votive candles dotted the vines. Andy's jazz mixed in with the sounds of nature.

"Let me help," Mom suggested. "What do you need?"

"I don't even know yet." That was true. "I just want to make their visit perfect. I want them to feel welcome and like they're part of the family."

"They are." Her eyes held a knowing gleam.

"I know. I guess I realize that even more with having had Ramiro here for more than a month. I'm putting myself in her shoes and I'm so grateful that she's willing to share him with us, and I want her to know that and also see that he's in good hands with us."

Mom placed her hand on her heart. "It's a true test of how wonderful she is as a mother. If we do our jobs right, our kids step out of our hearts and homes and into this great big world on their own. Also, honey, you don't have to worry about proving anything. Ramiro is clearly so well loved and cared for by you and Carlos. A stranger on the street could see that."

I leaned my head on her shoulder. "Have I said thank you for that? You never said a word to sway me from going to culinary school and then halfway across the globe. It must have been so hard for you."

She kissed my head. "I would never hold you back, but not so secretly, I'm still over the moon that you've chosen to make Ashland your own—on your own terms. That's the difference. I could have never lived with myself if I felt like I had tried to shape your path for you. My goal was to give you the foundation and let you chart your own course."

"You succeeded."

I brushed a tear from my eye as the first guests began to roll in. I circulated the tables, stopping to chat and catch up with old friends as the wine flowed and everyone rolled up their jeans to stomp in the large vats of grapes. Abby and her husband came. She brought me a plate of snickerdoodles for Ramiro, who had opted to go to the football game with a new group of friends. I took that as a good sign that he was already fitting in.

I felt a tap on my shoulder as I made my way to the wine table to pour myself a glass of merlot.

"Well, don't you look like a vision tonight, Juliet Montague Capshaw," Lance said with a playful grin. He offered me a glass of red wine.

"You're a mind reader. I was on my way to get a drink."

"I know." He looked smug. "I beat you to it. I had to show off my superior sleuthing skills. I sensed that you wanted wine, and I found you wine."

I took the glass from him with an eye roll.

"Now there's no need for the attitude. A simple thank-you will suffice."

"Thanks."

He tapped his glass to mine. "Here's to another successful case. We solved a murder and put a killer behind bars, not bad for a week's work."

"I'm not sure we can take credit for solving the case and putting Elisa behind bars." I tilted my head toward Mom and the Professor, who were dancing under the flickering lights strung between the trees and sunshades. They made a striking couple, Mom with her petite frame, the Professor with his solid grasp around her narrow waist. "I think the Professor, Thomas, and Kerry might have a rightful claim to that."

"Nonsense," Lance scoffed. "The credit is ours. Where would our intrepid detectives be without the input and sage insight provided by yours truly? Nowhere, darling. That's where."

Arlo came up behind us and cleared his throat. "Am I interrupting anything important?"

Lance leaned into him. "Never. I was taking a moment

to congratulate my partner in crime for another successful venture into the nefarious world of sleuthing."

"Oh, dear." Arlo caught my eye. "My apologies. Lance struggles with self-confidence. It's a skill we've been trying to improve, but I see there's more work to be done."

I laughed.

Lance pressed his lips together tight and wrinkled his nose. "Don't you two dare try to team up against me. It will never work."

Arlo smirked. "It could, am I right, Juliet?"

"It really could."

Lance huffed. "Listen, we're here for a night of merriment. Enough chitchat, let's go round up that Spaniard of yours and get our feet dirty. I was promised a traditional grape crush and I'm not leaving without grape seeds sticking between my toes."

"When you put it like that, it sounds so appealing," I replied, scanning the vineyard for Carlos.

"You missed an opportunity for a pun there," Lance said, reaching for Arlo's hand. "It's at the top of my brain. Something about peeling grapes . . ."

"Oh, wow." Arlo shot me an apologetic smile. "It's going from bad to worse, isn't it?"

The truth was, I was happy for their company, Lance's inflated sense of our involvement in the murder investigation, and even his cheesy puns. It meant that things were returning to normal again. For that I felt a deep sense of gratitude.

We went to recruit Carlos to stomp with us. He didn't take much convincing. In a flash he abandoned his wine glass and tore off his shoes. "Come on, mi querida, I've been waiting for this."

I followed suit, removing my sandals. I'd worn a pair of capri jeans for the occasion, knowing that it was likely I was going to get my feet in the mix.

Carlos helped steady my hand as I got into the barrel with him. The four of us erupted into fits of giggles as we competed to see which couple could pound their stash of grape bundles into a juicy pulp faster. Grapes exploded beneath my feet. Squishing through our well-earned harvest felt like the perfect culmination of the past year. We had nurtured the very first seedlings on the vine and seen them through every stage of their maturity. It felt a bit like the growth and change that Carlos and I had experienced together from the moment he said he was giving up his nomadic life at sea to cultivate a new start here in Ashland with me.

Like our vines, we had stretched toward the sun while grounding ourselves to each other and the Rogue Valley, allowing our roots to run deep and settle below the surface.

I caught Carlos's eye. "What is it?"

"Nothing, I'm just so happy. Blissfully so."

"Me too, Julieta. Me too."

It was the tiny moments like this that mattered. Letting the joy seep in. Embracing the now. Fully living, without hesitation about what might come next.

The atmosphere remained lively through the night as stars filled the expansive sky. Laughter reverberated through the crisp late September evening. Andy's throwback playlist was a hit, as were our charcuterie boards and grape-inspired desserts. He spun in a mix of modern tunes, too, which got Sterling and Steph on their feet. I couldn't help but wonder what was next for the two of them. I hoped that Torte would remain home for them a while longer. I could also fully picture what their future restaurant might look and taste like. Steph's alternative artist touch would be evident in the moody design—purples, blacks, rustic candles, and geometric wallpaper. While Sterling would put his mark on the food, elevated soups and plates of pasta served with love, just like he'd learned from his mentor.

Maybe I wouldn't have to worry about it in the near future. They seemed content to shine in their roles at the bakeshop for the moment.

I loved watching grown adults' faces turn childlike as they smashed the grapes that Carlos had watched over like a newborn infant for these many months, with their toes. Grape juice splattered everywhere, and no one seemed to care. Most guests left with their ankles still stained purple, like they were going home from a night-clubbing with a temporary tattoo, proof of the night's revelry.

It was a salve for my soul after the last week. I didn't realize how desperately I needed a reminder that while there might be a sour grape or two amongst the bunch, the masses were sweet and juicy. Just like the people I loved. The people I surrounded myself with in Ashland. Friends, family, neighbors, strangers—this was the heart of our community, our connection. While the lightness of our collective spirit might have been tested by Maddy's murder, I felt grateful that we had gathered again to celebrate the harvest and the changing of seasons. To celebrate a year of labor and hard work and experience nature's bounty firsthand, or maybe first foot.

This is why I had made Ashland my home. Mom was right that I had had to find my way. I was glad for the pitfalls and hurdles on my path to finding where I was meant to be. They had made me stronger. They had tested my resolve, and watching so many smiling faces against the backdrop of flicking candles and glowing grapevines, I knew without a doubt that there was no chance I was ever leaving again.

Recipes

Skillet Cookie

Ingredients:
1 cup butter, softened
¾ cup white sugar
¾ cup brown sugar
4 teaspoons vanilla
2 eggs
1 teaspoon baking soda
1 ½ teaspoons salt
2 ½ cups flour
1 10-ounce package of dark chocolate chips
2 cups walnuts (optional)

Directions:
Preheat the oven to 350 degrees Fahrenheit. In a large mixing bowl or electric mixer, cream butter, sugars, and vanilla until light and fluffy. Then add eggs. Once the eggs have been incorporated into the batter, gradually add baking soda, salt, and flour, beating on low until well blended. Stir in chocolate chips and walnuts by hand.

Spread dough into a greased 15-inch cast iron skillet and bake for 20 to 25 minutes or until the cookie is golden brown. Serve hot with a generous scoop of vanilla bean ice cream.

Cowboy Baked Beans

Ingredients:
10 slices of honey-cured bacon
2 large white onions
4 cloves of garlic
2 15-ounce cans of kidney beans
2 15-ounce cans of black beans
2 15-ounce cans of great northern beans
2 14-ounce cans of diced fire-roasted tomatoes
1 tablespoon chili powder
2 teaspoons paprika
1 tablespoon brown sugar
1 teaspoon salt
1 teaspoon pepper
2 sprigs of fresh rosemary
1 cup breadcrumbs
1 cup grated Parmesan cheese

Directions:
Place strips of bacon in a Dutch oven or large stock pot and cook on medium heat, turning so that both sides of the bacon are cooked through. Once the bacon is slightly crisp, remove it from the pan and place it on a paper towel or plate. Drain most of the fat, reserving a tablespoon. Dice onions and garlic and add to the Dutch

oven. Return the pan to the heat and fry onions and garlic for 5 to 10 minutes. Drain beans and tomatoes, add to the Dutch oven, and stir everything together. Then add chili powder, paprika, brown sugar, salt, and pepper. Bring beans to a simmer. Place rosemary sprigs on the top, reduce the heat to low, and cover. Allow beans to cook slowly for one to two hours. Remove beans from the stove and take out sprigs of rosemary. Sprinkle breadcrumbs, Parmesan cheese, and crumbled bacon over the top and serve hot.

Caramel Apple Strudel

Ingredients:

1 package (2 sheets) of frozen puff pastry dough, thawed
4 Granny Smith apples (peeled, cored, and diced)
¾ cup white sugar
2 teaspoons vanilla
2 teaspoons cinnamon
1 tablespoon flour (plus extra for rolling out dough)
1 egg, beaten
1 tablespoon Turbinado sugar

Directions:

Preheat the oven to 400 degrees Fahrenheit. Add apples, sugar, vanilla, cinnamon, and flour to a large mixing bowl and stir ingredients together. Sprinkle more flour onto a large cutting board and roll out puff pastry sheets. Spoon the filling into the center of the dough. Fold over the left section of the dough and brush with the egg. Do the same with the right section of the dough. Brush the top of the pastry with the remaining egg, sprinkle it with Turbinado sugar, and place it on a parchment-lined baking tray. Bake for 25 to 30 minutes or until the pastry is puffed and golden brown. Allow the pastry to cool for 10 to 15 minutes and cut into 2-inch slices.

Chicken Pot Pie

Ingredients:

1 package (2 sheets) of puff pastry dough, thawed
¼ cup butter
2 cups cooked and diced chicken breast
½ cup chopped celery
½ cup diced carrots
1 cup diced onions
½ cup frozen peas
½ cup frozen corn
½ cup peeled and diced potato
½ cup flour
3 cups chicken stock
¼ cup heavy cream
1 teaspoon salt
1 teaspoon pepper
1 egg yolk, beaten

Directions:

Preheat the oven to 375 degrees Fahrenheit. Melt the butter and brown the diced chicken in a Dutch oven or large stock pot. Add the celery, carrots, onions, peas, corn, and potato. Cook over medium heat for 5 minutes.

Then add the flour and chicken stock. Slowly bring to a boil and let simmer for 15 minutes. Stir in heavy cream and salt and pepper. Remove the filling from the heat and allow it to cool. While it's cooling, roll out the first sheet of puff pastry dough and place it in a greased baking dish. The dough should be 2 inches larger than the dish. Allow the sides to overhang and add the filling. Roll out the second sheet of pastry dough and lay it over the top. Crimp the sides together around the rim of the baking dish. Brush with the egg wash and cut 2 1-inch slats on the top to allow steam to escape. Place the baking dish on a cookie sheet and bake for 30 minutes until the filling is bubbly and the crust is puffy and golden. Allow the pot pie to rest for 15 minutes before serving.

Lemon Blueberry Muffins

Ingredients:
For the muffins:
½ cup butter
1 ¼ cup sugar
2 eggs
½ cup buttermilk
Juice and zest of one large lemon
2 cups flour
2 teaspoons baking powder
1 teaspoon salt
2 cups fresh blueberries (tossed gently with 1 tablespoon of flour)

For the lemon glaze:
1 cup powdered sugar
4 tablespoons fresh lemon juice

Directions:
Preheat the oven to 375 degrees. Cream butter and sugar together in a mixing bowl. Add eggs, buttermilk, and the juice and zest of one lemon. Slowly incorporate the flour, baking powder, and salt. Once the batter is smooth, fold in the berries, careful not to damage them. Scoop into greased muffin cups and bake for 20 to 25 minutes. Remove from muffin tins immediately. Allow the muffins to cool for 10 to 15 minutes. While muffins are cooling, make the glaze by whisking powdered sugar and fresh lemon juice in a bowl until silky smooth. Drizzle glaze over the cooled muffins and serve.

Ode to September Latte

Andy's favorite fall coffee creation is the perfect way to welcome the season.

Ingredients:
2 shots of dark roast espresso
1 teaspoon caramel sauce
1 teaspoon bourbon extract
1 teaspoon butter pecan syrup
½ cup oat milk

Directions:

Add espresso shots to a coffee mug. Stir in caramel sauce, bourbon extract, and butter pecan syrup. Steam the oat milk, add to the espresso, and serve hot.

Read on for an excerpt from
CATCH ME IF YOU CANDY—
the next Bakeshop mystery by Ellie Alexander,
coming soon from St. Martin's Paperbacks!

Chapter One

They say that things are not always what they seem. For a long time, I might not have agreed when it came to my idyllic hometown of Ashland, Oregon, where neighbors helped neighbors and there was a strong sense of community spirit. But my perspective shifted a few days before Halloween this year, when a strange turn of events left me unsettled and made me question whether I was sugar-coating how sweet life could be in our little corner of the Siskiyou Mountains.

The first sign that something wasn't quite right started amid the pre-holiday frenzy. We had been preparing for the upcoming ghoulish festivities at Torte, my family's bakeshop. Halloween in Ashland was like stepping onstage at one of the most elaborate productions of the Oregon Shakespeare Festival (known locally as OSF). Perhaps it was due to the creative and artistic types drawn to the Rogue Valley or that OSF had an entire warehouse dedicated to costumes ranging from Greek and Roman times to the Renaissance era, full military regalia, 1960s beehive headpieces, and everything in between. The company rented costumes to theaters of all shapes and sizes as well as for film and TV. Living in a thespian mecca meant that All Hallows' Eve might be the biggest holiday of the year.

Kids and adults alike would spend hours crafting unique and clever costumes for the celebration. That was my favorite part of the Halloween parade—*everyone* participated. In fact, to call it a parade didn't really do the event justice. It was more like a costume street party. And Torte was right in the mix.

We would close shop to join in the revelry and then, as soon as the parade spilled into the plaza, reopen to serve sweets, coffee, and snacks late into the evening. Trick-or-treaters would receive special Halloween goody bags, a longtime tradition at Torte. Mom and Dad had started the trend back in the bakeshop's early days. They had partnered with other family-owned businesses in town to offer a safe space for little witches and pumpkins to traipse from storefront to storefront in search of treats. Every business in the plaza embraced the experience. At A Rose by Any Other Name next door, Janet would hand out bunches of colorful lollipops tied with silky ribbons to resemble a bouquet of flowers. Puck's Pub offered red and white striped bags of cheesy and spiced popcorn. The bookstore gave every youngster a free comic. There was always a long line at the Green Goblin at the end of the block, where servers roamed the sidewalk with trays of their signature garlic fries and lemon aioli dipping sauce.

At Torte we packaged hundreds of Halloween treat bags filled with our classic sugar cookies designed to resemble candy corn, ghosts, and spiders. We also included cider spice mixes, Frankenstein and eyeball cake pops, and mummy munch—our Halloween take on trail mix, with crumbled pieces of shortbread, toasted nuts, coconut, pretzels, and orange and black M & Ms.

In addition to the treat bags, our pastry cases would be stocked with chocolate cupcakes featuring fluffy buttercream ghosts, tiered cakes with festive Halloween sprinkles, and cauldrons filled with decadent custards. Many customers had already put in special orders for parties, but the parade and subsequent street fair would bring in thousands of costumed tourists to our little hamlet and we wanted to be prepared to keep them fed and happy throughout the evening.

On a blustery late October morning, I made my way along Main Street while the last of the stars flicked overhead. As was typical, I had snuck out of bed while Carlos was still sleeping. After pulling on a pair of jeans, tennis shoes, and one of our new Torte hoodies, I tiptoed downstairs and left him and Ramiro a note letting them know that I would see them later. Ramiro had been living with us since August. He was doing an exchange year at Ashland High School, and unless he was a master of deception seemed to be fitting in seamlessly. He was doing well in his classes, his soccer team had qualified for the state championships, and he had a date for homecoming.

I had been nervous about whether the transition from Spain to American schools would be difficult and whether things between us would feel awkward or forced. I wanted Ramiro to know that he was welcome and would always have a place with Carlos and me. Fortunately, his easygoing attitude abated my fears. It was as if he had grown up in Ashland with the way he had almost instantly made friends and learned his way around the Alice in Wonderland trails that connected from our house to Lithia Park and all the way to Mount A. Watching him compete in his red and white Grizzly gear brought back many happy memories of my time at Ashland High School, running cross country and helping build sets for our theater projects. Ramiro had yet to experience an Ashland Halloween, though. He had looked at me skeptically when I told him that the entire town plus a few thousand extra visitors would be in costume. I'm sure he thought I was exaggerating. He would have to see for himself.

Neighbors had already decked out porches with carved jack-o'-lanterns, black and orange twinkle lights, and skeletons. If Ramiro had doubted me, he need only take a stroll through the plaza. As vintage homes transformed into the Tudor-style buildings that made up downtown, the Halloween theme continued. Scarecrows, bats, and creatures that go bump in the night were propped in front of restaurants and shops. Silky gold banners announcing the parade hung from the antique lampposts that lined the street. There were window displays with retro candy, advertisements for a midnight showing of *The Rocky Horror Picture Show* at the movie theater, and jewel-toned masks for sale at the costume shop.

I was glad for my hoodie as the breeze kicked up leaves on the sidewalks. A faint hint of woodsmoke lingered in the air. There was nothing like Ashland in the fall. To be fair, there wasn't a bad time of the year to visit our village nestled amongst the endless mountain ranges of the Rogue Valley, but autumn put on a glorious show of color. Every tree in the plaza looked as if it had been painted by hand. Deep maroons, mustard yellow, and burnt orange leaves glowed under the dimming starlight. I drank in the view and the early morning calm as I crossed the street in front of the police station and headed toward Torte.

Our family bakeshop sat on the corner of the plaza. Its cheerful red and teal awning and large bay windows always brought a smile to my face. I paused for a minute to take in the Halloween window display that Steph, our cake artist and recent college grad, and Rosa, one of our new bakers who managed the dining room, had created. They had turned the bakeshop's front windows into an inviting and slightly spooky scene. Black and white bunting and twinkling lights hung from the top of the window, below which hung a six-foot-wide spiderweb. Steph and Rosa had stretched fake webbing from it in each direction, creating a gauzy effect. Cake stands at the base of the window displayed skull-shaped Bundts and red velvet cakes pierced with bloody knives. Somehow, they had managed to strike the right balance of whimsy and just a touch of creepiness.

The vibe on the plaza was the same. At this early hour, fading moonlight illuminated the trees, casting moving shadows on the ground. The Lithia Bubblers gurgled steadily. A crow circled overhead, cawing its greeting to the morning. Most of the other storefronts were still dark, except the Merry Windsor Hotel, which looked like it should have been named Hotel Transylvania instead, with its crumbling faux-stone façade and dusty windows. Nothing about the dilapidated exterior, however, was an effect for Halloween. The owner, Richard Lord, just refused to spend a dime modernizing the hotel.

I made a mental note to tell Steph and Rosa how much I loved their display as I continued downstairs, unlocked the basement door, and went inside. Being the first person in the kitchen helped set the tone and center me for the day. My first task was to light a fire in our wood-burning pizza oven. Almost immediately the basement began to warm and the scent of applewood wafted into the workspace. Mom and I had designed the commercial kitchen with stations for baking, decorating, and making our savory breakfast and lunch items. I loved our modern revamp with bright overhead lights for the painstaking task of piping detail work on cakes and the easy flow between baking and prep stations. Prior to expanding downstairs, our entire operation had been crammed into the original kitchen upstairs. By far my favorite thing about the space was the exposed brick wall and wood-burning pizza oven that our contractor had unearthed in the remodeling process.

After hanging up my coat and turning on the lights, I didn't bother to brew a pot of coffee because I knew that Andy, our head barista, would be arriving soon. Instead, I washed my hands, tied on a fire-engine red Torte apron, and gathered the ingredients I needed for devil's food cupcakes. I wanted to get a head start on our specialty bakes. We had multiple orders for dozens of custom Halloween cakes, cookies, and cupcakes. The baking was relatively easy, but the task of piping dainty bones or devil horns would be much more arduous. If I could get all of the baking done before Steph and Bethany arrived, that would give the cupcakes and cookies plenty of time to cool before they began to work their buttercream and royal icing magic.

I began by incorporating vegetable oil and sugar into our industrial mixer. Then I added vanilla and eggs. I sifted flour, baking powder, salt, and dark chocolate in next, alternating with a splash of buttermilk and espresso powder. Once a thick chocolate batter had formed, I scooped it into cupcake tins lined with blood-red and ghostly white wrappers. We would use the devil's food cupcakes for a variety of Halloween designs, including actual devils made with a chocolate ganache glaze and pieces of red licorice for the horns. White meringue ghosts would top some of the cupcakes, and others would get drizzled with melted white chocolate spiderwebs.

As I was sliding the first batch of cupcakes into the oven, Andy came in through the basement door, the howling wind following him. He clenched his stocking cap and tried, unsuccessfully, to smooth down his unruly hair.

"Whew, it's really kicking out there." His youthful cheeks were flushed from the wind. He yanked off his coat and hung it on the rack near the door. "If it keeps up like this for the rest of the week, the trick-or-treaters might get blown away."

"Somehow I don't think they'll mind." I smiled and then turned to the pantry to get the ingredients I needed for our pumpkin cream cupcakes. "As long as there's candy, right?"

"Fair point, boss." He licked his index finger and pressed down a strand of wild hair.

Andy had taken to calling me boss instead of Jules or my given name, Juliet Montague Capshaw. I didn't mind. I knew it was a term of endearment, and quite honestly, growing up with such a Shakespearean moniker had its own issues. These days I appreciated that my namesake was arguably the most romantic heroine in all of literature; however, there had been a time when I was convinced that I was destined for a life of unrequited love thanks to my name.

"When I was a kid I didn't care if it was pouring rain on Halloween," Andy said, coming into the kitchen. "Give me the candy and I'm good."

"Same here." I set pumpkin puree and a trio of spices on the counter. "What's on the coffee menu?"

Andy had been roasting his own beans lately. After much deliberation, he had decided to take a break from college and football to focus on his passion—coffee roasting. Mom and I supported him in sending him to regional training and serving his specialty roasts. Part of me worried about him giving up the stability of a college degree, but then again, I had followed my dream of going to culinary school and becoming a pastry chef. That choice had sent me around the world and landed me back in Ashland. I'm a firm believer in living authentically and pursuing a passion. Andy had won a number of roasting competitions and installed his own setup in his grandmother's converted garage. He was definitely on his way to something bigger, but in the meantime, I was so glad that we were the beneficiaries of his quest for the perfect brew.

"I'm not going to give anything away yet, but let's just say that I have a few tricks up my sleeve." He winked and rattled the container of beans he had brought from home before heading upstairs.

"Am I going to get to taste these tricks?" I called after him.

"You know it. Hang tight, I'll be down in a few with my mysterious brew."

While he went upstairs, I returned my attention to the pumpkin cream cupcake batter. No Halloween pastry case could be complete without pumpkin on the menu. For these, I creamed together butter and sugar until it was light and fluffy, then incorporated the pumpkin puree, spices, eggs, flour, salt, baking powder, and sour cream to give the cupcakes a slight tang. Once the cakes cooled, we would core out the center and fill them with our cream cheese frosting. These would be finished with cinnamon buttercream and topped with pumpkin-shaped candies.

While I waited for Andy's coffee of the day and the rest of the team to arrive, I managed to finish a vat of sugar cookie and snickerdoodle dough as well. There was nothing quite as satisfying as checking off tasks on my morning to-do list.

Sterling and Steph showed up about thirty minutes later. They had been living together for a while, and I was curious about what would be next for the young couple. Sterling had worked as our sous chef and his skills continued to blow me away. Steph graduated from Southern Oregon University in June with a degree in design. Buttercream had been her muse lately, but I had a feeling that, like Andy, they were destined for their own culinary adventures. I wasn't sure what that meant, but I knew I had to appreciate every moment with them.

"I love the new tattoos," I said to Steph. "They're perfect for Halloween."

She tapped a skull cupcake on her forearm and then shot Sterling a triumphant grin. "That didn't even take a minute. I win. You're making dinner tonight." Her violet hair was in two braids tied with black rubber bands.

"I always make dinner," he countered.

"We had a bet how long it would take for someone to comment on my temporary tattoos," Steph said to me.

"Those are temporary? They look so real." I leaned in to get a closer look. Steph's left arm sported a collection of tattoos, both baking- and Halloween-themed. An anatomically correct heart with tendrils of purple and red veins with tiny heart shapes stretched from the top of her right shoulder to her elbow. "Wow, that heart is incredible."

Steph's eyes sparkled beneath a layer of black and violet eye shadow that perfectly matched her hair. "I was going to save this reveal for Bethany." She patted her arm. "I wear my heart on my sleeve. Get it?"

"Well done. Well done." I clapped.

Sterling rolled up the sleeves of his hoodie to reveal his collection of skin art. "I told her once she goes temporary, she's going to do the real thing."

"Never." Steph made a slicing motion across her neck. "Just the thought of a needle makes me want to pass out."

"It's not that bad. You hardly feel it," Sterling replied.

Marty came in to save Sterling and Steph from their tattoo debate. "Happy almost Halloween," he called out as he joined us around the island. "It sure feels like a good morning for bread," he said with a broad grin. "Warm bread, hot soup, a fresh-from-the-oven cookie—what could be better on a cold autumn day?"

"Coffee," Andy interrupted, coming down the stairs, balancing a tray of diner-style mugs on one arm. "Always coffee."

"Do we get to know what your roast is before we try it?" I asked, wiping my hands on my apron.

Andy set the tray in the center of the island. "I'm calling it Burial Grounds, get it?" He waited for a reaction. "Burial *grounds*."

"Oh no." Marty rolled his eyes. "Where's Bethany when we need her?"

"Still on the road with her celebrity crush." Andy's normally lighthearted tone turned a touch bitter, like a coffee that had sat in the pot for too long.

Bethany had landed an opportunity to partner with a celebrity chef, Jeremy DeSalt, who'd discovered her on Instagram thanks to her witty captions and artistic eye for styling food photos. Jeremy's show Pass DeSalt was hugely popular. He had rolled into the Rogue Valley with his decked-out traveling food truck for a few weeks and then invited her to continue the journey, traveling to Portland, Bend, Seattle, and BC with him. She was due back on Halloween and I knew I wasn't the only one excited about her return.

"What's the roast?" I changed the subject.

Andy passed around coffees. "It's my darkest roast ever. Like pitch black, strong and spicy, but so smooth that it will fool you going down. Fair warning, there's enough caffeine in this beauty to keep you kicking, so this one is a slow sipper. Unless you're wanting to fly high all morning."

"Yikes." I grimaced in anticipation of taking a sip. "Does it need to come with a warning label?"

"Probably." Andy held character, keeping his eyes narrowed and his brows furrowed. "It's dark, deadly, and delicious."

Marty pushed up his sleeves and took off his watch. "It sounds like this is going to have us howling at the moon."

"That's the goal." Andy raised his mug in a toast. "Let's see who's brave enough to handle these grounds."

"I feel like we need to make some graveyard pudding cups to accompany this," I said, taking a tiny sip. I half expected his highly caffeinated fuel to be bitter, but Andy was right that the coffee was smooth and easy to drink. I tasted notes of black tea and molasses with a spicy finish.

Sterling pounded his chest like a gorilla. "This will put hair on your chest, man."

"Or turn you into a werewolf," Marty countered.

"That's the goal. It is Halloween week, after all. We've got to keep the thrills and chills coming." Andy tipped his mug to take a large gulp.

"Hey, on that note, I know we've closed Scoops for the season, but I was wondering what you think about offering a couple of Halloween concrete specials?" Sterling asked.

Scoops, our summer pop-up ice cream shop in the railroad district, had been a hit with locals and tourists. We didn't serve an extensive menu at the outdoor spot, but rather stocked it with to-go options like sandwiches and cookies for picnics and daily "concretes," thick, creamy ice cream made with seasonal fruits and berries.

"We could turn our dark chocolate concrete even darker by adding extra cocoa powder and charcoal, and serve it in waffle cones with chunks of candy bars," Sterling continued. "And we have to have something pumpkin. Everyone loves pumpkin ice cream this time of year. I can level it up with chunks of pie crust and cinnamon crumble topping."

"I love it," I replied. "What are we thinking for lunch today?"

Marty leveled flour to add to his sourdough starter. "I was planning to make batches of breadsticks to serve with Sterling's soup of the day and for our annual mummy dogs."

Mummy dogs were a favorite amongst adults and kids. We wrapped natural organic Angus beef hot dogs with our breadstick dough to mimic mummy bandages. Then we baked them in the pizza oven and finished them off with mustard eyes and house-made ketchup for dipping.

"I'm doing a black bean stew with fresh avocado and cilantro," Sterling said, as he tied an apron around his waist. "I was also thinking of mac and cheese with toasted herbed breadcrumbs in ramekins to go with the mummy dogs."

"Can it be lunchtime now?" I gave the clock a wistful glance.

"If nothing else, I can have tastes ready soon." Sterling tossed a dish towel over his shoulder and prepared his workstation.

We went over the rest of the schedule and custom cake and specialty treat box orders. Soon the kitchen was alive with energy. As much as I enjoyed my early solo baking, I thrived on collaborating with my staff as we blasted a Halloween playlist and went to work on our own individual tasks. Running a bakeshop was like choreographing a scene for the stage. We each had our own marks to hit, but once everything came together it was a fluid display of edible art.

By the time we were ready to open the front doors the pastry case was filled with purple, orange, neon green, and black stacked cakes, sweet and savory breakfast pastries, hot-from-the-oven cookies, scones, and muffins, and loaves of freshly baked bread.

My phone dinged as I took a spin through the dining room to make sure everything was in order. The text was from Mom. She and her Mahjong group were meeting at her friend Wendy's house later. She had forgotten that she was supposed to bring dessert and wondered if she could reserve a Halloween treat box.

I could do better than that. I could deliver a box to Wendy's house personally. It was only a few blocks from the plaza and it would be fun to see Mom's gaming crew. She and her dear friends Wendy, Janet, and Marcia had been playing Mahjong for as long as I could remember. Their monthly gaming sessions were really an excuse to get together for a long lunch and an afternoon of catching up.

I shot her a text back to let her know that I would swing by later and then went to open the bakeshop. The next few hours were a blur of activity as Andy and Sequoia managed the continual line at the espresso bar, doling out orange spice lattes and cups of Andy's Burial Grounds roast. Rosa and I rang up orders for ham and swiss croissants, pesto egg breakfast sandwiches, and toasted almond pastries. Within thirty minutes of opening, every table upstairs and downstairs was filled with customers sipping coffee and enjoying leisurely breakfasts.

I couldn't contain my happiness watching friends linger over Earl Grey tea while the trees shed their leaves outside. The blustery winds bending branches and sending orange and yellow leaves scattering like confetti made it feel like Halloween. I still had plenty of work to finish in the kitchen and a costume to put together, but it was impossible to ignore the palpable excitement of the upcoming holiday. We were going to be in the center of the action, and I couldn't wait. What could be better than our entire community parading in costumes down our charming Main Street? I wasn't worried about ghosts, ghouls, or things that go bump in the night. This was Ashland, Oregon, perhaps the most idyllic place on the planet. Nothing could go wrong.